# Other Books by Joel B. Reed

THE JAZZ PHILLIPS MURDER SERIES

*Murder in the Choir*

*Murder by the Board*

THE COWBOY McKEE INTRIGUE SERIES

*Angels Fight Dirty* *

*Black Seraph*

*Children of Dust* *

*Devil on DOS* *

OTHER GENERAL FICTION

*Lakota Spring*

*Ravenwolf* **

*Paul Radford's Private War*

*Abbas Barabbas* *

*Not currently in print.
**Available July 2006

# MURDER IN THE KIRK

## A Jazz Phillips Mystery

by

### Joel B. Reed

## White Turtle Books
### Canby, Minnesota

The fathers have eaten sour grapes and
their children's teeth are set on edge.

JEWISH PROVERB

ISBN 978-1-933482-40-8
Library of Congress Control Number 2006923731
Printed in the United States of America

Cover design © 2006, TLC Graphics
*www.TLCGgraphics.com*
Cover design by Jim Zachs
Interior design © 2006 Joel B. Reed
www.whiteturtlebooks.com

# In Appreciation

There were several people involved in the production of this book that I need to thank. First, and foremost, is my wife, Noell, whose constant good humor and patience has carried me over the twists and turns of getting the thing written. Then there is Marge Freking who edits all I publish, and whose suggestions I usually take. The flaws in this work are probably those I did not. Add Bobby McFall, whose eagle eye and memory for detail have prevented several major blunders. The Mustang on one page that mysteriously becomes a Trans-Am four pages later comes to mind.

The wonderful thing about being in this labor of love called publishing is getting to know these folk and others like them. Jim Zach, whom I have never met in person, comes to mind. His art graces the covers of this trilogy of Jazz Phillips stories, as does Tamara Dever of TLC Graphics, whose masterful coordination gets things done.

To all these folk, and others I may not have mentioned, I dedicate this imperfect work.

Forward through the murk!

JBR

# 1. Killing In Cowtown

I was in town when the bishop went down. So I was in on the case from the beginning. This was unusual. I don't investigate normal homicides these days. These cases are pretty simple and local detectives can do a better job than I can. They know the turf and they know the players. They have their own sources of information and their own personal networks. There are favors they can do and markers they can call in, and they clear a lot of murder cases following standard procedure.

When they call me in is when the ship hits the sand. Sometimes it's because an investigation of an important case has been botched. No one likes to admit he's made a mistake or gotten in over his head without knowing it and this is true in spades with cops. We like to call ourselves professional, but the truth is that most of us are neither well trained nor educated beyond the basics. So a lot of us get by on macho and bluff, and admitting a mistake is hard to do.

Yet mistakes are made, even by the best of us, and smart cops know when to ask for help. This is particularly true when a case draws a lot of media flash and the powers that be start pushing hard. A smart chief of police can call in someone like me to fade the heat. The chief gets the credit when I sort things out, and if I don't, I carry the blame. Either way, by hiring me at my outrageous rates, the chief has shown good faith and due diligence.

Even so, most of the homicide cases I'm called into involve multiple murders. Over the years I've developed a reputation for nailing serial killers or people who commit multiple homicides. There is a difference. A multiple killer is someone who finds it necessary to kill more than once and the motive is usually fear or greed. Multiple slayers kill to protect themselves or to gain power, like a mob boss. The victims stand between the killers and what they want and there is not the same intense emotional involvement with the victims. With a serial killer, like Jack the Ripper, the victim is what the killer wants. Murder is how they take possession.

It was over the years I spent with the Arkansas CID, the state Criminal Investigation Division, that I developed a reputation as an expert on serial and multiple murders. This was not something I chose. Nor was it a matter of luck. Yes, I was the investigator on tap when my first serial case came up, but I was also behind the political eight ball. One of the governor's cousins overextended himself pilfering state money and I caught the case. I was brand new and they must have thought I'd never figure it out. Even if I did, they never thought I'd make a case. When I did both, aforesaid cousin went to prison and the governor was pissed. The director of the CID was led to understand my presence was no longer desired.

The quickest way to ditch someone is to have them blow a major case. So I was the man for the job when one of the nastiest serial cases in Arkansas history broke. The plan was to throw me in over my head long enough for me to make a major mistake, and then to give it to another investigator to make sure it got solved. After that, they could either fire me or send me back to the highway patrol.

It might have worked if I hadn't been lucky. I was thrown together with a young medical examiner named K.C. Jones, who was in as deep caca with his boss as I was in with mine. When Casey was asked to do some things he thought were more than a little out of line, he gave me a heads-up. The plan was to nail us both at once by sabotaging lab results, but Casey was smart enough to cover his ass using an independent lab. The state made Casey pay the expenses out of his own pocket, of course, but he saved my job as well as his own. When I solved the case with Casey's help, it set off a political fire storm that shook up the CID and got us a boss who was more focused on enforcement than politics.

That's how I got started with serial killers. The next time a serial case came up, the new director handed it to me and Casey and we busted the hell out that one, too. After that, the director let me have my head and between serial cases I pursued my real passion, which is corporate crime. The irony is that it was that very passion that led me to the governor's cousin in the first place.

The rest of the story is pretty simple, but it's funny how things worked out. After I retired from the CID, I made the mistake of writing down what I know about murder by the numbers. I even called it that. It started as a simple article for a police journal that turned into a long book. To my surprise, it became a best seller among other investigators, and I found myself in demand as a consultant.

I was also much busier than I wanted to be, but I can't complain too much. It brought in enough money that we never had to touch anything I put away for retirement. It also gave Nellie and me time and money to travel, and it kept me from getting underfoot around the house the way some retired husbands do.

So I was in Cowtown when the bishop got hit and Chief Joe McClellan drafted me right away. Nor was there any way I could gracefully decline since I was already on his payroll for the week. The chief had brought me in for a training session with his junior investigators and I jumped at the chance to get out of Ft. Smith for a while. Dee and I were going through a slow time after an incredibly busy two years. There was not enough to keep us both busy. What cases we had fitted Dee's talents much better than mine.

Even so, there was a more urgent reason I wanted to get away. To put it simply, the house has never been the same since Nellie died. There are too many memories gathered there over too many years. Even after all these months now I still expect to see her smile when I walk into the kitchen in the morning or come home at night. And that's when it gets me, early in the morning and through the long evenings. So I work a lot and I travel and it helps.

Yet, staying busy doesn't always work and there is a downside to travel. There are always the empty hours after class and every time I explored all the wonderful places Ft. Worth has to offer, I couldn't help wishing Nellie was there to share them.

The afternoon the bishop got shot, I was having an early dinner by myself in a well known local place. About halfway through the meal, I caught myself starting to ask Nellie how she liked the food. It damned near broke my heart when I remembered she was gone and I choked up. I don't normally lose it in public, but that time I did. This got me some odd looks but I told the waiter in a louder voice than necessary that I was all right. I told him I'd bitten my tongue and everyone relaxed. I paid the bill and left a hefty tip. Then I got the hell out of there.

I was just walking in the door of my motel room when the phone rang. It was the chief asking me if I'd like to ride along to check out a crime scene. I was tired and felt wrung out, but I heard myself agreeing to go. This surprised me because I've never gotten used to the harsh realities of a crime scene. Nor do I understand people who have. Yet at that point, anything was preferable to spending another evening alone with my ghosts in a strange city. The second anniversary of Nellie's death had come and gone the week before and they were riding me hard.

The chief picked me up in his white Crown Victoria. I had to smile when I got into the car. Except for leather seats and the usual police equipment, it was a twin to my own car in Ft. Smith. I always get a chuckle out of the way other drivers hit the brakes when they see me coming, and looking like a police car has its uses in dealing with rude truckers. A car salesman once told me cops sit on their taste buds when it comes to cars, but that's not true. We do tend to be conservative but most of us will tell you that a Jaguar is pure sex on wheels and we'd love to drive one. The problem is the Jag doesn't fit departmental budgets or what we need in a car. (Try cramming someone big and handcuffed into a two-door coupe.) The Crown Vic works well and cannot be beat for reliability and comfort. We put a lot of miles on our cars and we don't need something that's always in the shop.

Chief Joe McClellan is not a cheerful soul and his mind was apparently on his own dark thoughts. We drove most of the way to the crime scene in brooding silence. Yet as we drove up a broad avenue to the crime scene, he surprised me by chuckling, though it sounded more like a sneeze. "See that big-ass church up there, Jazz?" He snorted, pointing. "That's where we're headed. Hell of a place for a crime scene, isn't it?"

I looked where the chief was pointing. High on a hill overlooking several acres of lawn was one of the largest churches I'd ever seen. Later on I found out this was a common mistake. The setting made the church seem much bigger than it was. The neighborhood where it sat was an older part of the city and the houses around the church were much smaller than most houses today. The church architect must have taken this into account, for the clean Gothic lines of the structure accentuated the height of the building. The whole effect was like a European cathedral, built for the ages, solid and unmoving.

Somehow, the sight of the church reminded me of a well known hymn, but I was still trying to figure out what it was when Joe interrupted my thoughts with another snort. I wondered if he was one of those strange people who found murder cheering.

"You know what local pastors call that big barn, Jazz?" he asked. I shook my head. "They call it Ft. God," he told me, snorting again.

For a moment I thought Mac had read my thoughts. The hymn I'd been trying to remember was "A Mighty Fortress." Then I laughed, too. "I can see why. All it needs is cannon ports. What is it, Catholic or Episcopal?"

"Neither one," Joe replied, clearly pleased to have information I did not. "It's not even Lutheran. It's honest-to-God Presbyterian."

I looked at the building again. The stone facing was a tawny color favored by many of the wealthier Presbyterian churches I've seen, but the red Spanish tile used on the roof of the nave seemed a little gauche for staid Calvinists. Even at this distance I saw the building was shaped in the cruciform favored by catholic traditions.

"Sure looks Spanish to me," I said. "Maybe Anglican."

Joe McClellan laughed again. "Looks Catholic as all get-out to me. They use a lot of tile like that in Santa Fe. Wait until you get inside. They got stained glass windows all over the place. They're the old fashioned kind with lots of lead and angels spearing devils. The only thing missing is all the statues." He must have realized how his remark might be taken. "No offense, Jazz. You're not Catholic are you?"

I assured him I was not and that no offense was taken. "Did I misunderstand?" I asked. "I thought you told me a bishop was killed."

"That's the odd thing," he answered. "The victim is a bishop. Not Catholic but an Episcopal."

"Any idea what he was doing in a Presbyterian church?" I asked.

"Not a one," the chief told me. "The first officer on the scene didn't know and the detectives weren't there yet when I got the call."

"Do they normally call you out on a homicide?" I asked. While the chief would know about the death through the chain of command, some micromanage more than others. I doubted this was standard procedure in Ft. Worth, but I needed to know.

"Almost never," McClellan answered. "They called me because this one is going to raise some heat." He gave me a jaundiced look. "Political heat."

That explained why he asked me along. "You mean because he's a bishop?"

Joe looked at me and grinned. It looked like he was baring his teeth to bite. "No, because this particular bishop is a real asshole and very public about it. And you didn't hear me say that, either, Jazz."

"Didn't hear you say what?" I asked, grinning back. Seven years as head of CID made me glad this was McClellan's problem and not mine.

"I'm going to let the investigators fill you in," he answered. "I want you coming in with a fresh mind."

"I don't want to get in their way, Joe," I answered. "They may resent me being dumped on them."

"They won't," he reassured me. "I gave you Adams and Kowalski. You know them from the course this week."

I had a vague impression to go with the names, but not much else. "All right, but they get credit for any collar," I said. "All I am is a consultant."

McClellan looked at me with surprise. "Hell, Jazz, I hoped you would head this one up all the way. On the job training for my best boys."

"I'm not a certified peace officer in Texas," I explained. "The law has changed and I'm not sure exactly what it is here."

"You are certified in Arkansas, aren't you?" McClellan asked. "You said you were current there. That's good enough."

"Yes, that's my deal with the state there," I answered. "As long as I consult with them I'm carried on the rolls as an active officer and I can carry a gun. I don't know how that translates here, or if it does."

"Aw, hell, Jazz," Joe replied. "You don't need to pack a pistol for this one. You got two officers to take care of you if you get in a crunch."

I was having trouble believing my ears. A common sense rule of law enforcement is that when you go after a murderer, you go armed. Some departments require their people to carry a pistol at all times, even off duty. "Let me get this straight. You want me to go after a murderer unarmed?"

The chief gave this some thought. "Yeah, you're right," he said. "I'll write you out a temporary permit when we get to the office. I guess you'll need a gun, too."

I was liking this less and less the more I heard. I know how things work and I know how lawyers are, particularly ambitious prosecutors. The problem would not come in carrying a weapon. The problem would occur if I had actually had to shoot someone, even in self defense. Thank God, I never had, but it's not reasonable to carry a gun if one doesn't accept that possibility. I certainly didn't want to get left hanging out to dry over a murder charge in Texas.

"Come to think of it, that's not necessary," I answered. "I'll carry a walking cane."

McClellan gave me a strange look, but nodded. At that moment I was tempted to get out of the car and thumb my way back to the motel. I hate manipulation and it felt like I'd just been had. I decided to push back. "One thing you need to understand, Joe. This is over and above the training fee. I'll have to charge you full rates and for extra expenses, too. My minimum is three days. Agreed?" Up to that point, I didn't have a minimum, but he didn't know that.

It was clear McClellan had been counting on a freebie and I was glad I'd put it on the table now. He didn't like it much, but he nodded.

"Good," I told him. "You can type me out a letter of intent when we get back to your office." I smiled reassuringly. "Don't worry. You'll get your money's worth." When I said it, I had no idea just how true that would be.

# 2. Crime Scene

The perspective from the road may have made the church seem bigger than it was, but when we arrived, the physical presence of the building was overpowering. Part of this was in the landscaping, particularly the trees. Several varieties of oaks are native to this part of the world, but live oaks are the only ones I know which are evergreen. I'm told they shed their leaves every year in the spring, when the new buds push the mature leaves off their branches, though I've never seen this. What I do know from seeing it is that live oaks and juniper are the main source of greenery through the deep winter season. There is little snow here, but things turn a universal tan and gray like they do in Arkansas, and the deep green of live oaks provides some welcome color.

I'm sure this must have been something the architect had in mind in choosing live oaks for the church grounds. Another could have been their slow rate of growth. I've seen huge live oaks in deep eastern Texas, but it takes a century or longer for them to reach the size of a twenty year old sweet gum in Arkansas. So I'm pretty sure the architect chose live oaks to accentuate the size of the building for a long time.

Whatever the reasons behind the choices, I was impressed. The church reminded me of European cathedrals whose designers intended the buildings to dominate the landscape and intimidate the people living under its shadow. It was a clever way to keep the peasants in line, reminding them every time they saw it of human transience and insignificance in the face of eternity.

As we pulled in, there were the usual assortment of police cars and crime scene vehicles parked near the massive front doors of the church. I counted three patrol cars, an EMS service unit, two sedans like the one we were in, and a fire truck. I was surprised to see the fire truck and asked the chief about it.

"I can't remember exactly why they do that," he told me. "It has something to do with Texas fire law. Every time one of our EMS buggies heads out, so does a fire unit. Seems like a waste of time and manpower to me, not to mention fuel."

I looked at the massive doors as we entered the building. They looked like solid brass, though I'm sure they were not. Even if they were hollow, it must have taken a crane to lift them into place. They were at least twenty-five feet high and fifteen across the bottom, and arched to a point. Every inch of their surface was decorated with what looked like biblical scenes. Again I wondered whether the massive gates were designed primarily to decorate or dominate. They clearly announced to the world that this was the Big Guy's house.

The chief saw my glance and read my thoughts. "The price of those doors could run my whole department for a long time," he laughed. "You wouldn't know these folk were Presbyterians, would you?"

"Calvin and Knox must be spinning in their graves," I said, laughing.

The chief gave me an odd look. "The guys in the funny papers?" he asked.

I was able to catch myself before I laughed out loud. "No, they were both big wheels back when the Presbyterian Church got started."

The chief nodded. "Ah. That must have been before my time."

About four hundred and fifty years, I thought, but I said nothing.

We crossed a massive expanse of flagstone and entered the church through a small set of doors set in the center of the massive cathedral gates. There was a wide, broad narthex floored in the same stone just inside, and an ornate carved wood and glass partition separated the narthex from the nave. I glanced up and saw a flat ceiling at least fifteen feet above us. Two ornate brass fixtures hung from the ceiling, barely providing enough light for us to see where we were going. Two stairways leading up on either end of the narthex told me we were probably beneath the choir loft.

One would think that with this kind of staging, I would have been prepared for what I encountered on the other side of the open nave doors, but I wasn't. There are places in this world where the sense of spiritual presence, both good and evil, is as tangible as a summer breeze. This church was such a place, filled with a benevolent presence that not even the subdued working of the crime scene crew could displace. Someone lived here, Someone or Something far beyond human understanding, and I understood why people came here. Even in the presence of murder, there was an overwhelming sense of peace. I felt tears coming to my eyes.

"Kind of hits you doesn't it," the chief murmured softly. I glanced at him and saw a hint of moisture in the corner of his eyes, too. He was looking upward at a vaulted ceiling seemingly so high above us it was hard to make out details. I later discovered this was another part of the architect's art, a deliberate softening of lines in the detail work to enhance the sense of height. Nor did this discovery diminish my appreciation for what the architect had accomplished. As Pablo Picasso pointed out, art is the lie that reveals whatever truth we are capable of understanding.

The chief sighed and looked at me. "I guess we better get to work," he said, I thought with a touch of reluctance. This was a side of the man I'd not seen and I decided I needed to revise my somewhat pejorative assessment of Mac. There was much more to Joe than he let on.

I decided to file this and think it through later. I almost made myself a note to do so, but refrained. The chief had learned about my habit of making myself notes and sticking them into my shirt pocket. I didn't want to have to explain that this one had nothing to do with the case.

One of the uniformed officers had seen us enter and was headed our way. "Sorry, chief," he said when he met us. "They needed my help for a minute." Clearly, he didn't want to be reprimanded for leaving his post by the door.

"All right, Morgan," the chief growled. "Just don't let anyone else in who doesn't belong here. The last thing we need is some reporter getting pictures."

The group standing in the transept moved aside when we arrived and we could see a body lying across the carpeted steps leading to the altar gate. It looked like it had been casually thrown there, as if a giant child had tossed aside a rag doll which no longer held its interest. There was no question it was dead. Even at this distance I could sense it. The body was like a deserted house. No one was home.

This doll, however, was a white male of middle years. From what I could see, he looked fairly tall, but quite muscular. He was dressed in black wool trousers and black socks extending above the raised cuff line on one leg, and his feet were covered in high gloss wingtips. They were black, but not patent leather, and someone had invested a good deal of energy in getting that shine. We learned later on it was a professional job.

The body was also wearing a well cut suit jacket that matched the pants. The jacket was open and we could see a red bloodstain on the shirt just above the bottom of the sternum. The stain looked about the size and color of an eggplant, and there was a dark spot the size of my finger at the top center of the stain. The size of the spot and what looked like torn fabric around it suggested the victim had been stabbed, though I couldn't see any sign of a weapon near the body.

What was unusual about this corpse was the color of the shirt, which was dark pink or maroon, with a wide white dog collar enclosing the neck. Even with the bright crime scene lights, it was hard to tell the exact color of the shirt because of the light filtering through the stained glass windows lining the narthex and at each end of the transept. They were mostly shades of dark blue and green, with accents in red and yellow, and in the light reflected from the tan stone walls and floor, people's faces took on an odd pallor.

"Can we take a look now?" the chief asked one of the crime scene photographers standing idly at one side.

"We're done until the medical examiner gets here," the photographer answered. "So you can look, but don't touch," she added, earning herself a glower from the chief. "I'm sorry, sir," she apologized. "It's automatic."

"You're just doing your job," I assured her. "No problem." The photographer smiled gratefully, but I saw she was not convinced until the chief looked at her and nodded.

"How long have you been waiting for the ME?" the chief asked. He leaned over the corpse for a preliminary look, taking out a small black flashlight and turning it on. The bright beam seemed unnaturally white.

"About forty-five minutes, sir. The ME was in court."

I took out my own flashlight and turned it on. When I did, something on the stone floor to the right of the body caught the light and I moved forward to see what it was. I felt something grate under my foot when I moved and there was a scraping noise, but I couldn't see what I'd stepped on.

"What do you see?" the chief asked, turning in my direction. I waved for a place marker and a technician handed me one. He was careful to move between the pews rather than straight across the transept floor. "Looks like a piece of colored glass," I said, placing the V-shaped marker over the glass. "About the size of a pea." I looked around and saw other pieces of glass between me and the body. They were barely visible in the dim light. "There's more all around here." The technician handed me more markers and I placed them over the biggest pieces of glass. When I was done, I was standing just a few feet from the victim.

When I looked back at the markers I'd laid down, I saw a pattern. They were spread out like a fan half way down the transept, with the large piece I saw first at the point of the fan. I glanced up to see where they might have come from and my eyes were drawn to the large stained glass window at the end of the transept. The bottom of the window was about eight feet above the flagstone floor, and I thought I saw a bright spot near the bottom.

To keep from disturbing the glass, I moved back up the center aisle a couple of rows and made my way between the pews to the base of the window. I stepped back a pace and looked up. Sure enough, there appeared to be a hole punched through one of the larger pieces of stained glass. What was odd was it was shaped like a figure eight, with the top of the hole visibly larger than the bottom.

"Looks like a bullet hole here," I called to the chief. At that point I understood why the hole in the victim's shirt was so big. Any bullet striking heavy stained glass would tend to flatten out and could even tumble, making a much larger entry wound. It could also have carried fragments of glass into the body. This would also explain why the stain on the shirt was so big and the edges of the fabric were frayed. "You think he was shot?"

"Almost certain," the chief called back. "Come over here and look at the body."

I made my way back across the pews toward the center aisle when I saw a large, familiar figure striding through the narthex doors. I stopped and waited for the man to reach me. "Hello, Simon!" I greeted him. "When did they let you out?"

"Jazz, baby!" Simon greeted me warmly, extending a hand that could envelop half a cantaloupe. "I heard you were in town. I see Mac has you doing some honest work for a change."

Simon Smyth is one of the legends of forensic medicine. He must be in his late sixties by now, maybe older, and there are different theories why he chooses to remain in Ft. Worth. I know he has been offered tenured positions on the faculty of prestigious universities where he often lectures. At a seminar I was giving in Boston I overheard one of their deans complaining that Simon had turned them down.

"What would I want with Boston?" he replied when I asked him about this the next time I saw him. "I don't sip tea and I don't snob all over town. Yes, I get a fancy car there, maybe even a BMW. But there I can't drive my old pickup. There I can't wear my cowboy hat. There I got to clean the cow shit off my boots. Here, I got what I love. Here I got real people, Jazz. Here I get respect and country music. Where else can I live called Cowtown? Bean Town just don't pack it."

I followed Simon up the main aisle to the body, having to almost trot to keep up. When we got there, Smyth stopped and looked over the scene, taking in every detail, no matter how small. Even though his photographers would take several rolls of film, and Simon insisted on film, not digital images, Simon rarely used these images except for evidence or to show someone else a critical detail only Simon had noticed.

Once he was done memorizing the scene, or "Simonizing" it, as his assistants called this, Smyth waved for Mac and me to join him at the body. He reached out a huge paw and picked up a large ornate gold cross flung back over the victim's right shoulder. I had not noticed the cross before, though I'd seen the heavy gold chain across the victim's neck. "Would you look at that!" he said. There was a large hole about the size of the one in the shirt punched through the center of the cross. "Dead center. You should pardon the pun."

I reached out and took the cross. It was thick and very heavy. I guessed it must be made of high carat gold. Slipping on my reading glasses, I examined the back carefully. The hole was oblong, not quite round, and the raised lips were very sharp and irregular. I pointed this out, and Simon nodded. "So what does that tell you?" he asked, challenging me.

"Not enough evidence, Simon," I chuckled, dodging his trap. "It helps explain the tears in the shirt fabric."

Simon beamed at me with approval. "No galloping senility for you, Jazz. Turn it over now."

When I did, I saw why the hole was oblong. There was a deep round ring of flat metal for mounting what had been a large stone. "Billiards!" declared Simon. When I looked up for an explanation, he continued. "Eight ball in the hip pocket. Bullet hits stone and punches out gold, right through the sternum. My guess is we will find gold lodged in the heart and pieces of stone all over the lungs. God only knows where the bullet ended up or if anything is left of it."

One of the plain-clothes people looked at us like we were speaking Mandarin, so I translated. "It looks like the bullet hit whatever stone was mounted here and punched through the back, knocking a piece of gold into the heart. The stone was probably shattered and hit the lungs like birdshot." I shook my head. "I can't figure out how it did all that damage after punching through the window." I pointed to the hole in the stained glass.

"Ah, your eyes are sharper than mine, Jazz," Simon said. He squinted. "I didn't see the hole there until you pointed it out," he complained. "I must be going blind. So all that must be glass," he concluded, pointing at the fan of evidence markers on the transept floor.

I nodded and Simon thought about this a moment. "No!" he said. "Maybe, but I don't think so. How could he see where he was shooting? And what kind of bullet holds together through glass but shatters when it hits stone? Or maybe it didn't. Maybe it lodged inside. But how did it have enough power to do all this?" He shook his head. "I think there is something not quite kosher here. We'll see when we get the body to the lab."

Even though he talks like a Jew from Brooklyn, I happen to know Simon is a very devout Catholic who grew up in San Francisco. Yet over the years, the things he has said leads me to think there is a Jewish connection somewhere in the family. I would guess it was one of his grandmothers who lived with his family while he was growing up. Even though Scotland is two generations back in my own family, I spent a lot of time with a grandfather who was born there, and I can drop into a soft Midlands burr without knowing it. I also think Simon finds it useful to be a real character. Cowtown is full of these, which is one of the reasons I like it there, but Simon is unique. Even the local characters describe him as a real character.

Simon reached down and gently turned the body over. As he predicted, there was no exit wound in the back, but to make sure, he went over it carefully with a powerful flashlight. He also felt the surface of the coat with his palm, I think for projectiles that lodged just under the skin. It's odd how often that happens in shooting cases.

Skin is very tough and very plastic. It's hard to penetrate from either direction, particularly by something like a bullet with a rounded nose.

Simon rolled the body back into it original position and looked more closely at the face. "A heavy drinker," he said. I looked for whatever evidence might have led him to this observation, but couldn't see it. "Just a guess," Simon answered me. "No hard evidence at this point, but there will be. I'm almost sure of it. He has the look."

"The look?" Mac asked. "I don't see any broken capillaries."

"Not veins," Simon answered. "Stress. Alcoholics have a very tight, stressed look. It's quite unique once you recognize it." He grinned. "Want to bet he doesn't have bad hemorrhoids?"

We looked around a bit more, but nothing caught our attention. I had noticed a pair of plain-clothes officers in the crowd when we came in and was aware of them watching every move we made. I knew they were not long out of the squad car and both of them were attending my investigation seminar. I had nodded to them when we came in, but we had not spoken. They had kept a respectful distance when the chief and I were talking, and after Simon arrived, listened carefully. Now one of them touched my arm lightly. "Excuse me, Dr. Phillips," he said softly.

"Yes... Adams, isn't it?" He nodded, pleased I'd remembered his name. "And that's Kowalski, right?" I pointed to the other new officer. He nodded again. "Why does she have that stepladder?"

"That's what we wanted to ask you about," Adams said. "We thought it might be helpful to look at the bullet hole. You know, back along the line of sight."

"You guys are on the ball," I said, wondering why they were asking me about it rather than the chief. "Why don't you set up over there by the window?" I pointed to the one with the hole. "Just check the floor out carefully before you set up."

The chief looked up when Adams and Kowalski moved across the nave toward the east transept and started to say something. Then he looked to me, his brows raised in question. I nodded and he went back to what he was doing. Again, I wondered why he looked to me and not to whoever the senior investigator might be. I decided to ask him about this.

The chief was standing by himself looking around the church, so I walked over to him. "Who is your lead investigator for this case?" I asked.

The chief looked at me, surprised. "You are, Jazz. I thought I made that clear in the car."

"We've been through this, Mac," I reminded him. "I don't have official standing here. I'm just a consultant. I'm not a sworn officer in Texas and I'm not a resident. I'm not sure I can even make a citizen's arrest. I don't mind helping out, but you need someone local to sign off on the legal stuff."

"I thought we settled that," Mac replied. "I'll deputize you."

"Mac, listen to me. Can you imagine what a defense lawyer could do with that? I don't want to lose a case over a technicality. Do you? The media would have a field day at our expense."

I think it was that last argument that got the chief to see the light. He nodded but frowned. "We're stretched pretty thin now, Jazz. I don't have any senior guys who I can shift over."

"Which one of the two has seniority, Adams or Kowalski?"

"Kowalski," he said. "She's been on the force a couple of years longer, but she's as green as he is. He made detective a couple of days ahead of her."

"Then designate her as lead investigator and let me supervise," I suggested. "Is there some reason you wouldn't want her as lead?"

"No, she's as sharp as they come. She should have been promoted three years ago. My predecessor was a little old school about women cops. He wasn't too fond of Hispanics, either." He thought for a moment. "All right, I'll tell them."

Mac called the two investigators over and explained our roles. "You're lead officer on this one, Kowalski," he told her. "But consider this a training exercise. Jazz will be your supervisor, so do everything he tells you."

I was watching Adams closely while the chief spoke. He nodded when the chief told them this, and I had the impression he was relieved. From the start, Adams had struck me as a man who was more comfortable following than taking the lead. There also seemed to be good rapport between him and Kowalski.

"Now," said the chief, "what did you find over by the window?"

"We're still looking," Kowalski told him, falling into the lead. "One thing we did spot was a possible source for the shot." I noticed she was very careful to include her partner as she reported. "It may not be a straight line, but it seems to match the line of fire better than anything else."

"Yeah?" the chief said. "Let's take a look."

We made our way over to the end of the transept and the chief climbed the step ladder, stooping to peer out the hole in the glass. "Well, I'll be damned," he said. "The water tower. Good work! You guys get over there and see what you find."

Kowalski was careful not to look at me. She and Adams started to take down the ladder, but I stopped them. "Let me take a look, if you don't mind," I said. The chief looked surprised, but stepped aside.

"I see what you mean," I told Kowalski, looking out the hole. "It's slightly out of the line of fire, but I guess it could have be deflected by the glass. What did you make of the holes in the glass."

"The break looked funny to me," Kowalski replied. "The hole is pretty jagged, but I guess that could be from irregularities in the glass. It's not a flat surface."

"You think it could be two holes?" I asked.

"I wondered that," Kowalski replied. "So did Jim." She nodded toward Adams.

"Yeah," said Adams. "It looks almost like something hit it from inside after the bullet came through."

"You never know with stained glass," the chief interjected. "My wife works with the stuff as a hobby and she's always complaining about the strange way it breaks. Old glass is worse than new."

"Any idea how old these windows are?" I asked.

"They are only five years old, officer," a voice came from behind us. "The glass may be older, but we had the windows made for us five years ago. They look old because that's what we asked for, a medieval look."

We all turned around. The speaker was a tall, distinguished man in a suit that was obviously tailored for his lanky frame. His face was tanned, despite the season, and carefully groomed grey hair swept back in a distinctly European cut. Under his suit jacket he wore a simple black mock turtleneck that probably cost more than three of my dress shirts. Even though he had gray at the temples and streaked through his neatly trimmed Van Dyke, I would have guessed he was in his middle thirties.

"Who are you?" Kowalski asked before the chief could speak. I hoped she didn't get too badly bruised exercising the lead she had been given. On the other hand, the chief had put her in charge. I glanced at him and saw a smile teasing the corners of his mouth.

"Oh, excuse me, officer," the man said. "I thought you knew. I'm Karl Mann. I'm the organist and choir director here."

"What brings you here this afternoon?" Adams spoke up, following Kowalski's lead. His tone was courteous but required an answer.

"I was the one meeting with the bishop," Mann answered. "We were planning the ordination of his suffragan next week. Who are you?"

The man was entirely too assured for someone who had just been doing business with someone else who had just been shot. Kowalski made introductions quickly, then asked, "Were you here when he was shot?"

"No, thank God," Mann said. "That would have been awful. I had gone back to my office to get some sheet music. Then I got stuck on the phone."

"How long were you gone?" Adams asked. He reminded me of a bull terrier I had as a kid, pleasant and easy going until he got his teeth into something.

"I'm not sure. Five minutes, maybe. Eight or ten minutes at the most."

"What was the phone call about?" Kowalski wanted to know.

"It was strange," Mann told her. "I was told it had something to do with my car insurance being revoked, but then I was put on hold.

I must have waited for four or five minutes. Then I called my agent and asked him to look into it."

"Who is your agent, sir?" Adams asked politely. He carefully wrote down the name and phone number Mann gave him. "Have you heard back from him?"

"Yes," Mann replied. "I just got off the phone with him. The whole thing was some kind of mistake. The home office knew nothing about it."

Kowalski looked at me and I shook my head. She was doing fine. The insurance call might have something to do with the case but more than likely it did not. These things seem to happen quite often these days, probably as a result of corporate downsizing. On the other hand, someone needed to check.

"Were you the one who found the body?" Adams asked.

"No, it was our sexton. I'm afraid it gave him quite a shock. He has heart trouble, you know." Again, it seemed to me that Mann was far too calm for someone who had been so close to sudden and violent death.

"When did you come in?" Kowalski asked.

"I came running when I heard Greg shouting for help," Mann replied. "I thought he was having a heart attack. I'm not sure he wasn't. It must have been quite a shock to see the bishop lying there all bloody."

There was a brief pause. "Is he lying where you first saw him?" I asked, pointing to the body.

"Yes, pretty much. I'm afraid we may have moved him trying to see if he was still alive." Mann shook his head. "He wasn't, of course. I knew right away that he was dead, but we had to check."

"How did you know he was dead?" Adams cut in.

"I haven't been a musician all my life, officer," Mann answered. "I earned my way through music school working at a mortuary."

That went a long way toward explaining why Mann was so calm. Depending on the mortuary, he had more than likely seen more than his share of violent death. It loses its power to shock after a while, and having had to help with funerals, Mann would have had to learn to suppress his own feelings. I decided to take a shot in the dark. "You seem very calm for someone who has just seen all this, Dr. Mann," I observed.

For a fleeting moment there was a very bleak look in Mann's eyes. "That's just my professional training, Dr. Phillips, mortuary training. I don't give myself the luxury of falling apart until I'm alone. I imagine you understand what I'm saying."

"Of course," I replied. "I had to ask."

Mann gave me a wintry smile. "Yes, I know. What else can I tell you?"

Kowalski and Adams kept after him for a while longer, but there wasn't much else Mann could tell them. They were a bit too thorough, the way new investigators tend to be, but I didn't fault them for this. They were going by the book. I knew because I had written it.

One thing that surprised me was when they asked for Mann's prints. Nor was there any mistaking his displeasure when they asked. "Is it really necessary?" he asked, looking at his hands. "It's so messy and it's hard to wash off the ink."

"Not a problem, Dr. Mann," Adams said cheerfully. "We use electronic scanners these days." He called out to one of the lab technicians who brought something over that looked like a small laptop computer. The technician cleaned the screen and had Mann place his hand flat on it. A scanning light came on and moved across the screen quickly. Then the technician had Mann place his thumb flat on another area of the screen. When that was scanned, the technician cleaned the screen and the process was repeated with the other hand. I'd heard of these things, but I'd never seen one in action.

"There, we're all done," said Adams. "No muss, no fuss. No ink residue."

Mann looked at his hand. "All right. What more do you need from me, officer?"

Kowalski told him they were done for the moment, but that they might have more questions for him. She and Adams headed out to check the water tower. What little light remained from the day was going fast, and they didn't expect to find much, but they needed to take a preliminary look. Since Simon would be doing the first session at the seminar the next morning, I arranged to have Jim Adams pick me up on his way to work early the next morning. Kowalski lived on this end of town and would meet us at the water tower at first light.

I drifted back up the aisle toward the body. The forensics team was bagging it for the morgue and Joe McClellan was talking to one of the uniformed officers. Simon was supervising the bagging and stopped for a word with me on his way out.

"I didn't get to say it before, Jazz, but I was really sad to hear about Nellie."

"Thanks, Simon," I replied. "I really appreciated your note and the flowers."

"That's what your letter said. I just wish I could have been there. Claire, too. She and I really thought the world of Nellie. How you doing?"

"All right, Simon. There are good days and days not so good. I try to stay busy."

"So I hear," he answered. "I hear you are doing some good work for a mutual friend of ours back East. A real cowboy."

I glanced at Smyth, trying to hide my surprise. He laughed. "I know, us spooks ain't supposed to talk about it. Or should I say 'consultants'?" He chuckled. "As if they would let us know anything important. Sam is very worried about you. Not about your work, about you, personally. He asked me to check with you while you were here."

Sam McKee, the acting head of a shadowy quasi-governmental organization I only know as the Agency, is a new friend. He goes by the sobriquet of Cowboy, and I've seen him ride roughshod over what he considers bureaucratic foolishness. Yet, he is someone I've come to respect highly for who he is as well as for how he does things. He did me a great service putting me to work in the area of my real passion, which is organized corporate crime.

Nor was this charity on McKee's part. He understands clearly that corporate multinational crime is a far greater threat to the free world than terrorists ever will be. Networks like Al Qaeda will never hold a candle to crooked boardrooms, and the scariest are the ones we know nothing about.

What McKee has kept me busy with is a cartel of multinational crooks called the Cadre and I've spent a lot of the last year in Washington. Yet, I also suspect Sam was instrumental in my being offered a number of consulting jobs with police departments outside my own professional network. These days I do a lot of seminars with departments I've never been in touch with, like the one I was doing in Ft. Worth. While I realize that part of this is because of my books, I also know some of it has been McKee looking out for me.

Even so, McKee had not told me Simon would be in touch, so I was very careful how I answered. The last thing I wanted to do was cause McKee trouble. "There are lots of cowboys in this business, Simon and I seem to work with a lot of them." I gave his hat a pointed look and reinforced this looking down at his pointed boots. "Dee and I've been pretty busy this last year."

"DiRado?" Simon asked. "I heard he retired and bought a bait shop."

I laughed. "He did, Simon, but you know Dee. After the first season he was climbing the walls, so I pushed some business his way. He was always sort of a computer guy, at least by my standards. He handles a lot of the research I don't have patience to learn to do." What I didn't add was that Dee also did a lot of research for McKee.

Simon nodded and gave me a searching look. "So what do you do for fun, Jazz? You can't work all day every day."

"I'm still chasing light," I told him. "I had one photo that won a national prize this last year. What the judges didn't know was it was from a crime scene. You remember the Smiley Jones case a couple of years back?" Simon nodded. "It was from a photo I took for that case. It was no good for evidence, but it turned out stunning."

"I guess it's too early for you to be seeing someone?"

I nodded. "I don't even think about it much, Simon. Something is missing. I think it's called a heart. I'm not sure I want it back."

Again Simon nodded. "I was that way after my first wife was killed, even though I was only thirty and still full of hormones. It was like something switched off inside me. Then a couple of years later I met Claire. It was like in those movies when the warden throws the big switch to the electric chair." He smiled. "Thirty years now, and it's still that way. Give it time, Jazz. It will come back."

I had a momentary flash of Jeanne's face. I had not seen her since Nellie's funeral though her every feature was etched in my mind. This was followed by an odd surge of remorse. "As I said, I'm not sure I want it to. The memories are pretty rich."

"'The memories are ghosts that haunt us," Simon corrected gently. "I know, Jazz. I've been there. You need more than memories. You got too much life in you."

I didn't know quite how to respond. "I know. I know," Simon said waving a hand that could swallow a softball. "An old fart meddler, you don't need. But you come have dinner with me and Claire, all right?"

I agreed and Simon said he would call me to set a time if he didn't see me the next day. I agreed. I told him where I was staying and the room number. I laughed when Simon carefully wrote this down. "Why do you need to do that?" I asked. "You carry every single detail of every crime scene you've ever worked in your head."

"I know, Claire asks me the same thing," Simon admitted, embarrassed. "For phone numbers I've no head, not even for my own."

"Are you about ready to go, Jazz?" I turned to see Joe McClellan approaching us. I also saw something happen in Simon's eyes, though he was still smiling. For some reason Simon didn't trust the Chief of Police, and I wondered what lay behind it.

# 3. Ghosts In The Night

When I got back to my room, I felt depressed. So I changed into my running stuff. I don't run much these days, but walking is part of my continuing battle with gravity and I try to get in a couple of miles a day. Since this was not the best part of town to walk at this late hour, I went to the front desk and persuaded the night auditor to let me into the exercise room. After assuring him that I would only use the treadmill, and contributing a ten-spot to his welfare fund, he let me in. He insisted that I clip the safety line to my waistband and waited to make sure I was doing all right before he left. I think he was afraid this old man would have a heart attack on his shift, and I had fun imagining the story he might tell to cover his butt if I did. I decided he'd say the room had apparently not been locked, though he would claim to have checked it at the beginning of his shift.

Not that I had any room to judge the man, I reminded myself. After all, I was the one who offered the bribe.

After trying to wear out the treadmill at a fast clip for almost three miles, I had enough. I was sweating freely and breathing heavily, but I felt much better. However, I was also wide awake and I knew it would be at least an hour before I settled down enough to sleep, so I spent a few minutes making case notes on the murder. I also looked at my pocket notes, but there was nothing urgent there so I switched on the television. About all there was on at the time was heavy on sex and violence, or reruns I've watched too many times late at night. So

I switched off the television and sat there alone with my thoughts.

I'm not a religious person, but I do pray. It's an agnostic prayer, To Whom It May Concern, and I don't know if anyone is listening on the other end. Yet, it seems to help me make it through the long hours of insomnia, and over the years I've memorized a number of the Psalms. The crusty old chaplain I talk to about everything under the sun tells me the Psalter is the prayer book of the second Jewish temple, rebuilt after the Babylonian exile, and I've found a great deal of solace there. That night I found the opening lines of Psalm 130 drifting through my thoughts.

> *Out of the depths have I called to you, O Lord;*
> *hear my voice and let your ears consider well*
> *the voice of my supplication.*

This surprised me, as the Psalms often do, and I sat thinking why this particular passage came to mind. Then I remembered what had happened at supper earlier that day and I knew. A wave of human loneliness washed over me, so strong I could barely contain it, and despite the hour, I picked up the phone and called the old chaplain. He would grump about it with a lot of good humor the next time he saw me, directing his umbrage toward the Hound of Heaven for not tracking me down at a decent hour, but if he found out I hadn't called for fear of waking him, he would really be pissed. Nor would it be at the Hound of Heaven, but at me.

His phone went unanswered. The old codger refuses to learn how to install or use an answering machine, claiming his Boss will make sure any urgent call gets through. And until that night I couldn't disagree. Then I remembered Forster had told me he would be making an annual month's retreat in New Mexico, and had sent me a post card with the number where he could be reached in an emergency. The post card was resting on my desk in Ft. Smith.

I'm not one to panic. Yet, I felt very close to it for a scary moment. Nor could I tell why this hit me. Fear is something I understand very well. It goes with being a police officer and those who survive tend to be cautious. Blind panic is something else. It's like being hit by lightning. It comes out of nowhere and sweeps reason away like an avalanche plowing under a whole village, and the only thing to do is to get out of its path before it carries you away.

What I've found that works for me when panic strikes is to focus on specific fears. It's like bird hunting. Flock shooting rarely bags even a single bird. A hunter has to single out one target at a time. The paradox is that when you hunt this way, it is not at all uncommon to get two birds with a single shot. Facing one fear can resolve others.

What's the worst that can happen? I asked myself, as I've learned to do. The answer came back quickly. You can die unloved and alone.

What about Zilpha and the kids? They love me. But I knew the answer to that one, too. They can't hold you in the terrors of the night, Grampajazz.

I reached for the phone again, intending to call Jeanne, but my fingers froze half way through dialing. I picked up my planner and looked up another number, then dialed it quickly before I could change my mind.

"Hello?" said a familiar voice from the other end. I was relieved to hear no sleep in the voice.

"Hi, Lindy. This is Jazz. I hope I didn't wake you."

"Heavens no, Jazz. I'm a night owl since I stopped drinking and it isn't even ten here. Where are you?"

"I'm in Ft. Worth, on business. I just needed to talk to someone." I knew Lindy would hear what I left unsaid, someone I trust. Not only is she Jeanne's sister, she is also a licensed psychologist, both in Arkansas and in California where she lives.

"What's wrong?" she asked.

"Nothing urgent. I'm just feeling blue and a long way from home. I needed to hear a friendly voice."

"Nothing urgent at what, midnight where you are? Come on, Jazz, this is Lindy. Or do you mean Home with a capital H?"

"You got it. I feel like a stranger in a strange land, even in Ft. Smith."

"Have you talked to Forster about this?" Lindy asked. She knew I'd been doing a lot of counseling with the old chaplain. He is one of the few clergy she respects.

"No, he's on retreat at some monastery in New Mexico. I can't remember where and I don't have his number with me."

"All right. I'm glad you called. Hold on just a minute." I heard the soft music in the background stop suddenly. A moment later she was back. "OK, you have my full attention. It sounds like you're grieving. What's it been, almost two years now?"

"Two years last Thursday."

"And it's just now hitting you?"

I laughed bitterly. "It's just now hurting enough to call." I told her what happened at the restaurant.

"Yeah, it's tough carrying it alone. Cops have a pretty heavy burden with that."

As always, Lindy was right on target. Police are trained to remain calm in every situation. This helps us stay alive but it can come back to bite us in the ass when we try to macho our way through. Not many of us learn that when we don't deal with our own issues, they deal with us. When they do, they come at us sideways, from a blind spot. "I didn't know I was carrying it alone," I replied. "I talk to Forster."

"How often, Jazz? Every week?"

"Oh, every two or three weeks. Whenever I feel the need."

"When you let yourself feel the need," she corrected me gently. "Do you talk to anyone else, Jazz? Like a survivor's support group?" I admitted I didn't.

"That doesn't surprise me. Do you talk to anybody about anything but work? You know, fishing or stamp collecting or bitching about women or the president?"

I laughed. "I could do a lot of that," I answered. "About the president. There aren't many women in my life to bitch about these days. But, no, I don't talk to anyone about much besides work."

"You used to talk to Nellie about everything, didn't you?"

I tried to answer, but I choked. For the second time that day I lost it completely, but this time I let it out. I don't know how long I cried, but when I was done I felt completely spent. "Thanks," I said. "I guess I needed that."

"We all do from time to time, Jazz. It's just hard for men to let it go. I do have a question for you when you're ready."

"I'm not sure I can give an intelligent answer, but go ahead."

"Why are you talking to me?"

That stopped me. "I thought you knew. I trust you, Lindy."

"That's not what I meant. Why are you talking to me and not Jeanne?"

The silence grew heavy before I answered. "I started to call her just before I called you but it just doesn't seem right."

"Why not? She told me you called several of times before this. You called just last week, in fact. Why not today?"

I was overwhelmed with confusion. "It didn't seem quite right?" Even in my state of confusion I could hear what I said was a question, not a statement.

Lindy was silent for a moment. "What didn't seem right about it?" she asked.

"Calling her when I miss Nellie. That would feel like I'm using Jeanne, Lindy."

Lindy sighed. "Yeah, I understand how you could think that. Let me reframe it and say it another way. Calling her is what I'd call mutual support. There's nothing wrong with reaching out for support. I seem to remember both of us reaching out to you a while back. Or does it only work one way?"

I sighed. "I guess not, since you put it that way."

"No, Jazz!" Lindy almost shouted. "You really don't believe me, do you?"

The woman had me pegged. "Guilty as charged," I laughed.

"This is no laughing matter, Jazz," Lindy said gently. "You believe in your heart of hearts that reaching out to Jeanne would be betraying Nellie's memory, don't you?"

"Yeah, that's exactly how it feels."

"Do you honestly think Nellie would feel betrayed?"

I thought about our conversations in the last months of her life. "I don't know. She told me she wanted me to get on with my life when she was gone. I even had a dream about it. That was when I called

Jeanne the first time a few months ago. No, it's almost a year ago."

"Well, I got to know Nellie pretty well before she died," Lindy told me. "I know she loved you with all her heart and I know she loved Jeanne almost as much. She told us both to look after you."

"I didn't know that," I said. "She never told me."

"I know she left you a long letter," Lindy said. "At least, that's what she told me. She also told me she had written one to Jeanne."

"I didn't know that, either," I told her. "I found her letter, but I couldn't read it. It was just too painful."

"I think you need to read it, Jazz. I think Nellie left you some marching orders."

"You're probably right. No, I'm sure you're right. That sounds like Nellie. I just can't get my mind around it yet. It doesn't make any sense, I know, but I can't. I still feel married."

"Is it a religious issue?" Lindy asked. "Jeanne is a married woman. At this point, it's a technicality. You know how much she despises Henry. If he weren't in a nursing home I think she'd leave him."

"I don't think it's a religious issue," I answered. "I was raised a Southern Baptist, with all the baggage that goes with that. I don't believe that stuff in my head any more but maybe I do in my soul."

"I don't think her being married is the issue at all," Lindy sold me. "I think you know that if you asked, Jeanne would leave Henry in a flash. It's bad enough the way he lied to her, but the man's a Nazi and a serial killer."

"I couldn't ask her to do that," I replied. "That wouldn't be right."

"Why, because he's in a nursing home? Or because some of your friends like Walter might not approve? Think about it, Jazz. Henry hurt Walter pretty badly, too. He used him the same way he used Jeanne. I think if you asked Walter, he'd ask you what the hell you're waiting for."

I sighed. "I wish I had a sister-in-law like you," I said without thinking.

"That can be arranged," Lindy laughed dryly. "It doesn't even have to be legal. Look, are you going to make me get out my shotgun, Jazz? Call her, right now."

"She's sound asleep!" I protested.

"I don't care!" Lindy almost shouted. "Jazz, if you don't call her, I will! Then she'll call you, as sure as God made little green apples."

"You women!" I whined. "A guy can't win."

"You got that right, sweetie, now hang up and call Jeanne!" I could hear Lindy laughing as she rang off.

Two hours later, I hung up the phone. Even though I was exhausted, I knew I couldn't sleep. So I lay back and played the conversation over again in my mind.

When Jeanne first answered the phone, her voice was full of sleep and I froze. My voice just wouldn't work, and Jeanne became alarmed, thinking I was an anonymous caller. When I was able to gasp out my name, she became even more alarmed. "What's wrong, Jazz? Where are you?"

For the third time in less than twelve hours, the tears began to run. Somehow I managed to croak out, "Nothing. I'm just feeling lonely. I wanted to hear your voice."

"I've been hoping you'd call. Did you get my card? I mailed it last week."

"I must have missed it. I've been in Ft. Worth all week. I'm giving a seminar here."

"Cowtown!" she said. "That's my favorite city. You ever been to Billy Bob's?"

"Never have," I told her. "The closest I've come is the Spaghetti Factory in the old packing house."

"I wish I was there with you," Jeanne said, dropping into a nasal twang. "We could do some real country shit-kickin'. You like to dance, Jazz?"

I laughed. "I used to. I'm afraid I'm an old Arthur Murray slow dancer. I used to do a mean waltz."

"How about polka? You like to polka?" I snickered and Jeanne laughed, realizing what she'd just said. "My goodness, Dr. Phillips, you seem to bring out the earthy side of me."

"I'd love to have you here, Jeanne," I told her. "I'd love to hold you in my arms all night long."

"I can be there in four hours," Jeanne told me. "You just tell me where to come." She broke out laughing again.

"I'm on a case, Jeanne." I told her about the bishop's strange death. "I don't know how much time we'd have to spend together. Tomorrow is the last day of my seminar, but I planned to stay over the weekend."

"I don't care, Jazz. I'd wait all day at the motel just to hold your hand for an hour." Then she giggled. "Of course, a girl can't help hoping it would be more than holding hands. Seriously, Jazz, I want to be there, and I won't be a burden. I've got a world of credit cards that need filling and Dallas has some wonderful stores."

"Are you sure it's all right, Jeanne? I'd love to see you. I don't think this case is going anywhere and we could spend most of the weekend together."

"I could take you to Billy Bob's!" Jeanne giggled. "Would you let me buy you a cowboy shirt and some shit-kicking boots?"

Despite my concern, I laughed. Jeanne's delight was contagious. "I'd love it, but you better let me get the boots," I told her. "I'm a little hard to fit."

We bantered back and forth about that a while, and I wondered later why I had been so concerned about calling Jeanne. Yet, even as the question crossed my mind, I knew exactly why. Losing Nellie to cancer was the worst thing that ever happened to me. To let Jeanne into my heart and into my life would mean going through that kind of loss again. It might not be for a long time, but it would come. I was not sure I could survive it a second time. I wasn't sure I wanted to try.

Even so, being alive without that kind of love and intimacy is not really living. It's letting despair prevail, and that runs against everything I am. I understand the Irish custom of going into the fields after a funeral and making love until dawn. What better way to say, "Fuck you, Death! Up yours, Despair!" Yet, thinking such things is much easier than living the truth they embody, and I had to literally force myself not to turn Jeanne down.

As it turned out, Jeanne had never been to the Ft. Worth zoo or to the wonderful Zen garden just north of there. She had been to the Kimbell Art Museum and which had some recent acquisitions she wanted to see. Then she asked me shyly if I would take her to church there.

"Of course, Jeanne. I would be honored." I felt a twinge of guilt saying this because going to church together was something Nellie and I'd never done, mostly because of her experiences growing up in a strict Baptist home. I didn't have as tough a time, and while I may not be a religious man, I love the beauty of Episcopal services. I knew Jeanne was an Episcopalian. "Do you have one in mind?"

"Would you mind going to a black Baptist church?" Jeanne asked. "There's a gospel choir I'd love to hear."

That almost broke my heart. Going to hear gospel choirs was one of the few religious events Nellie would consider. She always left before the preaching began, which some consider rude, but she loved the music.

Jeanne sensed my hesitation. "We don't have to do that, Jazz. We can go to an Episcopal service if you prefer that. I'd just love being in church with you, even if I do have to keep my hands to myself."

I laughed. "No, I think we may need to go to a black gospel meeting." I explained my reluctance.

"I don't want to move too fast," Jeanne said seriously and I laughed so hard I almost fell out of my chair. "What on earth is so funny?" she demanded.

"Think about it, Jeanne," I told her when I could stop laughing. "Think about the first day we ever met. We almost jumped each other the minute I walked in the door. I don't know how much faster we could move."

We laughed about that a while and Jeanne told me about the little church she wanted to attend. "We'll have to get there early to get a seat," she said. Then she asked me about the case. "Speaking of church, what was the name of the bishop who was killed?" When I told her she said, "I don't like to speak ill of the dead, but I can't think of a more deserving soul than John Rufus Keller."

That was twice I'd heard ill of the man from entirely different sources. I asked Jeanne to tell me why she said that. "He's such a horse's ass," she told me. "Or, he was. Our bishop here in Arkansas is a real pastor. He's a decent, loving human being. Even the people who disagree with him will tell you that. He lives out the gospel and there's nothing fake about it. Keller was just the opposite. All he seemed to care about was power and being in the lime light. People were just there to serve him. You would not believe some of the horror stories that come out of the diocese there, Jazz. It's a real snake pit."

I asked her if she knew any of the clergy here who might be willing to risk talking to me candidly. She supplied a name without hesitation. "He used to be the priest here in Hope. He's the one Henry got fired. I think I told you about that. I needed someone to talk to and went to my priest. Henry got jealous and threatened to withdraw his contribution if the Vestry didn't get rid of Father Charlie."

"Yeah, I remember. You did tell me about him," I said, writing down the priest's name and where he was stationed. "Sounds like an honest man."

"He is," Jeanne replied. "He is a wonderful man. I'd like to look him up if we have time while I'm in Ft. Worth."

"Now I'm getting jealous," I laughed.

"I hope you're teasing, Jazz," Jeanne said seriously.

"Well, I'm a little jealous, Jeanne. You're a very desirable woman. On the other hand, I think I'm grown up enough to keep it from ruining things. How would you feel if things were turned around?"

"Who, me?" Jeanne giggled. "I'd be fine. I'd just claw the bitch's eyes out!"

"I think we'll be all right if we can keep laughing about it," I told her. "I hate to hang up, but I better let you get some rest. Will you be driving in or flying?"

"I'll be driving the biggest car you ever saw," Jeanne assured me. "I'll need it to bring all the booty back from shopping."

# 4. Vertigo

The ringing of my room phone launched me awake. Somehow I managed to get the receiver to my ear. It was Adams, there to pick me up. I told him I needed ten minutes and jumped in the shower, trying to wash away the cobwebs that gather when I get too little sleep.

When I got to the lobby, the clock told me it was still ten minutes before the time we had agreed on the night before. I looked at my watch to see if the lobby clock was running slow and discovered it was actually a minute fast. When I asked Adams if I'd gotten our wires crossed, he laughed and apologized. "It's a bad habit, I know. I'm usually a half hour early. I didn't want to be late."

I told him I was glad because I'd been out like a light. Since we were running early, I suggested Adams join me for the breakfast buffet, and I topped off my tanks. I read somewhere that the Eskimo say that food is sleep, and if this is true, I made up the lost hours of the night before at the breakfast table.

Adams is not a talkative soul, for which I was very grateful. Or maybe being in the presence of the august Dr. Phillips cramped his style. I know I was in no condition to give anything like an intelligent answer to the simplest question, and I appreciated the silence. I also like the way Adams drove, smooth and careful, with no sudden jerks.

I was almost awake when we met Kowalski at the base of the water tower a half hour later. The sun was just peeping over the horizon

37

and I thanked Whomever might be listening that Kowalski was not a chipper morning person who showered her co-workers with obnoxious good cheer. After a greeting us with the fewest civil words possible, Kowalski told us she had keys and we started up the steps right away. I gave her good marks for making sure we all had on vinyl gloves to preserve any fingerprints a shooter might have left.

Had I been fully awake and thinking, I believe I would have passed and let the others check out the tower. This was not the case but the circular stair leading to the top was at least on the inside and the lighting was dim. This saved me from vertigo until we were half way up and I made the mistake of looking over the top of the railing. The floor was only fifty feet below, but it may as well have been five hundred. Had we been on a ladder, I think I might have frozen. Thank God I didn't shit my pants!

As it was, I clamped my eyes shut tight and clung to the railing. Kowalski heard me stop and called down to ask if I was all right. At that point, macho kicked in and I told her I was just catching my breath. I told them the old guy would meet them at the top. I heard Adams chuckle, but there was no response from Kowalski.

After a couple of minutes I fixed my eyes up the stairs and continued the climb. I was even able to steel myself for stepping out onto the maintenance walk, and when I left the safety of the stairs, I kept my eyes glued to the horizon. Holding onto the rail with a Vulcan death grip, I walked around the tower until I could see the huge church about several hundred yards away.

When I saw the church, I knew right away that we would not find anything here. When a bullet is fired from a rifle, it does not travel in a straight line. It travels in an arc and can be blown around by the wind. While we could see the window with the bullet hole, we were almost on a level with the hole. Even with the flattest possible arc to its flight, no bullet shot from here could have hit the bishop as high as his chest.

Adams had noticed this, too. "The angle is all wrong, sir," he told me.

Kowalski nodded. "We're too high. Even lying on the floor here, the worst the shooter could do was mangle his ankle."

I nodded. "I think you're right, but that's uneven glass and we need to check it." I held my hand down at a shallow angle. "It's possible that if there's a slight ripple or a thick place in the glass, the bullet could be deflected upward. It's very unlikely, but we need to rule it out."

Kowalski nodded. "As long as we're here, we need to check this platform out for powder stains," she told Adams. She smiled for the first time that day. The exercise from the climb must have cleared her circuits. "We need to get our money's worth."

I made the mistake of looking down through the mesh floor of the platform. We seemed to be a thousand feet from the ground, and I must have gasped. Kowalski grabbed me by the arm. "Dr. Phillips, what's wrong?" she asked. I could hear concern in her voice but I couldn't see her face. My eyes were glued shut.

"Call me Jazz," I heard my voice saying. It sounded almost normal. "Dr. Phillips sounds like snake oil." I took a deep breath and let it out. When I opened my eyes, I kept them level. I was looking into two very worried faces.

"I'm all right," I told them. "It's only vertigo. I get it when I'm more than six feet up on a ladder. I'll be all right so long as I don't look straight down."

"Why don't you sit down here until we're done checking out the platform?" Adams suggested. "Then we can walk you down the stairs."

I didn't argue. I was very grateful for the respite. I sat down where I was with my back against the cool steel of the tower and closed my eyes. For the first time in many years I found myself craving a cigarette. I could almost taste the smoke of my favorite brand, which had not been sold in more than a decade. I could feel the rich smoke settling into my lungs, calming me down, and the craving became so sharp it set my teeth on edge.

Then the craving passed, as swiftly as it had come. After a couple of minutes I found myself beginning to relax and I opened my eyes looked around. I was careful to keep my gaze at a high angle, and as I sat there, I began to enjoy the view. The tower was one of the highest points in the city and I could see the outline of sky scrapers on the horizon to the north. There was an ugly haze from too many cars driving too many miles hanging over much of the city, but this seemed to be concentrated around the freeways. The air in this part of town was relatively clear and I could see the church where the murder took place quite clearly. The morning sun was high enough for the tan stone to catch the light, and the building looked bright gold in the distance.

I heard Adams and Kowalski talking and turned toward the sound. The wind kept me from hearing what they were saying, but Kowalski saw me watching and shook her head. "Nothing here, Dr....Jazz," she called out. "We think this is a dead end."

I laughed. "I like that. Dr. Jazz. It has certain lowlife ring to it."

They both laughed, though Kowalski looked embarrassed. "Are you about ready to go?" she asked as they walked over to where I sat.

"Believe it or not, I'm actually enjoying the view," I told them, pointing toward the church. "Any idea how far away we are?"

"Eight hundred and fifty yards, more or less," Adams answered. "I looked it up on an aerial map when I got home. It was a satellite image, actually. It looks a lot closer than it is. Depending on the particular shell, the elevation of the trajectory would have to be at least twelve inches, maybe more."

"Which means a shooter couldn't even hit the bishop's ankle without a ricochet off the glass," Kowalski added. "It's not something the shooter could count on for making his shot."

"It does seem unlikely," I agreed. Between the bishop's pectoral cross and the stained glass, most of the remaining energy should have been absorbed. From this distance it could cause a helluva bruise but I didn't think it would necessarily be fatal. It would be like being hit in the chest by a baseball bat, and if death occurred, it would be from concussion rather than penetration and tearing of tissue.

I shared these thoughts with the others and they nodded. "Something like a .338 magnum with solid nose might do it," Adams pointed out. "Thing is, you'd hear it from here to Dallas if the shot came from up here. I haven't ever heard of a full metal jacket for a .338. I can't imagine what you'd hunt with it."

I chuckled. "There's not much season for bishops behind stained glass, is there?" The other two smiled uneasily at my dark humor.

"Well, let's see what we find at the church," I said, starting to get up. As I did, my eye caught a dark smudge on the underside of the railing directly in front of me. "Look at that," I said, pointing. "We may have something here." I moved closer for a better look. "It looks like a powder burn to me."

I moved aside to give the other two a look. Adams took a small camera out of his pocket and took a few shots of the smudge. Then he took a sample of the residue with some evidence tape made just for that purpose. "We better seal this place for the crime scene crew when we get down," he said and Kowalski nodded. She called for a patrol car to guard the scene until the lab team got there.

We looked over the rest of the railing on that side of the tower very carefully, but there were no other smudges we could find. What is interesting to me now, thinking back, is how my vertigo disappeared completely after I discovered the residue. I'm not sure exactly why, but I imagine it had something to do with focusing on the hunt for evidence rather than on my fear of heights. It was only when we were getting into our cars that I realized I'd gone over the railing and the mesh floor of the walkway very carefully, looking straight down at times, and had made it all the way down the steps without a qualm. Now safe on the ground, I got the shakes, but it passed quickly. Go figure that one.

By the time we made it to the bottom, a uniformed patrolman was waiting to guard the site. Kowalski told him where we would be if the lab people needed to talk to us, and gave him her cell number. She told him it might be a couple of hours before the lab team got there and asked him to call if they failed to show up.

Adams met Kowalski and me at the church. At my suggestion, we looked inside first. The sun was well above the horizon and at about the same height as the middle of the water tower. I wanted to see where it would shine through the bullet hole. Fortunately, Kowalski had a key to the small door in front, and we had no trouble getting in. I could see the police seals put in place by the crime scene team the night before were still intact. I found it interesting they had sealed only the entry door and not both cathedral gates. When I pointed this out to Kowalski, she nodded and frowned. It was a small point, but that's the kind of thing a defense lawyer can use to establish reasonable doubt. Any new evidence we might discover today could be suspect.

When I got to the crossing of the transept and nave, I could see a bright spot of light from the morning sun on the stone floor. Sure enough, it was more than half way between the crossing where I stood and the east transept window. Walking over to the window, I climbed the stepladder, which was still there, and peeked through the bullet hole. The sun was just peeking over the top of the tower. We would have to check it out with a laser pointer to be absolutely sure, but it looked like Kowalski was right. Without a ricochet, the best our shooter could have done from the water tower was to hit the victim's ankle.

Turning back toward the crossing, I noticed something I'd not seen in the dim light the night before. About eighteen inches to the right of where the spot of sunlight shone on the flagstone was what looked like a shallow scratch or groove. The surface of the flagstone had been left unpolished when the church was built, so this might be an irregularity in the stone, but I doubted it. I hollered to Kowalski and Adams, excited as a hound that's just treed a coon.

"What do you have?" Kowalski asked. While she was not overbearing, there was no question she was the team leader.

"Look there," I told her, pointing to the shallow groove I'd seen. I handed Adams the laser pointer I used at the seminar, I asked him to hold the butt against the hole in the window and point the beam at the scratch. Then I went and stood in the middle of the crossing. The angle looked about right and I asked Kowalski if she had a pocket mirror.

"Every woman has a pocket mirror, Jazz," she told me, smiling.

"Watch your eyes." She placed the mirror on the floor and the red dot from the laser shone over my right shoulder. When I moved to the right, it hit my chin. "Stay there," Kowalski ordered me, removing the mirror. She pointed to the exact center of the scratch. "Put the dot right there," she told Adams, and when it moved, she replaced the mirror. The bright red dot was now six inches below my Adam's apple.

"Bingo!" I said. "Does anyone care to speculate?"

Kowalski shook her head, but Adams spoke up. "This doesn't make any sense if this was a deliberate sniping. Like Dr. Smyth said last night, how could the shooter see what he was shooting?"

"So the bishop was standing in the wrong place at the right time?" I asked.

"That's sure what it looks like," Kowalski said. "I don't like it, but that's how it fits with what we have. Maybe the ME has something else to tell us."

"Hold the laser steady for a second," I told Adams. I moved aside and looked at the point where the laser dot quivered on the other end of the transept. It lay in an area of shadow where two mitered pieces of carved wood came together. "I don't see anything there," I told them. "Let's look outside the window." Kowalski picked up her mirror. As she did, the beam of sunlight coming in the bullet hole hit the surface and flashed on the area where the laser dot had quivered at the other end of the transept. I was looking that way and for a moment I thought I saw something in the flash of the mirror. Yet when I moved closer and shined my flashlight on the spot, I could see nothing there.

Kowalski and Adams were looking at me curiously. "I must be getting old," I said. "My eyes seem to be playing tricks on me."

"Ain't nothing wrong with your eyes, Jazz," Kowalski assured me. "You're the one who spotted the residue on the tower."

"That's a new chapter for my next book," I laughed. "Vertigo: the new investigative technique." The other two laughed politely. They apparently weren't used to this kind of humor from a supervisor. "Come on, campers," I said. "T'ain't nobody here but us chickens. I ain't your boss. Let's look outside, then have some coffee."

The lawn had been mowed a couple of days before and the flower beds along the side of the building were raked spotless, which made our work easier. When we got to the spot below the transept window, Adams spotted something and pointed. It was a small piece of broken blue glass lying about six feet from the transept wall. Looking more carefully, we found several others not far from it. The farthermost from the wall was about twelve feet out.

"Anybody have a reading on this?" I asked, but both my partners shook their heads. I took a photo of the area and retrieved each piece of glass carefully. "This could throw a kink in the line," I told them. "What could cause glass to be on this side of the window?"

"Like Dr. Smyth said, a strange break in the glass could do it," Kowalski offered.

"Or a second shot from inside," Adams said, looking embarrassed. Kowalski's look told him what she thought about that, but she said nothing.

"Those are the only two options I can see," I told them, looking up and around. "I don't see any other breaks in the window and I doubt it was a bird passing kidney stones." Kowalski and Adams looked at each other, not knowing how to take my outlandish Arkansas humor. "You're supposed to at least smile when I say dumb stuff like that," I told them.

We found a brand name coffee shop a few blocks away and I insisted on buying. "It's on my expense account," I told them and they were glad to accept. Designer coffee is as expensive in Cowtown as it is in Seattle, and since I was on the city payroll, there was no question of graft.

After we ordered, Adams excused himself for a pit stop. "Do you mind a personal question?" I asked Kowalski. "There is something I'm dying to know."

Kowalski smiled. "You want to know what part of Spain the Kowalski family comes from, right?" I laughed and nodded. "Believe it or not, both sides," she told me. "My dad was born there during the second World War. His parents were on vacation there when Hitler invaded Poland and couldn't go home. Somehow they made it to Portugal, where he grew up, and he met my mother in Madrid after the war."

"I bet he speaks an odd brand of Spanish," I said. "So you were born in Portugal."

"No, I was born here in Ft. Worth," she told me. "My dad was studying at the med school and we ended up staying. He's an osteopath."

"Here I had you figured for Hispanic," I told her. "The genetic blend worked well with you. Are you bilingual?"

"Trilingual," she told me. "Although there isn't much demand for Polish speakers in Ft. Worth. I spent a lot of time with my dad's mother."

Adams rejoined us. He was talking on his cell phone when he reached the table. "That was Dr. Smyth," he told us when he hung up. "They recovered a lot of the slug that killed the bishop. It was from either a .357 or a .38, but get this. He thinks it was subsonic."

"Subsonic?" Kowalski asked. "That doesn't make much sense."

"It does if you're using a silencer," I said. "Anything going over the speed of sound is going to make a sharp crack as it goes by. It's a smaller scale sonic boom. So if you want to be quiet, you've got to keep muzzle velocity below about 1100 feet per second." I turned toward Adams. "Did Simon say what kind of bullet was used?"

"Yeah, it was some brand I never heard of. They make partition bullets so the front end will mushroom while the back end stays intact. This one was probably their 180 grain bullet fired from a .357 rifle."

I looked at Kowalski. "This isn't making sense to me. With a slug that big moving at about a thousand feet per second, the trajectory arc from the water tower would have to have been extremely high."

"The hole in the window didn't look like a .357 hole to me," Adams said. "I would have thought it was made by a .223, or a .308 at the largest."

Suddenly I had a sense of dread. While there was not much evidence, I had the feeling this case was getting far too complicated for a simple murder. Over the years I've learned to respect this intuitive sense. "This guy's playing with our minds," I said.

"What do you mean?" Kowalski wanted to know.

"I don't know for sure," I answered. "Maybe I've been in this business too long. I've the feeling we are dealing with more than a normal homicide."

"No shit!" Adams said. "So what do we do?"

"Normal police procedure," I answered quickly. "Always follow procedure, even if you're sure it's wrong. Chase down all the obvious lines of investigation and follow all the leads. When everything hits a dead end, then go outside the box. Otherwise you'll kiss your career goodbye."

"So we just shut off that part of our minds?" Kowalski asked. There was no question in my mind what she thought of this.

"Not at all," I said. "We keep out-of-the-box speculation to ourselves. I bet you can tell me exactly what course the chief will take with what we have so far."

Kowalski looked at Adams and they both nodded. "He will probably go with some accidental homicide theory," Adams said. "Assuming what we got off the tower is gun powder residue, he will most likely claim the bishop was killed by a ricochet fired by someone shooting at random from the water tower. It's a quick, politically clean solve and one the media will buy. They love random shooters. They can scare the hell out of the public and sell lots of papers." There was a raw edge of bitterness to his voice. This had apparently happened before while he was in uniform.

"Don't let it make you bitter," I advised. "This can be a real blessing. It takes the heat off so you can look for the killer as long as you need."

Kowalski looked at me and grinned, and Adams' face cleared. "Yeah, I didn't think about that. We'll have to be careful. Once the chief closes the case I don't think he will like us to keep looking."

"All right, then," I said. "Here's how we'll work it. Just to cover your six, we need to tell the chief everything we have, but not push it. Make it easy for him to sell the press on the random theory. Then the three of us can put things together as we get more evidence. I've got a line on the bishop I want to run before I leave town, so you two do the normal protocol and we'll touch base a couple of times a day. I've got to do my final session this afternoon and I plan to take most of tomorrow and Sunday off, but we can get together to compare notes. I'll brief you on what you miss at the session. Mostly, it's a wrap-up. Any questions?"

"How do we get in touch with you if something comes up?" Adams asked. I gave them my cell number. "That's my personal phone, so don't give it out. Not even to the chief if you can avoid it." I looked at them and smiled. "You guys are going to do well. Don't worry about the chief. I'll take the heat if we turn something up."

Kowalski gave me an appraising look. "You're up to something," she told me with a grin. "I can tell." Adams nodded.

"I have a date tonight and I'm as nervous as a cat," I admitted. "You guys are too sharp for this old man." That was not what I was up to, but they didn't need to know. Knowing could get them in trouble and that's the last thing I wanted.

Adams shook his head. "Not really. You should have seen your face a minute ago when you were talking about the weekend."

"Yeah," said Kowalski. "It was what my granny used to call a cookie-jar grin."

"You don't know the half of it," I said. "Let's get back to work."

Adams went by the church to check out the size of the bullet hole against the size of one of his nine-millimeter rounds. A standard nine-millimeter bullet is .356 caliber, a thousandth of an inch smaller than a .357. This is exactly the same size as what is called .38 caliber, and I've never figured out why the old police standard was not called a .35 Special. Even more confusing, caliber .35 rifle bullets measure .358 in diameter. Even so, a nine-millimeter slug was close enough to check the size of the hole.

When Kowalski and I got back to the water tower, the lab crew was just turning up, so I caught a ride back to the academy with the uniformed officer. This made his day. It turns out that he had read my books, too, and he was impressed as all get-out to be honored by giving me a ride.

For the life of me, I'll never figure out human fascination with celebrity. I guess I've put away too many celebrities for drugs, assault, and the other sundry troubles people with too much money and too much time on their hands seem to attract. These folk would be better off hiring doubles to do their public appearances and spend their days doing public service. Too many of them come to believe in their own public persona bullshit, and the money they receive by the truckload insulates them from reality. At least, it does up to a point. Then the sad result is that they often crash and burn completely. Janis Joplin comes to mind, as does Jimmy Hendrix, but there are dozens of others. What's so sad is that these are among our brightest and best people. There is something horribly wrong with the way we reward them.

I got to the academy just in time for lunch and brought the chief up to speed as we ate, knowing Kowalski would be reporting in later that day. As I suspected, Mac went for the obvious solution. "Sounds like accidental homicide to me," the chief said. "Some dumb asshole trying out his rifle and pretending he's a bad-ass sniper." He shook his head. "We see that kind of stuff all the time."

"There are some things that are inconsistent with that theory," I pointed out. "One is the subsonic loads and another is the glass on the lawn. There is also the size of the hole in the window, which looks a little small for a .357. I also have some information that the man may have had violent enemies, so we need to look at that. Let us have a couple more days to chase down the obvious leads to show due diligence. You don't want the media giving you grief over closing the case too quickly."

I could see the chief didn't like this, but he is far too political a cop to overlook the risk I was pointing out. He shrugged. "You said there was a three day minimum, so I guess I've a couple of days coming, anyway. Just be damned careful poking around Bishop Keller, Jazz. The man has some powerful friends in town."

"Are they clean?" I asked.

Joe McClellan laughed. "Do you know a wealthy man who is these days? Some of them got a shady start, but most of them are old Cowtown money. They're used to getting their way but I don't think there are any mob or cartel connections. Jesus! That's all we need, a dead bishop with drug connections. This is actually a pretty clean town."

I told him I had a prior commitment for Sunday and would start up Monday, but that I would be in touch with Adams and Kowalski before then. "They're a sharp team, Joe. They work well together."

"They should be," he told me. "They were partners on patrol for four years. They're closer than some married people I know." When he said this I wondered if he was not talking about himself. He sounded bitter.

# 5. Complications

I had trouble keeping my mind on the seminar that afternoon. For one thing, it was a recap of what we had covered over the week. For another, the last hour was a test over the material to see what had stuck. I always make these anonymous to take the pressure off my students, and they grade their own work, so doing this doesn't take much conscious effort on my part. I had far too much time to think, and while I tried to focus on the case, my mind kept easing back to Jeanne's arrival. I found myself worried about her getting there safely, and during the break I called to see if she had checked in yet. She had, but was not in her room, so I left a message that I might be a little late. When I hung up I felt as giddy as a teen on his first date.

The second call I made was to Charles Brighton, the former priest from Hope. His office said this was his day off but that he would be in the next morning. I left the message that I needed to talk with him and it was somewhat urgent. The secretary offered to call him at home if it was an emergency, but I told her I was tied up and it could wait. She took my name and cell phone number, but didn't ask what this was about. Nor did I offer any explanation.

There was time for a third call and I touched base with Kowalski. The lab crew was still looking around but nothing more had turned up at the tower. "As a matter of fact, Jazz, I find that a little suspicious," Kowalski told me. "There aren't any fingerprints at all on the railing inside the tower, not even smudges."

"What does that tell you?" I asked.

"It tells me someone wiped down the railing," she replied.

"That's what it tells me," I confirmed. "Listen, we're going to be out of here in about an hour. Why don't I catch a ride and meet you at the church? I want to poke around a bit more."

Kowalski hesitated, and I asked why. "I'm supposed to pick my daughter up from day care about then," she said. "Could we make it a little later?"

"What about Adams?" I asked. "Why don't you send the key and I'll meet him there? I'm tied up all evening."

"Ooh, that's right," she cooed, and I felt my face flush. "All right, we'll do it that way. He can tell me if you find anything."

"Did he say anything about the hole in the window?"

"Only that it seemed too small to him. He couldn't get the slug all the way through without scraping the edges. Something was wrong with the angle, too."

"He can fill me in when he sees me. Call me this evening if you need to."

"Not unless the station's burning down," Kowalski laughed. "Some things are more important than murder."

I couldn't have agreed more.

A squad car dropped me by the church and I found Adams waiting for me by his car. This was a battered old Plymouth that had seen far better days, but this is par for the course in most police departments. The senior people seem to end up with first choice for equipment. Adams told me what he'd found at the window and I had to agree with his assessment. It didn't look like a .357 had made the bullet hole.

When we entered the nave, I experienced the same feeling of benevolent presence I had the first time I came in. I walked straight up to the crossing where the body was found. There was a small dark stain in the carpet I assumed was blood, but other than that, there was no sign someone had met a violent end here. What remained was a deep sense of abiding peace.

Adams found the light switches and stepped aside to turn them on. Even with all the lights on, the large space was not well lit. I'm sure this, too, was the work of the architect, creating a reverent space that fostered reflection. Unfortunately, this wasn't useful for investigating a crime scene.

I turned on the powerful flashlight I'd brought along and adjusted its beam from spot to flood. This gave me a bright area about three feet in diameter and I stood where the body had been for a moment looking around the immense space.

"What are we looking for?" Adams asked, a little nervous. I wasn't sure if this was because of me or because of the building.

"Put yourself in the mind of someone who uses a silencer and hand-loads his own subsonic ammunition," I answered. "This guy wants to make it hard for us to find him, but he wants to rub our noses in it if we're good enough to understand what he's doing. He doesn't want to get caught, but he wants our respect for how clever he is." I looked at Adams and he nodded. "So he's got to leave us a message. The hole or holes in the window is part of it, as is the powder stain on the tower. Yet, I think he probably left us something else if we're clever enough to find it."

Again, Adams nodded, but I could see he was not on board yet. "We're working from the idea the bishop was shot from outside the building. The hole in the window is his message we're on the wrong track, assuming we are sharp enough to see it."

I stopped and looked around some more. "Assuming the bishop was standing here at the crossing when he was shot, what would be the best place for the shooter to be if he was shooting from inside? Remember, he's trying to stay hidden."

Adams walked up to where I was standing and looked around. Without hesitation, he pointed to the choir loft. Even with all the lights in the nave on, the loft remained dim. Only the area where the choir would sit was well lit, and the corners of the loft were in deep shadow. I had to admire the architect. With the right robes, the choir would look like a band of angels singing on high. It was a perfect perch for a sniper,

Then another thought crossed my mind. "Can you kill the lights in the choir loft?" I asked Adams.

"Sure," he answered. "They're on a separate switch in the stair-well." He headed up the center aisle.

"Why don't you go on upstairs and stand in the loft if you can get there in the dark," I called after him. A few moments later all the lights in the choir loft went out, except for two sets of bright spots on either side of the loft railing which were aimed at the chancel. These made it very hard to see anything in the loft.

"All right, I'm here," Adams called out a bit later. His deep voice seemed very loud in the silence. "Can you see me?"

"Is that you, Lord?" I asked, and Adams laughed. "Where are you, Jim?"

"Right here," he answered, turning on his flashlight. He was standing at the very top of the choir loft.

I had not heard him going up the stairs or walking across the loft. "Is the loft carpeted?" I called out.

"Sure is," Adams replied. "At least the walkways. The rest is wood floor. It would be an easy shot from anywhere up here. You don't have to shout, either. I can hear every word you say."

"How about this?" I asked in a low voice.

"How about what?" Adams replied.

"How loud are you talking now?" His voice sounded to me like he was speaking at a normal level. I kept my low.

"Not too loud. I'm not shouting but my voice is slightly raised."

"Turn on the choir loft lights," I told him. "I'll be right there. Glove up."

I pulled on a pair of latex gloves before I went up the stairway. When I got there, Adams was standing by the organ console, looking at something intently. I walked over to where he was. "Look there," he said, pointing.

The organ console was turned sideways to the center line of the church, and it was set on a level platform below and to one side of the choir risers. This gave the organist a clear view of both the choir and of the chancel area below. The top of the console also provided a wide, flat surface about six feet long that pointed toward the chancel. It was the perfect height for someone to lie across and use for a shooting rest. What Adams was pointing to was a dark, dull smudge about the size of a half dollar on the polished surface.

"This guy is really playing with our minds," I said. "We better get the crime scene guys over here right away."

Adams made the call and spoke briefly to Kowalski. "They can't get here until tomorrow morning," he told me. "They're on their way to another scene."

"Let me talk to them." Adams spoke to Kowalski again and handed me the phone. A moment or two later an impatient voice spoke from the other end.

"I know you have your priorities and procedures," I told the team leader. "However, this is a very high priority case and you're only five minutes away."

The voice on the other end demanded to know who the hell I was. "I'm the national consultant the chief assigned to this case," I answered. "If you want, I'll have the chief call you personally to confirm our priority. He won't like having to do it, either."

The team leader sputtered and spewed for a couple of more minutes before he gave in. When I handed the phone back, Adams was grinning. "Danny can be a real asshole at times," he said. "Nobody likes to work with him."

"I wonder why Simon keeps him on?" I murmured.

"He's a world class brown nose who gets the job done," Adams answered. "Anytime Dr. Smyth is around Danny is as nice as he can be. But I'd hate to be one of his crew members."

I looked at my watch. It was almost five-thirty. I called the motel and this time Jeanne was in her room. I told her what was going on and that I would get there as soon as I could. "What's it been now, Jazz, close to three years since we met? I think I can wait a couple of hours longer. There's no rush."

"Speak for yourself, woman," I told her. "I'm feeling rather urgent, myself."

As it turned out, I was not delayed as much as I thought. Once Danny was done grousing, his professional side kicked in and his team went after the choir loft like flies on a honey-wagon. Kowalski arrived a couple of minutes later and I asked her to give me a lift back to the motel. She had her daughter in the car with us, almost as cute as one of my own adopted grandkids, and Marcia and I had a wonderful visit while her mother drove. I showed her pictures of Zilpha and the kids, and if she wondered how this old white man had black grandchildren, she was too polite to ask. Or maybe she was just used to a lot of diversity, given her own family.

When I knocked on Jeanne's door, she beckoned me into her room, then came into my arms and buried her head in my chest. I could feel her trembling in my arms, but her own were tight around my chest. After a moment or two she sighed and I could feel her relax. We stood there quietly for a long time after that. Then she raised her head and smiled, and put her arms around my neck. "Before you called I was so worried something had happened to you."

"It did," I told her, looking into her eyes. "I fell in love with a lady from Hope." Then I realized she was not talking about my call today, but the one the night before. "I'm sorry I didn't call her sooner. I don't know why I didn't."

"It doesn't matter now," she murmured. "Here you are." Then she kissed me and things got rather urgent.

# 6. Digging Deeper

The next morning, we were up early, but it took us a while to get away. Jeanne had gone hog-wild at the western store, of course, and I had to try everything on. "I don't know which is more fun," she said as I was changing from one set of clothes into another. "Dressing you up or watching you take them off." This led to further delays and it was ten o'clock by the time we got under way to see Charles Brighton. I called ahead to make sure he'd be there.

Normally I would not have taken Jeanne along on an interview in a murder case. Yet, when I told her who I was going to see, Jeanne asked if she could come along, and I couldn't see why not. Her presence might even encourage the priest to be a bit more forthcoming.

We arrived at the church just before eleven, and the good padre was waiting for us on a bench by a flower garden to one side of the church, smoking his pipe. When he saw Jeanne, his face lit up and I felt a pang of jealousy. And when he looked at me, his eyes were full of questions, but I'm sure they were about me. I don't think there was any doubt in his mind about the nature of my relationship with Jeanne.

After Jeanne introduced us, they exchanged pleasantries for a while. Then the padre turned to me again, and I explained why I was there. I told him I was one of the investigators looking into the death of Bishop Keller.

"Am I a suspect? Do you think I shot him?" There was an edge of bitterness to the priest's laugh. "God knows, I certainly wanted to from time to time but I never got around to actually doing it. I don't even own a gun," he added. "I got rid of them all when the kids were little. Never had the time to hunt since."

"No, I didn't think you were a suspect, Father," I answered. "I need an honest opinion on the local church situation and Grant Forster told me once you are a no bullshit priest. Those were his exact words."

"Call me Charlie, Jazz," Brighton said. "I'm not big on titles. Coming from Grant Forster, that's high praise. Do you know him well?"

"Better than I want to sometimes," I admitted. "We spend a lot of time together and I guess you could call him my confessor. We do a lot of fishing."

"I suspect he's told you he's the fiend God sent to bring you to Jesus," Charlie said. "Damn, I miss him. What do you need to know?"

"All the scuttlebutt you know about the late bishop," I replied. "You don't need to stick to what you know as fact. More than anything, I need a sense of who the man was and who might have wanted him dead."

Brighton sighed. "I really wasn't kidding, Jazz. Put John Rufus Keller in my sights and I'd have had a hard time not pulling the trigger. He was one of the most vicious and vindictive assholes I've ever known. I fought his election here tooth and nail, but I was a new guy and no one listened to me. Since then, the people who elected him have pretty much turned against him, too. So if you want a list of who wanted him dead, start with the clergy roster of this diocese."

"Why did you fight his election?" I asked.

"I knew him in seminary. He was an arrogant asshole that came from an East Coast family with lots of old money. He was also very bright and manipulative, and he had a lot of the faculty convinced he could walk on water. Not many of his classmates shared that opinion." He stopped and gave me a level look. "Is the kind of information you want?"

"Yes. Even if it's inaccurate, it helps give me a general picture of the man," I told him. "Did you ever see anything that made you wonder?"

"Oh, yes," Brighton answered. "It was mostly small stuff, petty meanness. There were snide remarks and knowing looks, and the man could cut a weaker person to pieces without saying a word. I've seen him do that many times. I've seen him do it to the clergy of this diocese since he was elected. The man is damned clever and he is—was—very covert in expressing his hostility." Brighton paused and fiddled with his pipe for a moment.

"That was most of it, sort of like a threatening presence running along under the surface. Yet, there were two times I saw it come to the surface while we were in seminary. Once was while he and I were both serving on the student disciplinary committee. One of our classmates got caught with a playmate in his room after hours. Most of us were for giving the guy a severe warning. They weren't doing anything when they were caught, just sleeping together. Not John Rufus! He wanted to hang them both, regardless of the facts that 1) they were consenting adults, 2) neither of them were married, and 3) the other guy wasn't even a student here." He looked at me. "I don't know what you've read about the man, but Bishop John Keller is one of the most violent homophobes in the Episcopal Church. There are those of us who think it may be a simple case of self-hatred."

"You mean he was gay?" I asked. "That opens up a whole can of worms as far as his murder goes."

"Tell me about it," Brighton replied. "I'm sure you understand why I'm reluctant to even mention it. On the other hand, the most violent gay-bashers are often gay men themselves. Look at the late J. Edgar Hoover."

I thought about this for a moment. "You said there were two incidents," I reminded him. "What was the other?"

"One day I was asked to drop some books by his house my first year in seminary," Brighton continued. "John Rufus Keller never lived on campus as far as I know. He was married long before he went to seminary and he and his family lived in some ritzy apartments in a better part of town."

Brighton looked at me and asked, "Are you familiar with what gay men call window dressing?" I nodded. "I believe that's what his wife and children were for John Rufus. That and punching bags!" he added, clearly angry. "When I arrived at their apartment, Keller wasn't home, but his wife was. When she answered the door, she had a terrible black eye and bruises all over her arms. When I asked what happened, she told me she'd fallen down the apartment stairs."

"That's a pretty common cover," I said. "Did you notice it any other time?"

"No, and I was on the lookout, too," Brighton admitted. "I'd seen him in operation on campus and I would have liked to have nailed his balls to the pavement!" Then he remembered Jeanne was present. "Sorry, Jeanne. I guess you're getting to see a side of me I don't show much."

"You have nothing to apologize for, Charlie," Jeanne answered. "I would have ripped off his balls and stuffed them up his nose!"

Brighton blinked. "Now that would have been a sight to see."

"What about since seminary?" I asked. "Have you heard anything?"

"I ran into his oldest son at a youth event quite a few years ago. Wally must have been a senior in high school then, and maybe older. It was just before he ran away and he was pretty battered up—on crutches and with one arm in a cast. When I asked what happened, he told me he'd wrecked his car, totaled it out. A week later I saw him driving the same car he'd had for years, an old beat up VW bug. It was pretty obvious it hadn't been in a repair shop."

"So you think his dad did it?" I asked.

"I know for sure it was his dad," Brighton answered. "I can't tell you how I know or from whom, but I do know!"

"I'm not sure I understand," I said.

"Ask Forster," he told me. "He'll explain why I can't discuss this."

"Oh, sorry," I said. "I didn't realize what you were saying. Someone came to Forster and asked him to pass along some critical evidence to me a couple of years ago. They came to him as a confessor so he couldn't tell me anything the confess-ee didn't tell him to say."

Brighton laughed. "The confess-ee, I like that. It's much better than the penitent. I'm glad you understand." He glanced at his watch. "I hate to rush you but I have to make some calls about the funeral later this week."

"You mean the bishop's funeral?" I asked.

"I'm afraid so. His wife asked me to do it and that's not something one can refuse, as much as I might like to." He shook his head. "Part of me will be glad to plant him, but I sure hate what his family has ahead of them."

"It couldn't be worse than what they have behind them, Charlie," Jeanne said. She offered him her hand. "Thanks so much for seeing us. I'll call you later and explain some things."

"No need for explanation between friends, Jeanne," he replied, ignoring her hand and giving her a bear hug. "You seem to have made a very good friend here." He shook my hand warmly. I had the distinct feeling we had received his blessing.

We were back in the car and discussing where to have lunch when my phone rang. It was Kowalski. "Sorry to disturb you, Jazz. I just had a call from Dr. Mann, the organist we talked with. He wanted to know if we can release the building for church tomorrow."

"As far as I'm concerned, we can," I said. "Why don't you bring me up to date?"

"The crime scene crew went over the loft pretty thoroughly last night. Aside from the powder smear and enough fingerprints to keep us busy for a month, they didn't find anything. The organ console was perfectly clean. They even opened the keyboard and that was clean, too."

"What about the rest of the building?"

"It was the same as the choir loft. There were thousands of prints, but none in critical areas. I personally don't think they will help us much."

"Neither do I," I told her. "Fortunately, we don't have to run them all through the system at this point. Log them in the file to cover yourself but don't worry with them. I think the clean console is the shooter's way of thumbing his nose at us."

"I agree," she said. "I'm not sure where to go from here. I guess we need to talk to the bishop's wife and the people at his office. Any suggestions?"

"Yeah, I want to be there when you interview Mrs. Keller. It will give you a little protection if I am."

"Why do I need protection?" Kowalski wanted to know.

"It may get very ugly," I replied. I told her about our conversation with Charlie Brighton. "You might want to run John Rufus Keller through the system to see what you get," I told her. "Just for fun, run his prints through, too, but be careful. If anyone asks you why you are doing it, tell them that I said it was routine procedure. There should also be some directory or file that tells you where Keller was before he came to Ft. Worth. Check him out there, too, and pay particular attention to any domestic disturbance calls."

"This is going to take us more than a couple of days, Jazz."

"I know, but Mac has already made up his mind about the case. So do the obvious homicide investigation stuff first to clear that and then work on this other angle when you can. I've an idea it may take a while to run this killer down."

"You're not taking this personally, are you?" Kowalski asked.

"No," I laughed. "He's shooting us the bird, but it's not personal. I just like to nail the bastards. One other thing before I forget it, why don't you put out a query to other departments in surrounding states? This may be a regional killer who does clergy. Pay particular attention to any priests who may have been murdered."

"You really do think this is a serial case, don't you?" Kowalski asked.

"Let me put it this way," I answered. "When it smells like a cow and it sounds like a cow and it feels like a cow, then look out where you step. Seriously, I may be all wet and it may turn out to be accidental homicide like the chief says. Someone may come forward and confess. Right now that seems very unlikely."

"I just don't want to blow this," Kowalski told me. "This is our first case as a team, me and Adams. We've worked with other people, but not together. We'd like to keep it that way."

"I'll make sure you don't blow it," I assured her. Then something else struck me. "You know, one thing that bothers me is how the shooter knew where to set up if this was intentional. How did he know the bishop would be at the church? Or has he been stalking him for a while? Did he simply take advantage of the opportunity or did he create it? Why don't you and Adams run that down? Check out that phone call to Mann, too. See if that was for real. If Joe asks why you're doing any of this, tell him I asked you to clear those angles just to be safe. Tell him I said something about due diligence. That's a big issue now."

Kowalski laughed. "I think I'll tell him something else. Due diligence is not exactly his favorite phrase these days. The local papers have been giving him a hard time over it. I think that's why he brought you in to do the seminar."

"I wondered about that," I said. "People don't normally call me in until everything has gone south."

"Anything else?" Kowalski asked.

"Yeah, there is. Why don't you and Adams do that trick with the laser pointer again? Use the mirror and look around carefully where the red dot hits the far wall. I didn't see anything there yesterday, but check it out again. I've a hunch you might find something there."

"Like another bullet?" Kowalski asked. "That could really complicate things, couldn't it?"

"I'm thinking down the road," I told her. "I don't think this case is going to be cleared anytime soon, but I think it can be cleared eventually. If there's another bullet there, we need to have it now just to preserve a chain of evidence."

"What if the hole in the window was there before yesterday?" Kowalski asked.

"You really want to complicate the chief's life, don't you?" I said. Kowalski laughed. "You and Adams better nail down that one, too. Talk to the custodian and the pastor first, then to Mann. One of them should have known about it if the hole was there last week or even before. I don't think it was because the glass was still on the floor, but we need to check. Just be sure to tell them not to have it repaired until they clear it with you first. They may not like it, but it's key evidence either way the case goes."

"Anything else?"

"Yeah, get Adams and do a reverse of the light trick with the laser. Put the pointer on the scratch in the floor and aim it through the hole in the window. Then look east along the line of sight. Mark exactly where it points. It may or may not be on the tower."

I rang off and turned to Jeanne to apologize for the intrusion. She was looking at me with an odd expression. "What?" I asked.

"You're just so good," she said. "When you do your policeman thing it just really gets to me." There was no mistaking what she meant.

"Maybe we should stop by the room and clean up before lunch," I suggested.

She looked around the parking lot. It was deserted. "Maybe we should," she murmured. "Unless you want to risk being arrested for lewd public behavior at a church in Ft. Worth."

We had a late lunch and decided to put off our trip to the zoo until the next day. It might be crowded on Sunday afternoon, but I thought if we went early enough, we might beat the crowds. I suggested the Zen garden, instead, and Jeanne agreed.

"Oh, my," she said as we walked through the garden, hand in hand. "I could spend a week here."

"Why don't we?" I said. "I'm done with the seminar and I don't have much more to do on the case. How about you?"

"It sounds wonderful, Jazz," she answered, stroking the back of my neck. "I don't want to rain on our parade, but there are some things we need to talk about."

"Your list is probably the same as mine," I answered. "Why don't we take it a day at a time, and if something comes up, we'll deal with it then?"

"Just so long as we deal with it," she answered. "I don't want the past to poison the future."

"Have I told you today how much I love you?" I asked.

"You showed me pretty well a couple of times, but I don't think you actually told me," she answered laughing. "I hope I showed you."

"Maybe we ought to go over it again," I suggested.

"Well, we need to make it to Billy Bob's by eight," she told me. "After that I hear it's hard to find a seat."

My cell phone rang while we were on the way back to our room. I answered without looking at who was calling, wondering what Kowalski wanted now. It was Simon, calling to set up a time for me to come to dinner. He told me Claire had found some dead pig to barbecue and he had a new Mexican beer he wanted me to try. He asked if the next afternoon would be a good time.

"I think so," I said. "Just a minute." Muting the phone, I asked Jeanne how she felt about meeting some of my friends.

"I would love it," she said. "We can put off going to the zoo."

"That would be great," I told Simon, but there was no answer from the other end. Then I remembered to take the phone off mute. "That would be wonderful," I told him. "Can I bring something?"

"No," he said. "Just bring a good appetite." Then he paused, and I knew he was looking for the right words to ask me something. "You sound different, Jazz, happier, maybe. Has something happened?"

"Yeah, you could say that," I told him. "Definitely happier. I think the warden just closed that big switch."

There was silence for a moment before Simon remembered our conversation. Then I heard Simon's belly laugh. "All right!" he said. "Excellent! Then I can tell Claire you're bringing a guest?"

"Much more than that," I said. "I'll explain later." He was still laughing when I hung up.

No one who has never been there can comprehend the reality of Billy Bob's at the stockyards in Cowtown. I've no idea how big it may be but I understand it's not the largest country dance hall around. Yet, it's hard for me to imagine anything larger. I also find it hard to understand how that many people can gather under one roof and still be able to breathe.

Looking around after we came in, I estimated the dance floor would have to be measured in acres, and from where we sat, I'm not sure I actually could see the far wall. I was aware of a high ceiling overhead, with spotlights shining down on the band and dance floor, making bright cones through a smoky haze that stopped about ten or twelve feet above the dancers. The ceiling and air pipes must have been painted black, but through the haze I could see red blinking lights and dim outlines of what I thought must be air scrubbers, ionizing the smoke particles so we all didn't choke. I guessed that each of these scrubbers was about the size of a Buick.

What really amazed me, however, was the fact I could hear something besides the band. The musicians were on a high stand along one wall and banks of speakers, each on the scale of a clothes dryer, hung from the ceiling. There were even larger speakers on the stage to either side of them and I wondered how the musicians could stand the intensity of the sound night after night. Or had they become deaf over the years and had to play extremely loud just to hear themselves? I know that when we walked in, the sound level hit me like a crashing wave, and even where we stood, almost fifty yards from the band, I could feel my jeans vibrating against my legs.

We ordered a beer and took off for the dance floor. One song was ending but the lead singer announced a line dance and everyone cheered wildly, including Jeanne. I wasn't sure just what this was, but everyone lined up on the floor and the band struck up a lively chord. I had to watch for a minute or two to catch the step, but once I did, there was nothing to it. It was kind of like doing the Cottoneyed Joe by myself, but it was fun to simply drift and let my feet carry me where I needed to go. I only turned the wrong direction twice, almost knocking down two ladies. However, they were both well lubricated and this seemed to be part of the fun.

After that, the band played a couple of slow numbers, and Jeanne and I glided over the floor. Then it was a fast two-step, which I picked up quickly, and someone called for the Cotton-eyed Joe. That was a pretty simple step to pick up and it was easy to lose myself in the crowd as we promenaded around the dance floor shouting "Bullshit!" Then it was a mixture of waltzes and polkas and something I thought was called the schottische, and we didn't get a chance to sit down or talk until the band took a break. We could have continued dancing to the recorded music, but I was glad of the chance to sit down for a while. I try to stay in shape, but that first set was the most intense workout I've had in a long time.

The second set seemed to have more slow numbers and we stayed on the floor the whole time. I remember thinking at one point that the management was wise to have a cover charge at the door. They certainly didn't make much profit from us on drinks. All Jeanne and I had all night was a couple of beers apiece, and when we came back from the second set, another, older couple was sitting at our table. The man had a cane and it was clear they were there for the music.

When the other couple started to leave Jeanne insisted they stay. "We don't even want to sit down," she said. "Would you mind watching my jacket?"

I was seeing a whole new side of Jeanne I never knew was there. When we danced she moved with complete abandon, even though we'd not had time to finish our beer. When this almost ended in complete disaster on a couple of fast polka spins, she laughed in delight, and it was contagious. I found myself making moves I never knew I had as I tried to keep up with her. It amazed me how well we moved together, as if we had been partners for years, and I wondered who this stranger was that Jeanne seemed to bring out in me so easily.

Later I remembered something I'd read or heard many years before, that what matters most is not really how much we love or admire another person. These are both important, but what really matters is who we become when we are with them. There is a lot of truth in the old wisdom that intimates bring out the best and the worst in each other, but I believe that true partners bring out the very best. I liked this new man Jeanne brought out in me and just before we went to sleep that night, I told her so.

"Mmm," she said sleepily, snuggling even closer. I thought she had not heard me until she brought it up a couple of days later. "I don't know what the future holds for us, Jazz," she told me in a quiet moment. "What I do know is that being around you sets me free. I'm very grateful you were brought into my life. I hope we have a long time with each other, but the gift of today is enough."

"I'm greedy," I told her. "I want a lot of days like this, but I know what you mean. What we have right now is worth whatever happens later. I've been very blessed."

"Hmm," she laughed, raising herself up and pressing me down onto my back. "Let me show you what's about to happen."

# 7. Shabbat

The next morning I woke up stiff in all the wrong places, as an uncle of mine used to say. It took almost thirty minutes in the sauna to work out all the kinks and when I got back to my room, Jeanne was gone. Yet when I got out of the shower, she was back, fully dressed to the teeth and reading the Sunday morning paper. When I went across the room to kiss her good morning, she tugged playfully at the towel around my waist, then ducked around me when I dropped it and tried to grab her. "Silly man," she said. "We don't have time if we're going to get a good seat at church."

Then she sat there while I dressed, making bawdy comments. When I was done, she looked at me critically. "You sure clean up good for a country boy," she smirked, kissing me lightly on the lips. "Let's get some breakfast."

Jeanne was right about the church. We got there forty minutes early and the place was already two-thirds full. An usher in a waiter's tuxedo and white gloves showed us to a seat in the sixth row from the front, and handed us a program. I was tickled to see an admonition in the bulletin that said, "RESPECT THE PASTOR! Please remain in your seat until the preaching is done." I pointed this out to Jeanne, who smiled and murmured, "The wages of sin! The preaching's the price you pay for the music."

A lady in front of us heard her and turned around and smiled. She introduced herself as the pastor's wife and welcomed us to the church. "You'd be surprised how rude people can be," she said.

"Walking out in the middle of a sermon!"

Jeanne tried to apologize, but the pastor's wife waved it off. "He'll love it when I tell him," she assured us. "There's no doubt about his preaching," she assured us. "You'll see, especially if he gets the Holy Ghost." She invited us to have lunch with them but I begged off, telling her we were expected at a friend's home.

"I hope you weren't supposed to be there at noon," she replied. "We don't usually let out until one-thirty." I told her I would call and let them know and asked where the rest room might be. I didn't want to miss any of the music and I didn't dare try to step out during the sermon. Jeanne later told me that while I was gone, she was thoroughly interrogated by the pastor's wife. Nor was Mrs. Pastor surprised by our being there. "I wish as many people came here for Jesus as they do for the singing," she said when I'd returned. She was looking at me pointedly when she said it.

I don't know where the inspiration came from but I heard myself saying, "Well, if they are here, at least it gives God and the pastor a chance to get at them." For some reason, she found this hilarious. She was still chuckling about it when she introduced us to her husband after the service.

Kowalski was waiting for me when we got back to the motel. Adams had a family thing that afternoon and more than two of us might be too intimidating. We were due at the bishop's house at two-thirty and it was already a quarter of two, so I didn't take time to change. Between the dancing the night before and the singing at church, I was famished. Luckily, the Keller home was only fifteen minutes away, so I had time to grab a quick bite to eat.

Jeanne insisted that Kowalski join us while we had lunch in the dining room, and the two of them had some gentle fun at my expense. "You should have seen his face when he was telling us he had a date," Kowalski told her. "He looked like a high school freshman."

Kowalski and I were on our way at twelve past two and when she got us to the Keller home, we were five minutes early. Unlike Adams, Kowalski was an aggressive driver. I tried not to react, but approaching a hard turn, I found my right foot reaching for the brake pedal. I tried to catch myself but Kowalski saw me and laughed. "Jim does the same thing. He won't ride with me unless I let him drive."

"Don't mind me, I'm just praying," I told her. For some reason, this tickled her and she laughed so hard I thought she was going to lose control of the car. I was relieved when we pulled up into the Keller driveway without a scratch.

I know a fellow who has a photo collection of what he calls Texas Tacky. These are shots of things like large antebellum mansions with high white columns and little or no landscaping, all surrounded by fences made of unpainted steel wagon wheels. One of his finest is a seasonal greeting made of welded chain bent to form a message in irregular script: Joy At Xmas! Yet, the one I like best is a neat row of high-fin Cadillac sedans buried nose first in a flat field. The angle suggests they either fell out of the sky or were flown there by someone who consistently misjudged his landing.

The Keller home reminded me of this photo collection, although in a very tony way. The houses in this addition were all relatively new and so huge that they dwarfed their narrow lots. The houses were set next to each other cheek by jowl, with scarcely fifteen feet between them. The narrow sidewalks in front were set next to the street curbing, which made the front lawns look like postage stamps scattered between wide front driveways and generous shrub and flower beds along the front of each house. There were eight-foot privacy fences running from the front of each house to the back easement, and the only real deviation in the uniform appearance was the color of the brick and roofing shingles, or the age of the cedar used in the fencing. The color of the trim was almost uniformly dusky blue accented by cream, but what really sealed the tacky award in my mind were the ornate burglar bars on every door and window exposed to the street. The whole neighborhood looked like an upscale prison. It even had a high brick wall around the perimeter and armed guards at the entrance gates.

Kowalski seemed to read my mind. "How would you like to live here, campers?" she asked softly. "Welcome to Fort Nouveau Riche."

Then she remembered she was riding with me and not Adams. She looked at me with concern and started to say something.

I waved her off. "You took the words right out of my mouth," I laughed. "I'll never understand why people with this much money don't hire better architects."

As instructed by the security guard, we parked in an open space in the driveway. The house had a triple garage, but the doors were shut tight. There was a large black Mercedes sedan parked in front of one set of doors. I recognized it from the church parking lot Thursday afternoon. Across the left side of the rear bumper was a bright sticker with the words "DE COLORES!" spelled out in rainbow colors, but it was the vanity license plate that had caught my attention before. It read, "BP 606."

"Did you catch the license plate?" I asked Kowalski.

"Almost the number of the Beast," Kowalski answered. "I'm surprised he actually ordered it." She started to say something more, but the front door opened as we approached. A large African-American woman with the most soulful eyes I've ever seen invited us in. "Dr. Phillips?" she asked. "The guard phoned you were on the way. Missus Keller is waiting for you in the study."

Without acknowledgement of Kowalski or another word, she turned and led us down a wide hallway to a set of French doors that led into a surprisingly warm and comfortable family room. A large glassed fireplace faced French doors and a grand piano at the far side of the room. While I didn't recognize the work of the artists whose paintings decorated the walls, I knew these were the originals, not prints. What struck me most was the contrast of this room with the rest of the house, especially the front. This room was welcoming.

A pale and fragile looking woman of middle years rose to greet us when we came in. She was tall and far too thin, and her cropped gray hair made her look gaunt. She introduced herself as Amanda Keller and asked us to be seated. Then she offered us coffee or tea. We declined and Kowalski looked at me in question. I nodded and she began the interview as we had agreed on the way here.

"We are very sorry for your loss, Mrs. Keller," she said. "We know this is a very hard time for you, but we need to ask you some questions."

"That's what everyone says," the bishop's widow replied. There was more than a little irony in her voice, and I thought I detected more relief than grief in the way she spoke. "Please call me Amanda. Everyone does."

"I'm not sure what you mean," Kowalski replied. "Who is everyone?"

"Mostly people who don't know how things were. Are you here because you think I murdered my husband?" she asked abruptly. "Do I need a lawyer?"

"Not at all," I broke in, hoping to protect Kowalski if this went where it looked it was headed. As an outsider, I could survive the political fire storm. "Did you murder him, Amanda?"

Kowalski shot me a hard look but said nothing. I would have some explaining to do later. "No, I didn't," she answered. "I don't know anything about guns."

"Well, we didn't come here thinking you killed him," I assured her. "But since you suggested it, I had to ask." I was being very careful to keep any blame pointed at me and out of the corner of my eye I could see that Kowalski saw what I was doing. Her face cleared.

"I understand," Amanda told us. "Do you really think it was an accident?" She was looking at me but I looked to Kowalski for an answer.

"It could have been that way," Kowalski said. "What we have to do is make sure. What is it that everyone says?"

"How sorry they are for our loss. If they only knew how relieved I am he's gone!" As if challenging us she declared, "There! I've actually said it!"

Suddenly Amanda Keller burst into tears. I handed her a handkerchief, thankful I'd put a clean one in my pocket before church. Kowalski moved to the couch beside the widow and patted her on the arm. In a few moments Amanda stopped crying and wiped her eyes. "Excuse me," she said. "I need to wash my face." Kowalski looked at me but I shook my head and she remained seated.

Two minutes later Amanda was back. She looked more relaxed than when we arrived. I could see she had touched up her makeup. "I beg your pardon," she told us. "I didn't intend to dump on you. I guess I owe you an explanation."

"It might help us understand," Kowalski suggested.

"I am so tired of lies," the widow told us. "I don't want to hurt my children, but I refuse to lie any more. I hope you will keep what I say among us. I'd hate for them to read it in the papers."

"We will keep it as confidential as we can," Kowalski offered. "Of course, if it comes to court as evidence, then it will be a matter of public record."

"All I need is a few hours," Amanda replied. "I want to talk to my children and then you can shout it from the housetops for all I care."

"What is it you need to tell them?" Kowalski prodded.

"My late husband was a batterer," Amanda. "That's nothing new to my children, even though we don't talk about it much. What they don't know is that I was planning to leave him."

"Were you going to leave at some point, or did you have a definite plan?"

"I had a plan. I've been putting money away in my own name for the last couple of years. When my mother died last year I knew I would eventually have enough to live on without asking him. Mother's lawyer called last week and told me they've just settled the estate. I told him what I was doing and why. He set up a trust fund for me so my husband couldn't get at it, but I was dreading the confrontation."

"I can see why," Kowalski nodded. "When were you planning to do this?"

"Rufus was going out of town for two weeks next month and I was planning to make the break then. I wanted to be completely out of the house with the things that are important to me. Mostly it's the stuff in this room."

I looked around. There was enough in this room to furnish a large apartment well. All that was missing was a bed, and I imagined one of the couches might be a sleeper.

Kowalski looked at me and I knew she wanted me to take the lead. "Could you tell us about the abuse?" I asked. "When did it begin?"

"It began before we were married," she told me. "It was psychological at first and it didn't get physical until after our oldest son was born. And it didn't happen very often at first. Naturally, I thought I was at fault. I've learned most battered women do."

"What about the children?" I asked gently. "Did he hit them, too?"

"I think so, but I never saw it," she replied. "I think if I had, I would have left him. I think he must have known this. I was very protective of my children, and there were times I put myself between him and them." She smiled bitterly. "If you saw my medical record over the years, you'd see I've a lot of 'accidents' around holidays. For some reason, it was always worse then."

"Did anyone else know of this?" I asked. "Anyone on your side of the family?"

"My brother did. He came to see me in the hospital after one of my 'accidents.' I don't know how he heard about it, but I had to make Frank promise not to go after Rufus right that minute. He was still there when Rufus came by and I thought Frank was going to kill him. He told Rufus if he ever did this again, he'd be dead in a week." She shook her head. "That stopped it for a long time. Then Rufus got drunk and almost killed me. I was frightened to death Frank would find out, but he never did. I was careful to keep things from Frank after that."

"I'm afraid I'm going to have to ask you for Frank's address," Kowalski told her. "We need to talk to him."

A deep sadness came over Amanda Keller's face. "You won't be able to," she said. "He died three years ago." She looked at us defiantly through her tears. "I would never have told you about Frank if he were still alive. Even if he had killed Rufus and even if you put me in jail, too."

"Why do you call your husband Rufus?" I asked, more out of curiosity than anything. I also wanted to get us back to calmer shores.

"It was his family tradition. Rufus was named after his father, who was called John. Everyone in his family called my husband Rufus to avoid confusion. So our oldest child is called John." She smiled for the first time. "He calls himself Jack, partly because his father hates it. He's in town if you'd like to meet him. So are the other kids, except for Wally." She seemed sad again when she mentioned him.

I didn't see how interviewing each of the children would be fruitful at this point. Normally, we would need to check their alibis, but under the circumstances it seemed a bit risky. With the chief leaning so hard toward closing the case as accidental homicide, it was this kind of thing that could blow up in our faces. I decided it would be better to interview them as a group, but I wanted to clear this with Kowalski in advance since she was the lead detective. "Why isn't Wally here?" I asked.

"Wally was the first casualty of Rufus' violence," Amanda told us. "To my shame I took Rufus' word over Wally's. Rufus had not hit me yet at that point and Wally was placed with us as an older foster child. We'd been told we couldn't have children and I pushed for adoption. Wally was a distant relative in the Keller family and it seemed the thing to do, taking him in. He ran away when he was eighteen and joined the Marines. We have never heard from him since his discharge. Rufus assured me he had hired private detectives to find what became of Wally after he got out of the service, but I found out a couple of years ago that was a lie. I think that was the final straw."

"What's Wally's full name?" Kowalski asked.

It was clear that Amanda Keller didn't want to answer that question, but to her credit, Kowalski didn't push. The silence grew very heavy. Finally Amanda spoke. "Do I really have to give you that?" Kowalski nodded. "I wish I didn't have such a good alibi," Amanda told us. "I would much rather you blame me than Wally."

"Do you really think we can do that, Amanda?" I asked softly.

She shook her head. "No. I suppose you'll find out, anyway. His name is Walton Davis, Walton Davis Keller. We legally adopted him and Rufus had his name changed to ours." She snorted. "No, not ours, his! I plan to take my own name back."

"What is his birth date?" Kowalski asked.

"December 25, 1965. He was with us for eight years." She looked at us pleadingly. "Please, if you find him, tell him I know how wrong I was. Ask him to forgive me."

"We'll do everything we can to make sure you can ask him yourself," I promised. "I'm sure he has by now."

"God, I hope so," Amanda answered, crying softly. "He was my first child, even if I didn't carry him."

We stayed a bit longer, but there was not much Amanda Keller could give us. After we were done with her I had word in private with Kowalski. When I explained what I was thinking, she agreed with my assessment and we gathered the three remaining children in the family room. There were some pro forma questions we needed to ask that go with a homicide investigation and none of them seem surprised. They were very forthcoming and gave good answers. We would need to confirm the information they told us, but my sense was that their alibis would stand up. The only other thing we discovered was that all of the children were aware of the abuse their father had perpetrated on their mother. They had discussed it among themselves.

Only Jack was old enough to have much memory of Wally, and what he had surprised his mother. "Yeah, he got in touch with me a couple of years ago," Jack said. "We never got together but he called from time to time. He was my hero growing up. I was really glad to hear from him."

"When did he get in touch last?" Kowalski asked.

"Friday afternoon, just before I flew in here," Jack answered. "I told him Dad had been murdered and asked if he was coming to the funeral. He told me he couldn't get away right now. I think it had something to do with his work."

"What does he do?" Kowalski wanted to know.

"I don't know exactly," Jack replied. "When I asked, he told me he couldn't say much. I got the idea it has something to do with Homeland Security, but I'm not sure he ever said that."

Kowalski and I looked at each other. We both knew what the other was thinking. Homeland Security has been used to cover a multitude of sins. Often this has been by people whose only connection to a federal agency is being on the most wanted list or serving time. What better way to explain the possession of an assault rifle and body armor than to flash a bogus ID? This might be useless at an airport, where they use ID scanners that work the way credit cards do, but it might get a suspect by a routine traffic stop.

"Why didn't you tell me, Jack?" Amanda asked.

Jack looked at his mother sadly. "I think you already know, Mom. Wally made me promise not to say anything. He was afraid you would tell Dad. He didn't want Dad to know anything about him, not even that he was alive."

"Any idea where he was calling from?" Kowalski asked.

"Not really," Jack replied. "Wally wouldn't tell me and I'm glad he didn't. All I can tell you was that it was in a city somewhere. At least, I heard a lot of traffic in the background. I guess he could have been at a rest stop on a freeway, too."

"How did he sound?" Amanda wanted to know.

Jack laughed. "Just like Wally. He was worried about you, how you were taking Dad getting shot. I told him you were shocked, but doing all right." He shrugged, then shook his head. "No, I'm sorry, mom. That's not true. What I actually said was that you were probably relieved." He looked at Kowalski and me nervously. "I'm sorry if I'm spilling family secrets."

"Not at all, Jack," his mother smiled and opened her arms. Jack crossed the room to give her a hug. "I've always been proud of you for telling the truth." She looked at her children. "I've already told these officers I was planning to leave your father next month."

"Thank God!" Wendy said. She was the middle daughter. "We were afraid he was going to kill you." She began to cry.

The youngest daughter didn't share her sister's enthusiasm. "So you were just going to jump ship! What about your marriage vows? What about us? What about Daddy?" She was close to hysteria. I wondered if she had not been her father's pet.

"I was planning to take you all with me, Laura," Amanda said. "I found a safe place for us to live. You wouldn't even have to change schools."

It was clear the Keller family needed some time to themselves. I was surprised they were being so open in front of two strangers, but we needed to head out. "Excuse me," I said. "We're pretty much done. One thing I need is the most recent picture of Wally you have."

"Of course," Amanda said. She got up and walked to the fireplace. She took down a framed picture and handed it to us. "I don't know how much use this will be. Wally was nineteen when it was taken and he's close to forty now." She hesitated, then said, "That's the only adult picture of him I have. I really need to have it back."

"We'll make a copy and get it back to you this week," Kowalski promised. Jack showed us out.

"What do you think?" Kowalski asked me when we were in the car and driving away.

"I think Jack is holding something back," I replied. "Other than that, I found them pretty believable. I wonder what the relationship was between Laura and her dad?"

"I wondered that, too," Kowalski said, "but it isn't going into my report."

I called ahead to let Jeanne know we were on our way to the motel and studied the picture Amanda had given us as we drove. The picture was of a stern faced young man in a Marine Corps dress uniform. He was not wearing a hat and his hair was cut close on the sides. We used to call this "white sidewalls" when I was in the service, but the darker oval of hair on top of Wally's head was not much longer than the sides. I suppose it is a generational difference, but I wondered why bother with the top patch. Why not buzz it all the way across like we did more years ago than I care to remember?

There was something about the young man in the picture that looked very familiar to me, but I couldn't figure what it was. I've a good memory for faces and this really bothered me. I've heard it said that there are maybe a dozen standard faces most of us resemble, but there was nothing standard about Wally Keller except his GI hair-

cut. He had strong features, not unlike the young Rock Hudson, and
I found myself wondering if Wally was gay. I would have given odds
that Jack was, and given Rufus Keller's hard line on homosexuality,
there would have been no better way for Wally to rebel. Maybe that
was what precipitated the final split.

I also wondered if the real reason Wally hadn't wanted to come
home was because he was a victim of AIDS. One of the things that
really surprised me many years ago came on a visit to Washington,
DC. I was with the CID then and had been sent to a seminar no one
else wanted to attend. I think there was a major Razorbacks game
at home that weekend, and in Arkansas, football is as important as
religion, maybe more so. A lot of the guys in the CID had tickets to
that game and I didn't, so I was elected.

The original AIDS quilt was in Washington the week I was there.
This was the last time it would be on display as a single unit and Nellie was with me. We both wanted to see it, so we stayed over an extra
day. When I saw it lying there, spread out so people could walk between the squares, it was like seeing the Grand Canyon for the first
time. I was staggered by an overwhelming sense of loss and needless
waste.

What really struck me, however, was how many of the victims were
Marines. As I thought about this, though, it made a lot of sense. A
large element of gay male culture celebrates being manly, and there
is nothing more macho than being a member of the Corps. Nor is
there any uniform more elegant than Marine dress blues, complete
with a ceremonial sabre. What was their advertising slogan a few
years back? Something about it being hard to be humble when one
is the very best.

So I wondered if Wally was gay. Then something about the uniform caught my attention and I looked more closely. Sure enough,
there was something there that told me Wally had been a member
of the Marine Band. It took me a minute to realize what it was, and
when I did, I felt foolish. The uniform jacket Wally was wearing was
red, not blue, and it was completely unadorned. This was the uniform used when the band played at the White House and I should

have spotted this immediately. After all, my namesake was the Marine Band's most famous director.

"Did you notice the uniform?" I asked Kowalski.

"Yes," she told me. "It's the Marine Band. 'The President's Own.' A friend of mine plays in it." She grinned. "I tell him it's just because he likes the uniform."

"I wonder what Wally played?"

"The clarinet," she answered. There was no doubt in her voice.

"I didn't hear Amanda mention that," I said.

"There was another picture of him on the shelf by the piano. He was in a band uniform and he was holding a clarinet."

I shook my head. "I must be getting blind and senile," I told her. "Just drop me off at the nearest nursing home."

"Oh, I don't think Jeanne would like that," Kowalski said with a smirk.

There's not much to tell about dinner with Simon and Claire except that Simon's dead pig was excellent and Jeanne took them by storm. She and Claire clicked right away and on the way home that night Jeanne said, "You've got such nice friends, so unusual, too. Where do you find such interesting folk?"

I laughed. "Eccentric or weird would be better. We hang around crime scenes."

"You sure don't look Goth," she quipped. "Except in the dark."

"In the dark all cats are Goth," I responded. "They were very taken with you."

"Claire told me she and Nellie were good friends," Jeanne said. "I'm glad they accepted me. I told her about how we met. About Henry, too."

"Do we need to talk about Henry, Jeanne?"

"Yes, but not now." She smiled and took a deep breath. "It's been such a lovely evening. Let's stay with that."

"Are you saying the evening's over?" I asked, giving her a baleful look.

"Not for a minute," she responded, giving me a bawdy wink.

# 8. Fast Closure

The next morning came too soon. I was up early and spent almost an hour in the exercise room, still limbering up from Saturday night dancing. I was freshly shaved and just out of the shower when my phone rang. For a moment I considered muting it and letting whomever it was leave a message. Jeanne was still asleep, stretched out like a cozy cat on the oversized bed with the covers flung back, and I had a marvelous plan for waking her. Yet when I reached for the phone to mute it, old habits took over and I answered. It was Kowalski. She and Adams were there to pick me up.

I asked them to meet me in the dining room and gently woke Jeanne to let her know I was leaving. I asked her if she wanted to have breakfast with us and she told me she would be there in ten minutes. When she jumped out of bed and headed for the shower it was all I could do not to grab her and make us both very late.

When I got to the dining room, I could tell Adams was excited. He reminded me of a child waiting to open presents, but he restrained himself until I'd ordered and was sipping my first cup of coffee. Then he reached into his jacket and took out a clear plastic evidence bag.

I could see a single bullet through the plastic and held the bag up to look at it more closely. It was long and thin with a solid round nose, what the military calls a full metal jacket. Unlike expanding bullets used for hunting, various treaties require nations at war to use bullets that don't expand. This seems like a strange convention to me since these same treaties allow artillery shells that explode and tear off whole limbs, but I wasn't consulted when they put these things into effect. To me the whole concept of rules of war seems like an oxymoron.

The bullet I was looking at looked archaic to my eye, World War II vintage, if not older. I had a surplus rifle that shot this kind of ammo once. What I remembered was that I couldn't get a single round of the surplus shells that came with it to fire, even though I found the powder would still burn when I took the shells apart and the primers would pop when I heated them with a match. Yet, this was the weapon of choice of Lee Harvey Oswald, and at least one bullet like the one I held had been recovered from the assassination.

"Looks like it came from a 6.5 millimeter Mannlicher-Carcano," I said. "Or maybe a Norwegian Krag. Where did you find it?"

"It's a Carcano," Adams told me, trying to mask his disappointment. Police officers take a lot of pride in knowing about guns. It's not only part of our professional culture but it is also deeply embedded in the fabric of American society. No other nation on earth is as fascinated with personal firearms as we are, except maybe northern Ireland.

"It's two thousandths of an inch bigger than the Krag," Adams continued. "But it might work in the Krag with the right casing. It was buried in the crack between a couple of window moldings right where you told us to look."

I thought about this for a minute or two. Carcano ballistics aren't that good from a sniper's point of view. One of the bullets recovered in Dallas literally fell out of one of the people shot, the governor if I remember right. Or was it the president? I'd think a professional assassin would want a bullet that would destroy as much tissue as possible and deliver the most shock to the victim. This kind of bullet would require extreme accuracy. An expanding hunting slug gave lots of room for error.

Then another thought hit me. Maybe the shooter wanted this bullet found. The more I thought about it the more I was convinced this was why this bullet was used. I told the others what I was thinking.

"Goodness, you have a cheerful topic for breakfast." It was Jeanne, joining us and looking as radiant as any bride. I introduced her to Adams and she greeted Kowalski warmly. "Don't let me interrupt you," Jeanne added. "This is better than Court TV."

Kowalski snorted and Adams grinned. I explained to Jeanne what Adams had found and what I was thinking. "I thought there was a bullet in the victim," Jeanne said. "Did this go all the way through him?"

This called for more explanations, but when I stopped, Jeanne said, "I think you're right. I think your killer's messing with your mind. He sounds like Henry."

"Who is Henry?" Kowalski asked before I could jump in. I was caught completely off guard by Jeanne's candor.

"He's the serial killer I'm married to," Jeanne explained. Kowalski and Adams gave each other a strange look. "I know," Jeanne told them. "That sounds strange, doesn't it? Jazz caught him but we can't prosecute. Henry has Alzheimer's and is in a nursing home now and the evidence is not that good."

All I could do was laugh. "You better tell them the whole story, Jeanne," I said.

"The whole story, Dr. Phillips?" she asked in mock innocence. "Even the good parts?" I felt myself flush and despite their confusion, Adams and Kowalski started smiling. By the time Jeanne was done explaining my pursuit of the cat burglar who gave us the key piece of evidence, they were laughing hard.

"Anyway," Jeanne said. "It sounds like someone who does careful planning. That's the part that sounds like Henry, completely cold-blooded and too damned smart for his own good."

Kowalski and Adams and I looked at each other. Jeanne had put in words what we were all thinking. "The problem is the same as with Henry," Kowalski affirmed. "The evidence is not clear and the killer did a good job of muddying the water taking a shot from the tower hill." I must have looked surprised because Kowalski nodded. "That was the other thing we had to tell you. We think the shot came from a spot south of the base of the tower. The smudge on the railing was gray automotive primer."

"Three guesses who put it there for us to find," I said. "I wondered why this guy was going to so much trouble messing with our minds, and I think I know. He's been busy creating all these different scenarios to confuse the legal issues. He knows he's making it easy for the chief to grab the easy solution and he's setting up a strong case for reasonable doubt if he's caught. He's also having fun doing it. So where do we go from here?"

Adams looked extremely uncomfortable. "I'm afraid the chief is pressing us to close the case, Jazz," he told me. "He wants our final report on his desk by ten this morning. He's going to call a press conference."

"That's pretty much what we expected," I said. "The bishop's funeral is this afternoon and this will tie it all up at once. So file your report, but leave some wiggle room in case we find something later. I'll do the same." I held up the bullet in the case. "Be sure this gets entered into the evidence inventory and document where it was found. You don't need to give it any undue attention. I'll send you my report to slip into the file later. I'll follow up on my own and keep you posted. You can add it to the file as I send it. That way it's documented and everyone's ass is covered, particularly yours. Are you all right with that?"

Again, Kowalski and Adams looked at each other. An unspoken agreement was reached between them and Kowalski nodded. "Thanks, Jazz. We were afraid you might balk. The chief is moving the schedule ahead by a full day and we don't carry much weight in the department."

I handed each of them one of my cards. "Jeanne and I are going to be on the road for a few days, but you can leave a message on my machine. The other number is Dee, Steven DiRado, my partner in crime. You can call him in an emergency if you can't get in touch with me. He's as sharp as they get and you can tell him anything you'd tell me. He'll also know where to find me."

Adams and Kowalski took off soon after that but Jeanne and I lingered over our coffee. We talked about different things we might do in the next days and decided to drop my rental car off at the airport. I would ride with her back to Hope and pick up another rental to get home.

"I do need to check in with the nursing home every couple of days or so," Jeanne told me. "I'm the one they call if there's an emergency."

"Why don't you get a satellite phone?" I asked. "They're a little expensive, but that way you won't have to worry. Surely Henry can afford it."

"Henry could probably afford the whole company," she replied dryly. "I guess it's time for us to talk, Jazz."

"Only if you want to, Jeanne," I said. "I'm in no hurry. I intend to spend the rest of my life in your company on whatever terms you want."

Jeanne's eyes clouded up and she began to cry softly. "That's just it," she said. "I want to be Mrs. Jazz Phillips, but I can't leave Henry in the lurch. Yes, he lied to me, but I just can't abandon him. And I can't ask you to wait for him to die. It isn't fair."

"Life isn't fair, Jeanne," I told her. "Let's plan on a long engagement. I would love to give you a ring, but I guess that wouldn't be proper, would it?"

Jeanne chuckled. "We couldn't post it in the Hope paper but if you give me a ring, I'll wear it." She raised her left hand and pointed out something I'd noticed but not asked her about. "I'm not wearing Henry's rings any more. I haven't ever since I found out what kind of man he is. I put them in his safe deposit box and when the time comes, I'll put them in his casket!" Her voice was hard and flat as she finished.

Over the next couple of days we spent a lot of time shopping. There are scads of jewelry stores in the Dallas Metroplex, but I was looking for just the right thing. We finally found it at a small shop in Oak Cliff that specialized in custom designs, and the young man who made their jewelry told us we were lucky. "It's hard to find Colombian emeralds with this particular quality and color," he told us.

"I think you're going to be very pleased how it turns out."

When Jeanne picked out the setting she wanted, a very ancient looking design in white gold, he was even happier. "This is going to be fun," he said. "The light will catch it perfectly. When I'm done your ring will look like something that came from a sunken Viking ship."

"You hear that, Erik?" she quipped, looking at me.

"The real treasure will be the hand wearing the ring," I assured the jeweler.

The young man smiled and Jeanne turned bright scarlet. She was at a loss for words. "Thank you," she murmured in my ear when we were back in the car. "You'll never know what this means to me."

"It's my pleasure," I told her.

Since Jeanne was driving, I put a call in to Jack McKee, Sam's brother. Jack is Sam's electronics guru and I reached him at their ranch in Wyoming. I asked him about satellite phones and he told me a lot more than I needed to know. Most of what he said was lost in the vast reaches of my electronic ignorance, but he did recommend a specific system. He told me exactly where to find it in Cowtown and he gave me a number for the shop. "Remember," he said, "Ft. Worth is Tandy's home office. That's where Radio Shack has its headquarters."

I called the shop and found out we needed an appointment. I scheduled one for the next morning and we decided to have supper early in Dallas. Jeanne had heard of a place she wanted to try. It was called the Blue Mesa and was in the northern part of Dallas. Their specialty was gourmet Mexican food.

This may sound like an oxymoron to any Tex-Mex purist familiar with the fine food offered by small cafes from Cowtown to Albuquerque. I discovered very quickly it was not. Where the local cafes were excellent, the Blue Mesa was superb. I ate far more than I knew was good for me, but the food was so good I couldn't help cleaning my plate. I would have eaten even more if I could have.

The next morning we were up early. I spent an extra fifteen minutes in the exercise room trying to make up for the havoc the Blue

Mesa made in my diet. When I got back to the room, Jeanne was packed and ready to go, and she entertained herself while she waited by making remarks about my love handles. I threatened to ravish her if she didn't hush up and she laughed. "You're still too full from last night," she snorted. So naturally, I had to prove her wrong.

The satellite phone shop was much like the jewelry store in Oak Cliff, small and quaint and tucked away around the corner from a major street. The young man who opened the door didn't look much older than a college freshman, but he turned out to be the owner of what Jack McKee told me was a very successful business. When I explained what we needed, he brought out two systems. He told us they were about the same and that he himself preferred the less expensive one. "The instruments are better and so is battery life. The other company is running on its reputation."

"The Avis principle," I said. Jeanne nodded, but the shop owner gave me a blank look. "The rental car company," I told him. "They used to advertise that even though they were the number two service, they tried harder." He nodded vaguely and I felt all my years. I realized they had used that ad when I was a kid.

Jeanne saw my response and tried to kid me out of it. "It's all right, daddy," she said sweetly. "I remember them."

I had to laugh, not only at myself, but also at the look on the phone man's face. "We have interesting relationships in our family," I said blandly, and Jeanne roared.

I saw the shop owner's jaw tighten. "We're laughing at us, not you," I told him. "We're, um, newlyweds."

"We just haven't made it to the church yet," Jeanne giggled.

The phone dealer clearly had doubts about us, but when he checked Jeanne's credit rating, his manner changed completely. He wasn't exactly gushy, but it was clear the smell of money had greased the skids. That sad refrain from an old song went through my mind again. When will we ever learn? I began to understand from the inside how life must be for people who have great wealth. How can they ever be sure they are loved for themselves and not their money? No wonder so many of them become so cynical.

We walked out of the shop with the phone and all the accoutrements needed to use it on the road or in the depths of the Amazon jungle. Jeanne even picked up a small solar powered battery charger, and she couldn't wait to use it. As soon as we were in the car, she plugged the phone into the power outlet. It was all I could do to convince her she really needed to let the battery charge overnight before using the phone. "I need to call the nursing home," she told me and pretended to pout when I handed her my phone and told her to pull over. Cell phones and driving don't mix in heavy traffic and I took the wheel.

"Can I call Lindy, too?" Jeanne laughed when I started the car. She dialed her sister first, without waiting for my answer.

The satellite phone was one of the best suggestions I ever made. It gave Jeanne not only a sense of freedom, but also the gift of privacy. I suppose satellite records could pinpoint her location within a hundred feet while she was on a call, but in this age of caller ID it made it hard for callers to know exactly where she was. The rates were more expensive than standard cellular service, but as Jeanne pointed out, Henry could afford to buy the whole company.

"This is just wonderful," Jeanne said one day after checking in with the nursing home. "We could be almost anywhere in the world and still manage what we need to." At that moment we were in Washington, DC, eating our lunch at a bench on the mall. I was working on a project for Sam McKee and Jeanne wanted to see the new World War II memorial. We were staying in a large apartment the Agency kept for people like me, and Jeanne loved it there. It was easy walking distance from McKee's office and had easy access to public transportation.

Now Jeanne sighed. "I suppose I'll have to go back to Hope sometime soon, Jazz. If I'm gone much longer I'm sure there will be talk."

"I'm sure there already is," I told her. "It's been what, six weeks since you came to Ft. Worth? Have you ever been gone that long before?"

"Not quite," she said. "I spent a month in California with Lindy a couple of years ago. There was talk then, but I was sure to bore the right people with pictures I took of strange people on the beach."

"Just out of curiosity, what have you told them about where you are now?" I was not particularly concerned, but gossip in small towns can get quite vicious. Nor do I have trouble telling an outright whopper to those who snoop. Jeanne, however, has trouble telling even the smallest white lie, and she has a hard time dealing with nasty people. I admire this, but the truth can get you killed. The asshole that just broke into my house doesn't need to know the shotgun I'm holding is empty. I consider small town gossips scumbags, too. They steal an honest person's hard earned credibility and they assassinate good character.

"I told someone I wanted to spend some time visiting old friends," she said. "You qualify, don't you?"

"Well, I'm old enough, if that's what you're saying," I replied, pretending to be hurt.

Jeanne wasn't fooled for a moment. "I know, ancient one. What I don't understand is how you make the switch with that randy young stud I find in my arms."

I laughed. "You could always play the Betty Ford card. That would give them stuff to talk about for years. I'm sure it's something they could relate to in a moment of honesty."

"Wouldn't that frost their cake," Jeanne laughed. "I don't know why I care what they think. Maybe I should just tell them the truth. I mean about Henry. Do you think they'd believe it?"

"I doubt it," I said. "They have a lot invested in Henry the way they want to see him. I think they would trash you instead."

"Maybe I should just divorce him," she said. "I don't need his money."

This was news. When I first met Jeanne three years before, I gathered that she was a struggling widow with children when she and Henry met. I asked her about this.

"You have the best memory!" she said. "I was having a hard time right then. I had three kids and the job I had didn't pay much. It took most of our savings to pay for Ken's funeral, even though the Navy eventually reimbursed me. Then his insurance company tried to keep from paying off his policy on some technicality. I got a lawyer, but it took years to settle. I was remarried by then, so I put it into a trust fund for me and the kids. Henry wanted me to invest in his company but I wasn't about to let us get stranded twice. I told Henry that was our parachute, including him, if his company went down."

"Makes sense to me," I said. A National Park Service Ranger was riding by on her horse just then and caught my attention. I grabbed by camera and managed to get a good shot of her with the reflection of the Lincoln Memorial in the background. The ranger smiled and waved.

I was getting used to a new digital camera then and when the shot popped up on the LCD display, I showed it to Jeanne. From what I could see on the tiny display it was going to turn out to be a keeper.

"You're the strangest man," Jeanne told me. "Here I tell you I'm independently wealthy and you don't even ask how much money I have."

"I don't even know how much money I have, Jeanne," I told her. "I seem to make a lot more every year than I need and a lot goes into CDs. I own everything I have."

"What about the monthly bills?" she asked.

"The bank takes care of all the annual insurance payments and stuff like that, and I've an accounting service that takes care of the routine things like gas and electric. I had to do that since Nellie died because I travel so much." I laughed. "It's funny how well the details from a case years ago stick in my mind, but when it comes to my own financial stuff, I always have to look it up. I think I grossed over two hundred and fifty thousand last year, but I had some pretty big expenses, too."

"Maybe that's what I need to do with the household bills, too," Jeanne said. "I've been paying them myself all these years, and I'm sure there are a lot stacked up for me in Hope." She was thoughtful for a moment. "That's strange. I started to say 'at home,' but Hope isn't home to me any more. I don't have any real friends there. I've met more people on this trip I now consider friends than I've met in the last fifteen years. That's sad, isn't it?"

I had to agree, although I was delighted Jeanne melded so well with the people I know. "Well, they're real people, Jeanne, and you are, too. They respect you for that."

"You're sure it's not just because I'm Jazz's lady?"

"Yes, I'm quite sure. Kowalski is a tough cop and you had her on your side in two minutes flat. The same thing happened with Simon and Claire."

I could see Jeanne was having trouble believing me and I took her hand and lifted it to my lips. The green stone of her ring looked like an ancient treasure. "How about me?" I asked. "Doesn't my judgment count?"

Jeanne laughed. "You're under undue influence," she said. "Lust at first sight."

I couldn't argue with that. "It's your beautiful soul that enthralls me," I quipped.

"Is that what you call it?" she shot back. "Now I know what those preachers were up to with all their talk about saving souls."

"Down by the riverside, no less. Seriously, Jeanne, it might be better to get things rolling. I don't want to ever be without you. As long as you're still married to Henry you'll always be torn. I don't want that to destroy what we have."

"I know, Jazz. I want the same thing. I just can't do it quite yet. Despite everything else, Henry did a lot for me and my children."

"Yeah, you're right," I said. "I didn't think about your children or how they might feel. Sorry, I just never had kids to take into account."

"Oh, they want me to leave him," she said, surprising me. "I don't hide things from my children. After I found out, I told them all about Henry the next time we were together. They were pretty shaken up. Then a month later, they all showed up at the house again. They had been talking among themselves and thought I needed to get out. They told me to find a new life." She laughed. "That's something grown children do, you know. They tell their aging parents how to live their lives."

"So have you told them about me?" I asked.

Jeanne blushed. "I was too embarrassed. I asked Lindy to tell them. She did it a couple of weeks ago."

"Have you heard from them?" I asked.

"Yes, my oldest called. What they had to say was pretty simple." She stopped.

"I'm dying over here, Jeanne. Was it thumbs up or thumbs down?"

"Oh, it was definitely thumbs up, though they want to meet you soon. They said I should go for it." She smiled. "I think their aunt told them you walk on water."

# 9. Running Leads

At some point during our time in Washington, a package from Kowalski and Adams finally got to me. It was a copy of the case file, complete with photographs. Dee had gone over it first and knew I would want to see it right away, so he sent it to me in Washington by express messenger. It cost a bundle to ship but it was worth it.

Dee's sense of urgency was greater than mine, but I understood why he sent it on. It was as clear to him as it was to me that the case had been closed prematurely and there was a note from Simon in agreement. On the other hand, without more evidence pointing toward specific lines of investigation, it would be almost impossible to get the case reopened.

There were some things I found interesting, however. Had I been in charge of the case, I would have pursued them. One was that Kowalski and Adams had run into a dead end trying to track down Walton Davis Keller. Two years after his discharge from the Marine Corps he was reported killed in an apparent robbery in southern Arizona. No body was ever found but the area in and around his car was saturated with blood, enough of it to satisfy the county coroner. DNA testing was still in the future when the crime was committed, but the blood was the same type as Wally Keller. The case was still open, but the file was gathering dust. For some reason the family had never been notified and I made a note to find out why.

What I found most intriguing about Wally Keller, however, was in a footnote Adams added to the report. His conversation with the sheriff in Nogales revealed that Wally had been working as a gunsmith at the time. There was some suggestion he may have been dealing in illegal weapons and died from a deal gone bad.

I made a note to have Dee find out if Wally had ever gone to gunsmith school and, if so, where. A fellow I know retired from police work and attended a gunsmith school in southern Colorado. His final assignment was building a gun from scratch, using stock metal and wood, and he showed it to me. What brought him to mind was the fact he had built a police weapon inspired by the Mac 10. Unlike the Mac 10, his rifle was bolt action and chambered for the .44 magnum shell. Even though it, too, had an integrated silencer built into the barrel, the accuracy was much better, even at close range, and it had far more knock-down power. The design was good enough to win several awards and could have been duplicated.

I made another note to call the gunsmith and ask if someone had ordered his rifle chambered for .357. I doubted if he would tell me if someone had, since such weapons are illegal to manufacture or sell without a special license. On the other hand, he might since there were legal ways he could sell both the rifle and silencer as parts without having to register them. I knew the market for such weapons was intense, though few of them ever turned up at crime scenes. They were very expensive.

The package also held a set of notes from Kowalski's interview with the custodian at the Presbyterian church. There were some small inconsistencies with what we had been told by Karl Mann, the organist, and if the case was still open I would have had Adams or Kowalski check these out. Most of the time such small inconsistencies are due to the way different people see things, but sometimes they open up a line of investigation. So they are worth checking.

Another odd note was that the organist was seen leaving the church late Friday evening. This was the day after the murder and he apparently used a small door at the back of the building. This was near the staff parking spaces, so it was not unusual that Mann used this exit. Nor was the reason he was there. There was a special music program planned for the following Sunday and he was there to practice. Kowalski had checked this out, and Mann apparently did this often.

What was strange was the fact Mann said he had not seen the bright orange crime scene seals on the doorway. The only light for the door was a security lamp between the church and the church offices in the next building. Yet this should have provided plenty of light to see the large seal.

Kowalski followed up and checked with the lab tech in charge of sealing the scene. The tech swore she had sealed the back door and made sure it was locked before she left on Thursday. Yet there was no sign of the seal except a small bit of sticky residue. Even this was in doubt because the spot where the residue was found was often used for taping notes or reminders to the door for the staff or clergy. There were several similar smudges on the door, as well as a watertight box of pencils, paper and adhesive tape. I found this quaint system interesting in an age of e-mail and high technology communication.

Kowalski and Adams had not learned much from a canvas of the homes nearby, either. No one had seen or heard anything unusual. This was not surprising since the walls of the church were thick and it was at least a hundred feet from the nearest dwelling. One neighbor did remember seeing lights on in the church late at night from time to time, particularly on Wednesdays, which was choir practice. However, none of them had seen anything on the Friday after the shooting. Or maybe none of them wanted to get involved.

I noticed one other thing reading over the report of the lab team that covered the choir loft Friday afternoon. One of the technicians had tried to look inside the organ console and noted that he had not been able to do so. The access panel of the console was secured by a special security lock and no one could find a key. The custodian didn't have one, and no one was able to reach Mann until the next day. The alternative was breaking in, but the console was walnut and no one wanted to be responsible for damaging the expensive cabinet.

The organist did have a key in his office and made a special trip to the church to open it for Adams Saturday afternoon. There was nothing in the console that seemed out of place. When Adams asked about the lack of dust in the cabinet, he was told it was vacuumed frequently when the dust filter was changed to prevent malfunction. The only thing Adams did see were some odd marks on the inside of the back panel, but Mann had no idea what caused those.

Adams also noted that at that point, there were lots of finger smudges on the polished top of the console. There was also a new stack of sheet music, which was no surprise, either. Choir lofts aren't known for being the tidiest places. What I found odd was that there were no fingerprints inside the rear panel.

I took out Simon's autopsy report and began reading through that. I'm always surprised at how such an eloquent and expressive soul as Simon can produce such dry prose, but I understand the necessity. Professionals cannot do their best work without keeping emotional distance from their subject, and the horrific nature of forensic work makes this even more essential. Then, too, a simple statement of the facts in unambiguous technical language is best. Lurid prose can give a defense lawyer a loophole broad enough to float a ship of reasonable doubt.

One thing I found fascinating was Simon's methodical affirmation of the bishop being in the early stages of chronic alcoholism. There may have been no red capillaries showing on his cheeks or nose, but there was some evidence of liver damage and other tissue pathology. Simon noted something he called long term "oxidative stress," and he also noted that the bishop showed signs of malnutrition consistent with substitution of drink for food. He also noted that the bishop's stomach was completely empty.

The bishop was also far from being sober when he went to meet his maker, though no one may have noticed. Some alcoholics are very good at hiding obvious symptoms. Keller's blood alcoholic level stood at .07 at the time of death. While this was not quite high enough to qualify as being legally drunk, it was enough to impair normal functioning. Nor was there any doubt the bishop had driven himself to the church. In my mind this tended to confirm Simon's diagnosis of alcoholism. I believe the appropriate phrase is self-will run riot.

Simon gave the cause of death as massive trauma to the heart and lungs from numerous fragments of gold and sapphire, any one of which could have done the trick. The bullet itself was lodged in the spinal cord and would have only caused paralysis from the waist down, though small fragments of lead were scattered throughout the traumatized lung tissue. The irony was that had the assassin waited a just a few more months, the bishop would have died a slow but certain death. There was evidence of incipient liver cancer, which Simon attributed to alcohol abuse. Given the bishop's lifestyle, it seems unlikely this would have been detected until far too late.

One thing I noted with a sense of satisfaction was that the angle of the wound indicated an elevated shooter, even though the large sapphire in the pectoral cross was deflected slightly upward. To me this meant the bullet had struck the bottom half of the stone, though it was still centered enough to shatter it. From the choir loft this would have been an easy shot to make.

I finished the autopsy report and set it aside. I glanced through the case file again and saw a hand written note from Kowalski. The writing was easy to read and stated that she and Adams had not been able to interview any diocesan staff. She included a list of the people scheduled for interviews the Monday following the murder, and noted that the chief had instructed her to close the case Sunday evening. She also included a number of questions she still had and a list of leads she and Adams had planned to follow up. I laughed when I saw this. It was Kowalski's way of getting a message to me without direct contact. It was also a way of protecting herself and her partner, just as I had advised.

As I looked over the leads Kowalski listed, I saw she had included a query to other regional law enforcement agencies about similar crimes. This was something I'd already asked Dee to follow up and I saw a separate envelope addressed to me from him. I set the file aside for the moment and picked up the envelope. As I opened it, I thought about everything I'd read and seen so far. There was something about all this that struck me as not quite right. Yet I couldn't quite figure what it was.

I scanned Dee's summary and then read through his notes. These were carefully typed, something I had insisted on with Dee from when he worked for me at the CID. Based on his writing, he would qualify as a physician. What caught my eye were his notes about similar crimes.

We had asked for information about any open murder files involving clergy in a twelve-state area, and indicated we were especially interested in cases involving priests as victims. We got six responses, which surprised me. Two or three was what I'd expected, if that many. Three of these cases involved the shooting death of a priest and the geographical distribution was intriguing. One of the priests was from Albuquerque, another was near Tulsa, and the third was from a small town I'd never heard of near St. Louis. Except for Albuquerque, these were all within a day's drive from Little Rock, most of it by freeway. So was Ft. Worth.

The remaining cases all involved Protestant clergy in California, which we had not queried. I wondered how they had heard of our query and why they had responded since the details of these cases were significantly different. There was a note from Dee suggesting I call there and a phone number was given. This was typed, too, but Dee had underlined the number with a highlighter.

Knowing I would want the information quickly, Dee followed up the responses with telephone calls to the first three departments. He hit pay-dirt right away. The small town in Missouri was not far outside St. Louis and the victim was an Episcopal priest. What really got my attention was how the padre was killed. A single shot from a .357 magnum had passed through a large silver pectoral cross while the priest was standing at the chancel crossing. He was found some time later hanging backwards over the chancel rail, once again by a custodian. Out of curiosity I checked, but the name of the custodian was different from the one in Ft. Worth. I made a note to make sure it was not the same man.

When Dee asked if the bullet was a 180-grain Nosler partition slug that had been fired from a rifle, he said the officer on the other end almost came through the phone after him. Later the officer called Dee back, asking why he had gotten such a cold reception from Chief Joe McClellan. When Dee explained the situation, the officer told him something else that convinced me the cases were linked. Several years before he was killed, the priest in Missouri had been suspected of domestic abuse while serving a church in one of the suburbs. Nothing ever came of this and no charges were ever filed, but the priest had been quietly moved to another church.

The officer had also caught wind of a rumor of sexual abuse of altar boys by this same priest, but there was no solid evidence. When the investigator had visited the diocesan office, the bishop refused to talk with him, and a subpoena of the priest's personnel records had been fruitless. There was nothing in the file but credentials and personal correspondence to and from the priest about routine matters.

The case in Albuquerque was not nearly as well tied to the shooting in Ft. Worth as the one in Missouri. Like the Keller case, the priest in Albuquerque had been shot at a church of another denomination. He, too, had been killed by a single shot from a large caliber bullet, either a .38 or .357, or possibly a 9 millimeter. However, he had been killed outside the church and was discovered by a squad car responding to a call. Nor did the officers know the victim was a priest until they checked his wallet, which was still in his hip pocket. It was a warm day and the padre had taken the white tab out of his black clerical shirt.

The problem was that this investigation had been given only a lick and a promise. No real forensic analysis was ever done. The priest was new to his congregation and was not politically connected. Nor was there anyone in his congregation who was. The fact that the shooting took place late in the evening in a rough side of town made it easy to write off as a drive-by shooting. One of the gangs in town favored all black for their clothing and it was assumed the priest was shot by mistake by a rival gang. For some strange reason he had been carrying a green bandana, local gang colors.

Dee had tried to follow up by running down the detective in charge of the case. He learned the man had retired and moved to

Oregon and had tried to phone him several times with no luck. So Dee had underlined the retired detective's name and number if I wanted to follow up.

Dee also tried to get in touch with the other detective assigned to the case. Yet the partner had died in a high-speed pursuit a couple of years before, so Dee set this one aside for me to decide. I understood why. While there were enough similarities to the Ft. Worth shooting to make this case worth following up if something more developed, there were also enough differences to raise questions about the connection. I had a hunch these three cases were all related to the bishop's death, but the link with this one was tenuous.

The third response was from Tulsa and involved a priest who had been suspended for a year from his duties for unspecified "indiscretions." I knew that in church-speak this can mean anything from being caught fondling the organist to pilfering the poor box to outright larceny or child molestation. This particular priest had been released from his suspension just weeks before he was shot and was filling in on Sundays for another priest on vacation.

The Tulsa priest had been found dead at the chancel crossing, too, although he had not been shot through his cross. He had been wearing a long, black cassock and one of those odd hats Irish priests wear. He was also wearing a purple stole and had been waiting to hear confessions before a Saturday evening service. Apparently there were never many takers aside from one elderly lady who was always there. She had been kneeling at the altar rail and was not aware the priest had been killed until she looked up to see why he wasn't responding. When she did, she had been so frightened she had to be taken to the emergency room. No one had seen or heard anything.

Dee got all this talking to the investigating officer. He also learned that the officer had excellent case notes that he was willing to share. Once again there had not been all that much forensic work done, mostly due to budget restraints. The forensics lab had determined that the slug came from a .357 and sent photos to the FBI lab. The report they got back indicated the gun came from an unknown manufacturer. This caught my attention and I made a note to follow up. At that point I was willing to bet the bullet came from the same gun that was used to kill Keller in Ft. Worth and was custom made.

There was a note from Dee asking me to call him about the other three cases when I had time. His assessment was that they were not worth too much time but I needed to check them out. When I reached him at his fishing camp in Mountain Home, he told me he had made one call and thought we needed to follow up with the other two.

"These guys were all shot and they were all involved in some form of child abuse," Dee told me. "That's how they picked up our query. They monitor the wire very closely. The guy I talked to works in Sacramento at state headquarters and he handles a lot of abuse cases. He was aware of the other two. When I told him about the Ft. Worth case he wanted to talk to you. He's also a member of your fan club."

"Why did I ever write those books, Dee?" I laughed. "I never wanted celebrity."

"Yeah, right. I bet you bitch about it all the way to the bank." He gave the number for the investigator in California. "You're not going to believe his name," Dee told me. "He goes by Mike or Lou, but his first name is George."

"I see why," I told him. "On the other hand, it's a fairly common name."

We talked about the cases a bit more and I finished going through the whole file from Ft. Worth. By the time I was done, my stomach was telling me it was time for lunch. I called Jeanne to see if she wanted to meet me somewhere, but she and Megan McKee were having lunch with some other ladies. "I hope you don't mind, Jazz," she told me. "It's been years since I had so much fun around other women."

"Be careful or Megan will recruit you," I laughed. There was an awkward silence from the other end of the conversation. "She already has, hasn't she!" I said. "That damned McKee bunch. You can't trust them for a minute."

"Actually, it was Martha," Jeanne told me. "Sam's sister-in-law. And I was under the distinct impression you're part of that damned

McKee bunch."

"That's what I mean," I told her. "You can't trust them. You better watch out or I'll get you in a family way. Have fun with the ladies."

"Now, wouldn't that be nice," she chuckled and rang off.

I glanced at my watch and decided to make a call to California. By my calculation, it was early morning there. Lieutenant Wallace would just be getting to his office and I wanted to catch him before he headed out for the day. I was in luck.

"Thanks for calling back so quickly, Dr. Phillips," he said. "Steve DiRado wasn't sure when you might have time."

"I always have time to nail serial killers, Mike," I answered. "I'm glad to help any way I can. And please call me Jazz."

"To be honest with you, what I'm going on with these three cases is a hunch they may be connected. I don't want to waste your time, but I'd appreciate a consultation. I don't have much budget for it, but maybe I can trade favors later on."

"Don't worry about it," I told him. "I'm always glad to make new contacts. What do you have?"

"The only real connections are that these killings all involve male clergy of about the same age who died from single gunshot wounds to the chest. They were all killed on church property and all three deaths happened within a hundred miles of San Diego. The radius is eighty-six miles to be specific. With each of these clergy there is some indication of previous sexual misconduct involving minors but no proof that would stand up in court. Two were white and one was African-American."

"What about denominational ties?" I asked.

"That's completely different," Wallace told me. "One was a Lutheran, another was a Baptist and another was nondenominational. The only other common tie I could see was that they all served very conservative congregations."

"Are you aware of the research connecting sexual abuse and fundamentalism?" I asked. "The link is pretty strong."

"Yes, sir, I am, even though I consider myself pretty conservative when it comes to faith. I hate to admit it, but what I've read makes sense. It also makes me sick. What I've seen in church has made it hard to go there sometimes."

I told him I could relate to that and asked if he had ever had to arrest a member of his own congregation. Wallace had the grace to laugh. "Well, not exactly," he told me. "That would be like busting a member of my own family. Let's say I just made sure the information got to the right desk and was very forthcoming when I was interviewed by the investigators. Maybe that makes me a hypocrite, but justice was served and what I guess you'd call my 'cover' wasn't blown. My kids go to church in a safe place now and I can help keep it that way."

"I never had kids, but I appreciate what you're saying," I replied. "How can I help you with these cases?" I'm never really comfortable talking about religion with other police officers, or with anyone who is not a close friend. Growing up in rural Arkansas I learned very early how strange normally sane people can get when it comes to belief and matters of faith. The older I get the more I've come to understand just how very little even the brightest human minds can comprehend. We just don't know much for sure and what we do know is warped by the limits of our imagination.

Wallace went over the cases quickly and professionally and I could see why he had gone as far as he had in the California system. Not only was he good with details, but he also had a good grasp of the larger issues and I began to see why he thought these cases were related. The details differed in significant ways, but the overall feel was the same. What bothered me was the geographic separation from my cluster.

I mentioned this to Wallace and he agreed. Most serial killers work an area or a region. This can be a wide area but it's a long way between St. Louis and Los Angeles and it's hard to move weapons across state lines except by ground. Yes, hunters can take their weapons to Alaska or Montana by air, but this creates a paper trail a serial killer would want to avoid. Traveling by auto was the simplest solution, particularly if the killer used a custom weapon. Yet this limited the range of the killer unless he went to considerable lengths.

I told Wallace what was going through my mind. "You know, we may be going at this thing backward," I added.

"What do you mean?"

"Well, we normally try to narrow things down. That works most of the time, even with serial killers. Yet, if these cases are connected, this is not the normal serial. This guy seems even more organized than usual. Maybe we need to widen our thinking."

There was silence from the other end. "All right," Wallace said. "Suppose we do. Where do we start?"

"Maybe we need to look at the weapon," I said. "From what you tell me, it sounds like the California killer never used the same weapon twice. Say he was smart enough to get rid of the weapon each time. That would be safer if he was ever caught, but it would also make killing more difficult."

"Yeah, I see what you mean. He'd have to get a new gun every time. Which means he'd have to buy it or steal it. It would be safer in one way but it would also increase his risk from another direction."

"Exactly," I said. "The guy I'm dealing with is very careful. He also has a unique weapon that's hard to get. So he has to take a lot of precautions to protect it."

Suddenly my mind made an intuitive leap. Arizona is right next door to California. "Maybe he makes them himself," I said. "What if he's a gunsmith? Or a gun runner?" I told him about Wally Keller.

"Too bad he's dead," Wallace said. "He sounds exactly right for it. I've wondered if we aren't after someone out for revenge. Nogales is a real hell-hole these days. You can buy just about anything there."

"How far away from Nogales are you?" I asked. "Could you check Keller out?"

"Looking at the map, I'd guess a little over five hundred miles, maybe more. It's not a trip I'd take without more than I have."

"No, but it would be fairly easy to do for a killer," I said. "What if our guy is like the Washington area snipers? What if he has a special rig? Would anyone notice a service van or a small camper? It would be a perfect setup for a street sniper."

"Let me call the sheriff's department down there," Wallace said. "I used to know one of the deputies pretty well. Maybe he can tell me something."

I could tell Wallace was reluctant to extend himself and I couldn't blame him. All we had was a very tenuous connection and Wally Keller was probably dead. The fact that his body was never found is not necessarily that significant. People disappear all the time along the Mexican border, and most of them are never found. On the other hand, Jack Keller told us he had talked to his adopted brother within the last year and I didn't think he was making it up. I could see how he might do so to comfort his mother, but if he did, he was a superb liar.

Wallace and I talked some more and I was able to point out a couple of lines of investigation he had not thought to pursue. Since the three clergy were about the same age, one possible connection was where they were trained, and Wallace promised to run this down. I also made a note to myself to do the same with the cases we had near Ft. Worth. This could be the connection between some of the cases.

I also suggested he might look for a special interest connection, like sports or even stamp collecting. Wallace had thought of that one and turned it inside out. The only connection of that sort he found was an area wide clergy action group that did lots of work for the poor and dispossessed. All three of Wallace's victims were active with this and it was possible the killer was among those they served.

Unfortunately, this widened the suspect pool considerably. It also made it almost impossible to investigate with the limited resources at our disposal. Most of the people the clergy group served were either homeless or had a less than cordial relationship with the police. While this doesn't seem to prevent any problems for television cops, it does for flesh and blood police trying to run down witnesses or suspects. Doing this requires a lot of time and effort, and most police departments have trouble covering even basic protection.

When I hung up I was surprised to see almost two hours had passed. I made it to the canteen just before they closed up, but the offerings were very slim. I settled for a plate of tuna and cottage cheese with Norwegian hard bread on the side. I'm sure it was quite healthy and very good for me, but it left me craving a banana split. Instead, I settled for a cup of flavored yogurt. That didn't help much, either.

I tried to get my mind back on the work I was doing for McKee, but it kept drifting back to the Keller case. There were things I would be doing if I was working on the case for a police department and it was frustrating not to be doing them. For my own peace of mind I called Dee and talked to him. He knew exactly what I meant.

"You know, Jazz, we are both sworn police officers here in Arkansas," he told me. "There is no reason we can't pursue this on our own."

"Who do we say is our client?" I asked. I don't like lying to other officers. It simply doesn't pay. The good ones have excellent built-in bullshit detectors and I don't care to work with those who don't. Integrity is the name of the game.

"Tell them it's something you came across on your own. You're not sure enough about it to blow the whistle, but you think there may be something there. That is the exact truth, after all." Dee shrugged. "Or you can tell them you're doing a favor for the California state police. Wallace will back you up."

"You see the issue, though, don't you?" I asked.

Dee laughed. "Jazz, at this point you don't have to be worried about coming across as a fly-by-night operator. You're pretty well established, wouldn't you say?"

"I don't want people saying I'm getting senile, either," I protested. "This feels like going in without backup."

"Hell, have them call me. I'm a pro bono deputy in Baxter County, and a game warden, to boot."

"I better not tell you about that venison in my freezer," I laughed.

"What!" Dee cried. "I better come over and help you eat up the evidence!"

"Thanks," I told him. "I guess I got things out of perspective." Dee has always had the ability get me back on beam, even since we were both troopers in the highway patrol. I seem to do the same for him. We're a good team and one of the reasons I sent work his way after he retired is that I miss not having him for a partner. With Nellie gone it's been even more important to have him present in my life quite a bit.

I outlined what I had in mind for him to do. I was pleased to learn Dee anticipated one of my questions and was running down the background information on Keller and the other clergy. He had even thought to call Grant Forster, the old chaplain, who had given him a shortcut. "Turns out the Episcopals have a clergy directory with all the basic biographical stuff," Dee told me. "The local padre only has an old one, but that ought to give us what we need. There's a recent copy we can use in Little Rock, if we need more recent information. I also got a phone number for their national office."

"Good work," I told him.

"Thing is, nobody I talked to had much use for Keller. Nobody really bad mouthed him except the local padre, who knows me, but I got the impression Keller wasn't too well thought of in Arkansas."

"He apparently pissed off one cowboy to many in Cowtown, too," I quipped, and this tickled Dee. He was still chuckling when I hung up.

# 10. The Clergy Connection

I worked the rest of the afternoon on McKee's project. When I called it quits, the siren call of the chocolate sundae was still there. It was just before five and I was supposed to take Jeanne to dinner later. I convinced myself a small sundae wouldn't hurt and promised myself I would do a few more laps the next day to make up for the added calories. So I headed for a small ice cream parlor not far from McKee's office.

When I got there, McKee was seated at the counter and he greeted me as if he hadn't seen me in years. "Hello, Jazz! How's police business?" he called out and waved me to a seat beside him. "You in town for the FBI thing?" There were only a couple of other people in the shop, but I'd seen them around the office. I figured they were two of McKee's guardian angels. He bitches about the necessity of bodyguards cramping his style but gives in gracefully when Megan insists. I gather she is the real head of the Agency and that McKee is just filling in until her family leave is over, but their oldest child must be almost five. It's a strange way to run a public agency, but it seems to work. McKee tells me the Agency is something like the Postal Service, a semi-private corporation that has a government charter.

I had no idea what FBI thing McKee was talking about, but charades in public are part of the games we have to play. "Doing some research for my next book," I told him. "The virtue of ice cream in serial murder investigation."

"I never had one with cereal," McKee quipped. "Megan won't let me have ice cream that early." We exchanged pleasantries for a while as we enjoyed our sundaes, but as I was about to leave, he asked if I had had a chance to see the National Cathedral.

I confessed I hadn't and he offered to give me a tour. I figured this was a way of telling me we needed to talk so I agreed. "Why not?" I said. "It will have to be a short one. I'm on the way home. I promised to take herself out tonight."

"Ten extra minutes," he said. "It's on your way. Besides, Megan called and I can promise you the ladies will be late." I knew the tour would take much longer than ten minutes, but it beat waiting around the apartment for Jeanne.

I have no idea what McKee was after that afternoon. Perhaps it was nothing more than companionship. He knew I headed up the Arkansas State Criminal Investigation Division for a good while, and even though I was a contractor, we were close enough in age and life experience to be friends. It does get lonely at the top and the older I get the more I appreciate the company of someone else who has lived through the same era. I find younger people respectful and working with them keeps me young, I guess. Yet with people like McKee I don't get a blank look when I mention someone like Angela Davis or Jerry Rubin. Somehow that's ever more important the older I get.

McKee was in good form that afternoon. He gave me an excellent nutshell history of the National Cathedral, established by the Episcopal Church as a cathedral for all Americans regardless of faith or creed. The services there were mostly from the Book of Common Prayer, but McKee told me no one was ever turned away from participation and there had been rites from other religions there, too.

Then something occurred to me and I felt really dumb. Back in Mountain Home, Arkansas, deep in Baptist country, Dee was trying to find an Episcopal clergy listing. Yet here I was at the national Episcopal cathedral. Surely they'd have what I needed right here. I asked McKee if he knew any of the cathedral staff. I told him what I wanted and why.

"Sure, Jazz," he said. "Let's ask one of these guys." He nodded toward a group of people in vestments waiting to start a service. He turned and ambled over to them, and spoke to the fellow at the back of the line. "We can have one in thirty minutes," he said when he came back. "They're about to start Evensong. I can pick it up if you can't wait."

I looked at my watch. "I'd actually like to hear the service. Like you say, I doubt if our wives are back from whatever they've been up to." Then I realized my mistake.

McKee saw my consternation and laughed. "They grow on us, don't they? I found myself doing the same thing before Megan and I married. She thought it was cute."

"That's how I think of Jeanne even though she's still legally married," I told him. "You know, I've been married more than half my life. Sam. I don't know how to think of Jeanne as my girlfriend."

"Why bother?" McKee replied, handing me a prayerbook. "I'd bet Jeanne doesn't mind a bit."

"I don't like to make public slips like that," I told him. "It's embarrassing."

"I imagine it's more than that for the guys you bust," McKee chuckled. At that moment, the organ began a prelude and McKee crossed himself and knelt down. I did the same and it felt good being on my knees and reaching out to Whomever might be there. Regardless of what one believes, kneeling is an act of humility, which is good for the soul. At least, it is for mine.

Evensong is a celebration of light. One of the opening canticles is the Phos Hilaron, so named for it's opening words, "O gracious light." The mystery we call light is one of those things that never tire me. It almost always fills my soul and I guess that's why I love photography so. Even on the darkest days, the play of light and shadows is full of wonder for me, and sometimes it feels like the light is teasing me, playing. I see a flicker of something that seizes my imagination, but by the time I get my camera to my eye, it's gone. Then I lower the lens and it is there again for just a moment, and then gone again before I can push the shutter. There is nothing to do at such times but to take delight in the moment and be thankful one is given these glimpses of something that lies beyond our words or understanding.

Dee is one of the few people I've ever trusted enough to tell this, and it took me a long while to do so. When I did, he smiled and shook his head. "Shoot, I've known this for a long time, Jazz," he told me. "When it comes to light you get downright mystical."

This is not exactly the way an Arkansas police officer is taught to think of himself, and it goes against the accepted norm. So I blew it off to Dee's imagination. Yet when I mentioned it to Nellie in passing later on, she agreed. "You are so intelligent when it comes to other people and so blind to yourself, Johnny. I've been trying to tell you that for years."

That night there was a visiting choir practicing in the cathedral and they sang one of the numbers they were doing the following Sunday. The choir loft is high in the rear of the nave and the acoustics are magnificent. Nor do I believe this is by accident. The voices filtering down from the heights were clear but sounded as if they were coming from a celestial distance. I thought of that old Christmas carol that begins, "Angels we have heard on high."

When the anthem was done I looked down at my prayerbook to resume the service and saw I was turned to the wrong page. I started to flip back to the front of the book but my eyes caught a wonderful phrase in rolling Middle English. "Therefore, with angels and archangels and with all the company of heaven, we laud and magnify thy glorious Name...."

I was taken completely off guard and snickered. When McKee asked me about it later I told him about the coincidence. His assessment was the same as mine. "Well, Jazz, if it isn't coincidence, Someone was having a little fun."

The guy at the end of the processional line turned out to be the bishop of the cathedral. He introduced himself and led us to his office. Taking down a large maroon volume about the size of a small city telephone book, he asked me who I needed to look up. When I took out my list and handed it to him, his face became grave. His dark brown eyes seemed to search the depths of my soul. "May I ask why you are looking at Bishop Keller?" he asked. "He's dead, you know."

I told him I was aware of that. "I'm investigating his death," I said. "It may be connected to some murders."

The bishop was surprised. "Oh? I thought he was killed by a random shooter."

"That was a politically correct conclusion to the case," I answered. "However, I still have some questions." I told him about the deaths of the other three priests and why I thought they might be connected.

The bishop looked deeply troubled when I had finished. "I wasn't aware of all the details of Rufus Keller's death," he told me. "I was never close to the man, but then I don't know who in the House of Bishops really was. What is sad is that he will not be missed. Quite the contrary, he was a very, um, challenging presence."

I knew he was holding something back and asked what it was. "It's the bullet through the middle of the cross," he said. "It's probably not related, but there was a priest in New Hampshire that was killed like that. Shot dead one Saturday evening as he was setting up for the Sunday service. He was single and no one found him until Sunday morning."

"Well, that may rule him out," I answered. "With the other guys there was some history of domestic abuse."

The bishop sighed deeply. He looked even sadder. "I'm afraid the young man I'm talking about was under something of a cloud, too. His wife had left him the year before and there was some hint of scandal involving the teen group. Nothing was ever proved, but it was there. After his death the matter was dropped."

"May I ask how you know about this?" I asked.

"Yes, and I can even tell you. His bishop was a good friend of mine. I used to be a lawyer before God retreaded me. Sometimes my colleagues call me for free legal advice. I always tell them to ask a real lawyer, but I sometimes I can tell them some things to avoid until they talk to one."

"So this priest's bishop consulted you?" I asked.

"Asked my advice as a pastor, actually," he corrected gently. "As a pastor to the young man and to the people in his charge, too."

"Was the murder ever solved?" I asked.

"Not to my knowledge. I talked with my friend a couple of weeks ago and the case was pretty much at a standstill." The bishop shook his head. "Even in a city that size it created quite a stir."

"Could you give me the name of the priest?" I asked.

The bishop wrote it out on a piece of personalized note paper. He also wrote down the name of his fellow bishop and looked up the telephone number. "You can tell him I referred you and why," he told me. "Why don't you let me make copies of the names you need?" He took my list and disappeared into another room with the maroon book.

"I hope I'm not keeping you, Sam," I said to McKee.

"I'm having fun," he replied, "You do this very well."

"One would hope I had caught on by now," I laughed.

The bishop apparently heard us because I heard him chuckle from the next room. A moment later he was back. "The copier's broken," he said. "Can you bring this back to me tomorrow morning?" He held up the clergy directory.

I promised to have it there before ten-thirty and thanked the bishop for his time. He smiled and corrected me gently. "You're the one we should be thanking, Jazz. You don't have an easy job dealing with stuff like this."

"Yes, but I don't have to deal with church boards," I told him. He thought that was hilarious.

The clergy directory turned out to be a key element in breaking the case. When I looked up the Episcopal clergy on my list, the connection among them quickly became clear. They were all trained at the same seminary and had all graduated within a three year period. Bishop Rufus Keller had been the first one there, but his last year overlapped with the first year of the priest killed in Oklahoma. Nor was it just four priests from that time period who had all been killed in the same manner, but five. It turned out later that the young priest from New Hampshire was actually middle aged when he died and graduated from the same place a year before Keller.

This didn't make any sense until I looked up the bishop at the cathedral. I found out he was now in his early seventies, but from the strength of his bearing, I would have judged him to be only a year or two older than me. So I understood his mistake. Age is very hard to guess as one grows older. Even to me, not far past sixty, a man in his early forties seems very young. I'd normally place him in his thirties. The young priest from New Hampshire was just weeks past his fortieth birthday when he died.

When I looked up the divinity school on the Internet, I discovered something very interesting. Located in Berkeley, it was part of a cooperative network of seminaries that shared common faculty and library resources. As I understood it, the faculty were all attached to specific seminaries but might lecture in their areas of specialty in all the seminaries at one time or another. This struck me as a very good idea, but I wondered how it worked in practice. Christianity has been dividing itself into armed camps from the beginning and the disputes have been as bitter as only family fights can get. There doesn't seem to be much tolerance for ambiguity or diversity or much middle ground.

To be fair, the same is true in law enforcement. I've seen otherwise sane officers take sides and get themselves overwrought over the pettiest issues. Quite often this is over turf, though we dress it up and call it jurisdiction. What does it matter whose case it is or who makes the bust? The point is to get the bad guys off the street and the turf wars among cops only benefits our common enemy.

I copied down the number for the seminary and placed a call to the dean. He was not in at the moment and when the secretary asked if anyone else could help, I asked to speak to the faculty member who had been there longest. This turned out to be one of the chaplains, a Dr. Olsen, and the secretary forwarded my call.

When I explained why I was calling there was a long silence from the other end. I thought the connection had been broken and asked if anyone was there. The answer came back quickly, "Oh, yes. Sorry, your question took me by surprise. I was in the thirteenth century.

Give me a moment."

The voice was that of a woman. When she came back on the line, she was all business. She asked who I was and asked if she could call me right back. There was nothing I could do but agree.

Ten minutes later my phone rang again. It was the chaplain. "Yes, Dr. Phillips?" she asked. "What can I do for you?" This told me she had checked me out. I had not mentioned my academic credentials. Whoever she called must have spoken well of me because her tone was cordial. I wondered who it was.

"What I'm looking for is background, Dr. Olsen. We have five Episcopal clergy all killed in almost the exact same way. They all went to school there and graduated over a period of four years. I wondered if you remembered any of them." I read off my list of names.

"Oh, yes, I remember them. They were something of an anomaly here. We didn't know quite what to do with them."

When I asked her to explain, Olsen replied, "You have to remember the history of this area. During the sixties and seventies it was a hotbed of radical action and that has remained one of our traditions here. We are on the liberal end of the theological spectrum and many of us take pride in that." She laughed. "I'm afraid we may also take ourselves too seriously. We see ourselves as the keepers of the liberal flame in a world of conservative darkness. Yet, considering the history of Christianity in this country in the last quarter century, there's some truth to this."

"That's odd. I thought all the men on my list were quite conservative," I replied.

"Oh, they were. That's just the point. I've no idea why they came to school here. They would have been much better off someplace like Pittsburgh. Yet, they may have been too conservative even for there. The prevalent theory among the faculty was that their bishops sent them to school here to loosen them up a bit. I'm afraid it had just the opposite effect. They found each other very quickly and circled the wagons."

"Oh, so they hung around together?"

"Very much so. They reinforced one another's prejudices. What was a real pity is that so many of them were so bright. With a little seasoning, any of them could have become strong conservative scholars." Olsen sighed again. "As it was, they wasted our time and theirs, too. I'm not saying they didn't get good training, because they did. On the other hand, they seemed to all grow harder rather than more compassionate."

"Rules over people?" I asked.

"Exactly! They had very little patience with human limitations, and as far as I could see, they were blind to their own."

"It doesn't sound like you disliked them," I observed.

"Goodness, no!" Olsen replied with feeling. "Rufus Keller was my favorite. He could charm the pants off a hanging judge."

"I don't know how else to put this," I replied. "There is some evidence that all these men were involved in sexual misconduct. Was there any evidence of it back then?"

"There were rumors," Olsen replied. "Things were different then and this tends to be a very tolerant place. So I'm afraid no one paid enough attention."

"So this doesn't surprise you?" I asked.

"Not really, though I hate to say it. What I saw expressed was some very strong homophobia. What I think now is that this might have been self-hatred more than anything else."

"You're not the first who has suggested that to me," I said.

"You must have talked with Charles Brighton," Olson laughed.

I was startled. "Why do you say that?"

"Charlie and I are very close. We always have been. I was his faculty advisor and we stayed in touch over the years. He called me when Rufus Keller was elected. He was so upset he was thinking about leaving the diocese right away, even though he had just taken the call to Arlington. I talked him out of it and I think he would agree that was the right course for him to take." I could almost hear her smile. "He was one of the people I called to check you out."

"Just out of curiosity, who else did you call?" I asked.

"Simon Smyth and I go back a long way, too," Olsen laughed. "He told me not to believe anything you said. Then he said you're the best he's seen."

I laughed. "That sounds like Simon. Is there anything else you can tell me about this group?"

"Only that there were many more members than the five you've mentioned. Rufus Keller was the ringleader, I guess you'd say. He had a lot of charisma and seemed to attract people who wanted to follow someone strong and unwavering. That was Rufus. He could be wrong at times but he was never in doubt."

"Were you his advisor, too?" I asked.

Olsen sighed again. "Only for the first semester. After that, he changed advisors. One of the things Rufus Keller didn't believe in was women priests. He was quite vocal about it, too. Since a lot of our students are women, you can imagine how this set with his schoolmates."

"You mentioned there were others in his clique. Could you give me some names?"

"Why do you want to know?" she asked, then stopped. "Oh. Do you think they may be in danger, too?"

"Or maybe already dead," I suggested.

"I think I would have heard about it," Olsen told me. "We've lost a lot of students in that age group, but it's that time in life, too. Those are the only ones I'm aware of who have been murdered. I don't know why I didn't see the pattern before now."

"No reason you would unless you were looking for it," I answered. "We only came across it now and we were looking. After all, Keller's death was considered an accidental homicide, as was the guy in Albuquerque."

"Tim," she told me. "That was so sad. It looked like he was getting his life together at last and then he was killed. He was the least rigid of them all. I heard that it was gang related. Is that true?"

I told her that was the official story, but that I had reservations about it. Olsen agreed. "Tim was very gentle," she said. "It was unfortunate he was so drawn to Rufus Keller, but that's the religious background Tim came from. His father was a priest, too, a real patriarch." The way she uttered the last word left no doubt she considered it a polite term for asshole.

I laughed when she said this and Olsen demanded an explanation. "It was just the way you said 'patriarch.' It sounded like you wanted to spit out the bad taste it left."

"That's putting it mildly," Olson replied. "As I said, we tend to be a radical bunch."

I asked if the Keller cabal had died out after his crowd had all graduated. "Not in our wildest dreams," Olson said. "I'm afraid it's become a tradition here. They call themselves the Honorable Opposition, but the other students call them Hell's Angels. If anything, they seem to have become even more rigid. They have grown in numbers, too, and they stayed in touch with Keller. He was their grand dragon, so to speak."

I laughed but couldn't think of anything to say. Nor was I sure Dr. Olsen was aware of the meaning of her words. Grand Dragon in Arkansas means the Klan.

When I didn't respond immediately, she apologized. "You seem to have drawn out all my prejudices, Dr. Phillips. I'm normally not such a bitch. I hope you don't have that impression."

"I don't," I assured her. "In my book, being friends with Simon covers a multitude of eccentricities. I hope that goes the other way."

"You are so diplomatic," Olsen said. "Are you married?"

I laughed. "No, but I hope to be soon. I'm spoken for."

"Too bad," she laughed. "The best ones are."

"Thank you," I replied. "Were you using a metaphor or was there some tie with Keller and the Klan? You know, when you called Keller their grand dragon?"

"I was using a metaphor. Nothing about that group would surprise me, but I don't think they're racist. They do have a number of minority students, mostly Koreans and Chinese. With them it's understandable. They come from patriarchal cultures and those tend to be abusive."

Even had I not been spoken for, Olsen was a little radical for my tastes. In my own experience, matriarchy is every bit as oppressive as patriarchy. This may be expressed in other ways, but the bottom line is who controls. The hard fact is that most domestic violence in the United States is perpetrated by women, not men. This is not generally acknowledged outside police circles since it flies in the face of popular prejudice. Yet it is based in fact. Women can be as violent as men. They just go about it differently.

Olsen must have been reading my mind. "I suppose that being a policeman, you disagree," she went on, not asking a question but making a statement.

"Not necessarily, but I don't see how going there will help me catch a killer," I said. "I don't find argument much fun. No one ever really wins. I'd rather do something I really enjoy."

There was another long silence from the other end of the line. "You're an unusual man, Dr. Phillips," she told me and it almost broke my heart hearing those words, for Nellie used to say the very same thing. "What do you do for fun?"

"I chase light," I told her, but there was a catch in my voice. "Sometimes I even catch it. Thanks for your help."

I sat for a while after hanging up, trying to stay in my feelings and to pull myself together at the same time. This was like being one of those Chinese jugglers who keeps a plate balanced on a cane in each hand. It took all my attention. Yet grief is like that. It slips up on us at the damnedest times and in the strangest ways. Nor does it help to ignore it, or to even try. All I've found that works is living through it and coming out the other side when it passes. That's the thing to remember. We may feel so awful we want to die, but feelings pass and we remain, changed, perhaps, but still there. When we resist, we only end up hurting more.

After a few minutes the feelings subsided. I thought back over the conversation as I reviewed the notes I had made. When I was done I added a few more and made a note to call Dr. Olsen back later on. There were a couple of questions I'd failed to ask in my grief. Nor did I give myself too hard a time about this. Once upon a time I would. Now I understand that like everyone else in this world, I'm rarely playing with a full deck. That's one of the reasons I pray, hoping to be given more than a clue.

I was about to ask Willie Dill if he wanted to grab lunch in the canteen when my personal cell phone rang. It was Wallace, calling from California, and I could hear he was excited. "I found a connection," he told me. "I made the calls last night and found out all my victims went to the same seminary."

"It wasn't the combined one in Berkeley, was it?"

"How did you know?" Wallace demanded.

"I got lucky this morning, too," I replied. I told him about the call to Olsen and what I'd learned. "It would be nice to know if all your guys belonged to the Keller cabal, too," I said. "Apparently it's membership was all over the Holy Hill."

Wallace laughed. "I haven't heard it called that before," he said. "But it is that. There are nine different seminaries working together in the same place. It's amazing."

I had to agree. As I've said, what I've seen of churches in operation tells me that they're much better at splitting up than working together. Mostly it's over what seem to me minor points of doctrine, but that's human nature. Our most bitter fights seem to be over the smallest stakes and churches aren't exempt. I said as much to Wallace and he told me that was his experience, too. He agreed to check out the connection between his clergy and the Honorable Opposition, and we set up a time to compare notes after Thanksgiving.

Lunch was pretty much picked over when I got to the canteen, so I had a salad to make up for the sundae I had the day before. I don't know why people play games with themselves like that, but we do, and for a few moments I convinced myself I was being virtuous. Michael Angelino, McKee's chief analyst was sitting alone, so I asked if I could join him. I'd not had much chance to get to know him outside specific projects.

Like me, Angelino was eating a salad. Yet when I compared his simple lettuce and vegetable creation with my spread of ham, cheese and croutons, I had to laugh. "There's not much low-cal about this, is there?"

Even though McKee's agency is run on informal lines, security is always an issue. So people don't talk much about work in the canteen. As a matter of fact, there's a big World War II vintage poster one can't help seeing on entry. It shows the silhouette of a ship going down and declares, "Loose Lips Sink Ships."

So I asked Angelino what he did for fun and discovered we share a lively interest in photography. Unlike me, who prefers the whole spectrum, Michael is a fan of Ansel Adams and spends a lot of time in the dark room printing black and white. He also uses older equipment and told me some of his best work was done with an ancient box camera that belonged to his dad. I mentioned the first camera I ever got, which I still have packed away somewhere, and we got into an animated discussion that almost made Michael late for a meeting with Sam McKee. He left the canteen at a dead run. A moment later I saw Sam leave the canteen. He was clearly amused.

I was pretty much done with that day's work for McKee, so I decided to take the afternoon off. I called Jeanne and suggested we play tourist. There were still a few places on our list we hadn't seen, and I was tired of looking at spreadsheets. After a while the numbers run together and I find myself having to back up and repeat what I just did a moment before.

This is one aspect of police work most people don't understand. A lot of time is spent in basic research, waiting for a pattern to appear. This is particularly true with investigating white-collar crime. Although I can get lost in ferreting out the significant thread of evidence in a mass of raw corporate data, I do get tired. When this happens, it's better to step away for a while. The temptation is to push even harder, but I've found doing so incurs a steep curve of diminishing returns. Sometimes it's faster to wait.

That afternoon, it was clearly time to play. Jeanne apparently thought so, too, and waylaid me on my way in the door. Then it was time for a shower, which involved even more horseplay, and we ended up sending out for Chinese.

"So what have you decided about Thanksgiving?" Jeanne asked, reaching for her fortune cookie. She laughed before I could answer and handed me her fortune. "You encounter many pleasant adventure," it said, and gave a string of numbers for playing the lottery.

I handed her mine and she laughed again. "Many blessing come in old age." That got us started on Confucius jokes, and the worse they were, the harder we giggled.

"I don't know," I said when we had stopped. "I'd love to be there but I don't want to mess things up with your kids. With all the grandkids, it's going to be a houseful. Like I said, it might be better if I stay at a motel."

We'd been over this before and Jeanne had her mind made up. "No, you need to stay in the house. The kids know how things are with us. They'd think your staying in a motel was strange."

"What about the grandkids?" I asked. "What will they think about granny staying in the same room with her boyfriend? Some of them are old enough to wonder."

This was the same impasse we had reached before. "I've been thinking about that," Jeanne said. "Since Lindy is coming, too, we're going to need more space. I think it's time to take Henry's land yacht out of storage. We'll put all the kids in that and the oldest can baby sit. It will be like going camping for them. Girls can stay in one end and the boys in the other. We'll just have to be discrete during the day."

"You mean quiet," I clarified. "You know, we could give Lindy and your kids a real gift. We could stay with the kids in the RV for the weekend. I could stay with the boys while you stay with the girls."

Jeanne blushed. "I guess I do get carried away," she said. "I don't know if I can keep my hands off you for three days."

"We can kind of store up beforehand," I suggested and Jeanne thought we better start right away.

# 11. A Deep Con

At some point in the middle of the afternoon, my cell phone rang but I was busy and hit the mute button. My intent was to check for messages later that day, but I got distracted and simply forgot. Nor did I remember to switch the phone off that evening and it was dead by the time I picked it up early the following morning. So I plugged it into the charger while Jeanne and I had a leisurely breakfast. By the time I left for the office there was enough charge in the battery to see someone had left a message, and I dialed into my voice mail from the apartment.

There were actually two messages. One was from Wallace, calling to let me know he had made some calls and discovered a connection between all his clergy cases and mine. While he kept his voice professionally calm, I could hear he was excited.

The second call was from Dee, asking me to call back at my earliest convenience. Those last two words are part of a personal code Dee and I developed over our many years working together. I knew he had something important for me, but nothing that could not wait. So I called Wallace first, but he was out of the office and I left word I'd returned his call.

When I called Dee, I caught him on the run. There was a fishing party due and he was getting their boat ready. He told me it looked like we had a match between the gun used in Ft. Worth and the one used near St. Louis, but there was no word back from Albuquerque or Tulsa. The identification was based on photographs forwarded directly to Simon Smyth, who was 98 percent sure it was the same gun. The twist in the barrel was unique, as were some of the marks made by the rifling. Simon would want to compare the actual slugs involved before going on the stand to testify, but he was sure the cases were tied together.

I thought about this as I walked to McKee's office, and when I got there I looked back through my notebook. Then I realized what had been bothering me. Wally Keller was reported dead in Arizona years ago, but his adopted brother, Jack, had told us he talked to Wally just after the bishop was killed. I'd made a note to myself to follow this up but never had, and I gave Jack a call at the Keller home in Ft. Worth.

It was Amanda, the bishop's widow, who answered the phone. She recognized my voice when I asked for Jack. "He's not here at the moment, Dr. Phillips." When I asked when he would be home, she laughed. "He's gone to New York with our high school band," she told me. "They were invited to march in the Macy's parade next week. May I ask what this is about?"

I told her I needed to ask Jack about his calls to his adopted brother. "Didn't he call you yet?" Amanda answered. "He was supposed to. Maybe he called that other detective. I can't remember her name but she gave us a card."

"Detective Kowalski?" I asked.

"Yes," she told me. "Jack was supposed to call you or her and let you know. I'm afraid Jack was making it all up, Dr. Phillips. There were no calls from Wally."

"Any idea why he would do that?" I asked.

"Well, Jack is just sixteen now, and not a very mature sixteen, I'm afraid. This is an issue he's been talking about with his counselor. Somehow Jack thinks if he really believes something, it will turn out to be true. We had trouble with him about that when he was very little. I thought he'd outgrown it."

"I know kids do that," I said. "Why would he start again now?"

"You have to understand Wally was Jack's hero. When he left, Jack was at that age when little boys like to believe in Batman. The counselor told us Jack made Wally into some kind of super hero in his mind. When Rufus was killed, the counselor says Jack regressed for a while and couldn't tell the difference between reality and what he wanted to happen. When he told us about Wally's calls, he really believed what he was saying."

"I see." I thought about this for a moment. It made sense to me. The human mind is very creative when it comes to protecting itself and I'd run across this behavior before. While it was with younger kids, not adolescents, we were dealing with a child, not an adult. With children the magical thinking associated with *dementia praecox,* the old medical term for schizophrenia, is normal. As Amanda said, children grow out of it, for better or for worse. The trauma Jack had been through, both before and after his father was shot, was more than enough to induce irrational behavior.

"Are you still there?" Amanda asked.

"Yes, thank you. Why don't you have Jack give me a call when he gets back? I don't doubt your word, but I do need to hear this directly from him."

"Please be gentle with him, Dr. Phillips," she replied. "He's been through so much."

"I will," I assured her. "You've all been through a lot. Tell Jack it's no big deal, just something I need to clear up for the record." I left my cell number.

When I rang off, I was still not satisfied. I called Wallace again, and this time he was there. "Great timing," he told me. "I just walked in the door and sat down. I don't have much yet. I did find out all three of my clergy went to school in Berkeley. I haven't been able to get in touch with some of the people at the seminary I want to talk to, but I will. It may be after Thanksgiving. You know how crazy everything gets around the holidays."

"Actually, I was wondering if you had been in touch with anyone down in Nogales." I told him about my conversation with Amanda Keller. "I don't think there's anything there, but it would help to rule Wally out completely."

"I talked to them again, but it was a wasted call. They aren't really interested in extending themselves at all. I can't say I blame them."

"I guess you're right," I told him. "There's something about all this that bothers me. I can't figure what it is."

"It's not getting personal, is it?" Wallace asked.

"Not really. I don't know any of the people involved personally. It's more like one of those Chinese puzzles. I can't seem to figure where to push to get it apart."

Wallace laughed. "I've had cases like that. I still wake up in the middle of the night thinking I've finally put it together. Then I can't remember which case it was!"

I wished him a happy Thanksgiving with his family and ended the call.

Since there was nothing immediate I needed to do for McKee, I told him I was thinking of heading back to Arkansas for the next week. "I'm surprised you're still here," he told me. "We're heading for the ranch tomorrow." He stretched lazily. "It's been too long since I've seen high country. Hopefully, I'll get to stay all week."

I wished him a good Thanksgiving, too, and wandered down the hall to see if Willie Dill was in, but I was out of luck. The only person around I knew well enough to visit was Angelino, but he was in the middle of something. I wasn't ready to go home yet, so I decided to take a walk.

The part of the District where McKee's headquarters is located can be confusing and it's quite easy to get lost. About twenty minutes after I started walking I realized I was right back where I'd begun. I decided to go back in and have a cup of coffee in the canteen, but my door pass wouldn't work. I tried it a couple of times before a man I didn't know opened the door and asked if he could help me. He was dressed in a security uniform and I showed him my plastic door key. He glanced at it and smiled. "I'm afraid we don't take credit cards, Dr. Phillips. Do you have a building pass?"

I looked down in consternation. Sure enough, the blue card I'd pulled out of my wallet was the wrong one. I replaced it in my wallet and pulled out the right one and handed it to the guard. He swiped it through the slot by the door and the small light by the slot turned green. The guard stepped aside for me to enter. "Don't worry about it, sir," he told me. "It happens all the time."

I went to the canteen, but no one was around. I picked up a daily paper lying next to the cash register and was reading the comics when McKee walked in. He didn't seem too surprised to see me. "How's the stock market doing?" he asked dryly.

"Peanuts up three points, sorghum down a quarter, and hog bellies are steady and holding," I answered, and he laughed. We visited a while and I asked where his ranch was and what kind of cattle he raised.

"It's out near Casper, Wyoming," he told me. "We used to raise registered Angus but it's mostly range cattle now. Raising breeding stock takes a lot of attention and our whole family seems to have drifted into security business now." He gave me a very direct look. "Care to talk about what's on your mind?"

"I hadn't realized it was that obvious," I chuckled. "The problem is that our best suspect is dead." I outlined what we knew and told him about my conversation with Jack Keller's mother.

McKee nodded when I was done. "You seem to attract these cases, don't you?" I asked what he meant and he said, "Well, you were on a case like that when we first met. I can't recall the guy's name but he killed Smiley Jones and some other folk near Nashville, Arkansas. He was supposed to be dead, too."

"Oh, yeah, the Posey case. But I think this guy really is dead. What bothers me is there wasn't a body. The blood was his type and there was apparently enough of it to convince a state medical examiner, but something about it bothers me."

McKee nodded. "I can see why. Let me make some calls next week. I may have some sources your guy in California doesn't."

We visited a while longer. Then McKee left to take a phone call and I headed for home again. This time I intended to go to the apartment, but when I saw the National Cathedral, I decided to go inside. When I did, I remembered something else I'd never followed up, the shooting death of the priest in New Hampshire. I made myself another note to call the number the bishop here had given me.

Someone was practicing the organ when I entered the building and I took a seat in the nave to listen for a while. One of the things about the National Cathedral is that it is a tourist site and there are people moving around the outer aisles most of the time. I'm not sure why they allow this, and I'm sure there must be times when they don't . Yet this is not as distracting as it sounds. The music was gorgeous and I found that after a few minutes my mind simply tuned out the sound of movement.

Even so, I was aware someone had entered the row where I was seated and taken a chair near me. When the music was done and I started to leave, I was surprised to hear a familiar voice call my name. "Dr. Phillips? Is that you?"

I turned around and was surprised to see Charles Brighton, the priest I met in Ft. Worth. "I thought that was you," he said, greeting me warmly. "What brings you to Washington?"

"Research," I said automatically. "How about yourself?"

"It's one of those many committee meetings I waste my life attending," he told me. "I'm sure you've attended your share. You know, the kind when everything is said and done, a lot more seems to have been said than done. How are you coming along with the Keller murder? Have you found anyone yet?"

"I'm not sure," I told him. "I actually need to talk to you if you have time."

"Sure," he said. He glanced at his watched. "I'm just waiting around for a plane. Will it take more than four hours?"

I thought about inviting him to the apartment. Then I decided against it. I wasn't sure how Jeanne would feel about it. Instead, I found a quiet corner with a couple of chairs where our talking would not be intrusive to others.

"Do you remember anything about the Honorable Opposition?" I asked when we were both seated.

"That's what the British call the party that is out of power," Brighton replied. He looked startled at the question.

I chuckled. "I was thinking of something closer to home. Do you remember a group that called itself that in seminary?"

Father Charles was very quick. "You think this is somehow related to the Keller shooting?" he asked.

"There are some things we don't understand yet. The case may be linked to similar cases. We check out everything."

"Well, I do remember hearing about something called that," Brighton nodded. "It was a bit after my time, but Keller was their guru. I think he actually had a following among the more conservative students in the other seminaries, too."

I took out a piece of note paper and wrote down the names of the clergy who had been found shot in Tulsa, St. Louis, and Albuquerque. As an afterthought, I added the name of the one shot in New Hampshire and handed him the list. "Do you remember any of these people?"

Brighton was clearly surprised. "Good Lord, yes!" he declared. "These guys were all part of Keller's clique. Why are you asking about them?"

"They were all killed the same way Keller was," I replied. I was watching him very closely when I said this.

"You don't mean it! All of them?" This was clearly news to him. I nodded and saw him reach the same conclusion I had. "You mean someone is after all these guys?"

I nodded. "It looks like it. I can't give you any details but they are all pretty much the same."

"I don't understand. Why would someone pick them?"

"That's the sixty-four thousand dollar question," I replied. "When I know that, I'll know who killed them."

"Church politics can get really ugly," Brighton told me. "Yet, I can't see how it would drive someone to murder. Mass murder, if you're right."

"Do you know anything else that connects these guys?" I asked. "Even rumors or gossip." Brighton frowned and I added. "I don't give gossip much credibility, but it sometimes holds a grain of truth."

"Mostly it's pure malice," Brighton answered. "Character assassination."

"Someone went a little further than character assassination with these guys," I replied. "Chances are it's connected to something they have in common, something on the dark side they would want to keep secret. If they were lawyers I'd be looking for drugs or gambling or a swindle."

Brighton looked very uncomfortable. "I hate to even suggest anything," he told me, but I knew he had thought of something.

"How about abuse or domestic violence?" The look on his face told me I'd hit the nail squarely. "What about child abuse?" I added. "We ran into that with Keller and picked up some rumors of it with a couple of the guys."

"I don't know anything for sure other than what I've told you," Brighton replied. "I do know their attitude toward women was awful. You know, the old vessels of sin and sources of temptation thinking that has nothing to do with the Gospel. At least, not as I understand it. Their wives were to be seen and not heard, and, frankly, I've never seen an angrier bunch of women. They had to hide it, of course, but it was there. I do know because a lot of them come to talk to me." He shook his head. "I'm afraid our diocese doesn't have women priests for them to talk to."

Brighton looked thoughtful and I waited for him to speak. "You don't suppose it's one of the wives, do you?" he asked. "I can't imagine any of them killing anyone beside their own husband. It sounds like your killer does a lot of planning."

"He is very well organized," I agreed. "But, no, I agree with you. I don't think it's one of the wives. Women don't tend to operate like this guy."

We talked for a few more minutes but there wasn't much else Charlie could tell me about the Honorable Opposition. He asked after Jeanne and I told him she had come to Washington with me. "I'm glad," he said. "That may sound strange coming from a priest, but I'm glad Jeanne has found you. I hope you treat her well."

On impulse, I asked Charlie his thoughts on my having Thanksgiving with Jeanne and her family in Hope. "I don't see any problem with that as long as you're discreet. I know the kids and they are

Jeanne's children, not Henry's. From what you tell me, it sounds like she's done a pretty good job of letting them know how things stand. So if it were me, I'd go."

I told him about the question of divorce and how Jeanne felt. "That sounds like her, all right," Charlie laughed. "I understand your feeling uncomfortable, but I think Jeanne is right. I think it would be bad for her if she divorced Henry. She'd tear herself apart with guilt. What would you do in her place, Jazz?"

"The same damned thing!" I growled, and Brighton laughed. "The whole thing is just so... ambiguous."

"I hear you," Charlie assured me. "I hope you can stand the ambiguity because I think you and Jeanne may be very good for one another. I think you may be God's gift to each other."

"That's what Forster says," I answered. "You didn't talk to him, did you?"

"Not about you, or Jeanne, either," he added. Then he smiled. "So I guess it's true. Great minds do think alike."

There were things that needed my immediate attention in Ft. Smith before the holidays, so I had a couple of days by myself up there while Jeanne got ready for the crowd in Hope. This was our first time apart in many weeks and I found myself missing her terribly. I did stay in touch, calling a couple of times a day, but it's not the same. When I finally headed my Crown Victoria south on US 71, I had trouble keeping under the speed limit. The trip seemed endless and when I finally got to Hope, I was so tense it took an hour in the hot tub to unknot the muscles in my back. Of course, Jeanne's massage didn't hurt, either.

Not all of my stress was due to wanting to arrive, however. I'm always uneasy with anything involving family visits and I try to find other things to prevent my having to go to family reunions. I don't dislike my relatives, but many of them still live in the same small town where I grew up, and we have very little in common. There is only so much that can be said about fishing and the same old family stories are told year after year. I try to stay in touch and stop by when

I'm passing through, but that doesn't seem to happen too often. The nearest major highway is forty miles away and the good pavement ends when it gets to town. Out in the countryside where my kin live, the roads are minimum maintenance. I heard a visitor from out of state describe them as rustic, and they certainly are that.

I arrived in Hope on Wednesday afternoon so Jeanne and I could have a little time to ourselves before the children arrived. Lindy was already there but that didn't seem to matter. We had fun working together and that evening Lindy excused herself to go to an AA meeting in Texarkana. I don't think her car was out of the driveway before Jeanne and I were in each other's arms.

There were some last minute things left to do Thursday morning and I was glad to have something to occupy my time. I was nervous as a groom and trying hard not to show it, which made it even more obvious. I suppose I could have taken a stiff drink, but the last thing I wanted was to meet the kids with liquor on my breath. So I stewed in my own juices until Lindy had pity on me. It took her a while to tease me out of the mood, but she did, and I was very grateful. Then Jeanne jumped in and before long we were so tickled we could hardly breathe. Every time we looked at each other we'd burst out all over again and when Belinda, Jeanne's eldest, arrived with her husband and kids, the three of us were laughing so hard we could barely answer the door.

I think Byron, Belinda's husband, thought we were drunk at first. He's a reserved soul, a college professor who's almost dour until he starts talking about his first love, molecular biology. I'm sure we startled him, and Belinda looked worried herself. Their three children stared at us wide-eyed from the hallway.

"Come in this house!" gasped Lindy and made the introductions. Somehow Jeanne and I managed to avoid looking at each other and pulled ourselves together long enough to greet them. Then Lindy's eyes met Jeanne's and they started laughing all over again. When I tried to explain, I got tickled, too and the kids started laughing at me. Then Belinda caught the bug and pretty soon even Byron was laughing.

"What in the world is going on here?" someone called from the doorway. I turned and saw a tall young man accompanied by two women about his age and two small children. "Has mother been in the sauce?"

The young man was speaking to Lindy and when she tried to answer, she burst out laughing. She pointed at me and said, "This is Jazzed." At that point, Jeanne and I lost it again, as did Belinda and the children, and pretty soon the newcomers were laughing at the rest of us.

When we all calmed down, Jeanne introduced me to her children, being careful to keep breathing normally and not look at me. The young man turned out to be Tom, her middle child, and Jeanne introduced the young woman who looked like his twin as Marian, her youngest. Tom's wife was named Rebecca.

Over the weekend I learned that Tom was a computer systems engineer, as was Rebecca, and they owned their own company. I'm not completely sure exactly what service or goods they provided, but it had done well and they had recently sold their business to a large corporation. Marian, it turned out, was a successful attorney with an old firm in Little Rock. Her specialty was intellectual property and her work was mostly related to computer software. At least, that's the impression I have. There are a lot of computer related occupations around these day I simply don't understand. I understand their words when people try to tell me about their work, but I walk away still in the dark about what they actually do.

One thing I do remember is that Marion was married to another lawyer. She was vague when she told us why he couldn't be there. It was something about a major estate being settled in Alabama, and I wondered if they were having problems. At this point Marion had no children, which was probably best. Or maybe it was the problem.

The laugh-in at the front door broke the ice and we had a wonderful Thanksgiving celebration. I visited a while with Tom and Byron after the ladies chased us out of the kitchen, and the kids were plopped down on the carpet in their pajamas watching the Macy's parade. Or was it the Rose bowl? I get as confused about football playoffs as I do about computer occupations. The passion is just not there.

There wasn't much passion that evening, either, at least not in Henry's land yacht. The kids were as delighted to be away from their parents as their parents were to have us baby-sit. The two couples retired early and Lindy and Marion joined us in the RV by nine o'clock. Nor would we allow the kids to go into the house to watch television. They moaned and complained about being forced to huddle around the small set in the RV but I noticed they weren't paying much attention to whatever was showing. Television seemed to only be a background to a board game marathon. Somehow I ended up with the most hotels on the best properties and I cleaned them out.

Friday morning I slipped away to have a talk with a gunsmith I knew. He was the one who won the design award for his .44 magnum with the integrated silencer. Tom and Byron had reserved a time slot for their annual Thanksgiving round of golf at the local links and Jeanne and the ladies were off to make their pilgrimage to the sales at the Texarkana mall. I was invited to go along to both, but I've never developed the vice of golf and Friday after Thanksgiving at the mall is a celebration I've carefully avoided all my life. I volunteered to stay in Hope with the kids, but they were as excited as their mothers about the mall and I was on my own.

There were the inevitable football games I could have watched, but I'd had enough of that the day before. Even though the kids and I hit it off well, I felt like getting out and being on my own for a few hours. So I gave the gunsmith a call and when it turned out he was going to be at home, I set up a time to come by. I gathered Wes was at loose ends, too. He sounded about as enthusiastic about the football lineup as I was, and told me he would be glad to see me. He had planned to spend the day catching up on his paperwork, too, and he wasn't too thrilled about it.

It wasn't far to drive. When Wes Miller retired from police work, he moved home to his native Arkadelphia. This was something he'd planned judiciously, being a careful soul, and his shop was located on old family land north of town. Rather than working himself gradually broke being a hobby farmer, Wes had turned his place into a private hunting preserve. He also built an indoor pistol range off one end of his shop, mostly for himself and his friends to use. Yet, the place had become so popular Wes had to hire help to so he could devote his time to making custom weapons. I know his hunting rifles sold for over a thousand dollars apiece, not counting the scope, but I had no idea what one of his police .44s would run.

When I got to the farm there was a big sign by the drive stating that the shooting range and store would be closed for the entire Thanksgiving weekend. Someone had hung a hand lettered smaller sign over one corner that read, "Gone Huntin'!" A sign further down the drive said that this property was protected by video cameras. The background of this sign was the outline of a shooter's target with three holes closely grouped around the center dot. When I looked more closely, I saw the holes around the center were actual bullet holes.

Two large dogs ran out to greet me when I drove around to the back of the shop like Wes told me. Their barking alerted Wes, who opened the door and said something quietly. When he did, both dogs stopped barking and sat watching as I got out of the car and went into the shop. I had the distinct impression that all it would take to get them after me again would be another quiet word from Wes.

The dogs and some distant cousins were about all Wes had for family and the dogs followed us into the shop. Once we were there, the dogs found their beds on the floor and quickly went to sleep. "Hellacious guard dogs, ain't they?" Wes laughed. "Hardly worth feeding." Yet there was a note of pride in his voice and I noticed neither of the dogs looked as if they had missed a meal. I also suspected that these now docile mutts could turn downright mean if they perceived a threat. "Just don't take out your piece if you're packing one," Wes told me. "Not without telling me first."

"Sneaky," I laughed and Wes' nod told me I was right. The dogs had been trained to attack without orders if someone pulled a weapon. I suspect they had been trained to do so silently and without warning. Nor could I find fault in this precaution. Anyone who is crazy enough to try to rob a gun shop at gunpoint is crazy enough to pull a trigger in spite. To give warning is to invite sudden death.

I'd given a lot of thought how to approach Miller and decided to be direct. I told him about the case in Ft. Worth and the similarities to the ones in Missouri, Albuquerque, and Tulsa. I mentioned my guess that the loads were subsonic and that the killer was relying on the weight of the heavier .357 slug. I also mentioned the fact that none of the forensic labs that had reported back were able to identify the weapon, and that the FBI experts suggested it was a custom rifle designed by an independent maker. I also mentioned my own idea that the weapon had an integral silencer along the barrel.

As I talked, I watched Miller's face. I saw it grow ever more guarded the more I filled in the details, and by the time I mentioned the integral silencer, it was an unreadable mask. "Why are you talking to me?" Miller asked.

"I thought someone might have either copied your design or stole one of your weapons," I answered. "I thought you might point me in the right direction."

"I've never made a .357 in that design," Miller answered. "I only do .44 magnums or an occasional .41 magnum for a police department. You can look at my list."

"Why did you settle on the .44 magnum?" I asked.

"Brute force," Miller answered without hesitation. "I wanted something to knock a perp down on the first punch. A .357 doesn't always do that, and even the standard .45 Long Colt is not as powerful. I redesigned it to automatic when they came out with the .44 auto mag."

That was a long speech for the taciturn Miller. I gave it some thought. "Why did you develop the bolt action first?"

"Accuracy," Wes replied. "That was the other issue with the .357. I had a hard time getting the twist right. I hit it right away with the .44." He reached over and pulled a paper target off the wall. In the dead center was a large hole that looked as if it had been made by three shots. It was about the size of a quarter, maybe slightly more.

"Nice group," I told. "What range?"

"That's a subsonic load at seventy-five yards," he told me. "I was using 240 grain soft nose Nosler partitions out of an eighteen inch barrel. They were moving at just under eleven hundred feet per second."

I whistled. "A lot of guys would like to shoot a three shot group like that with a .270," I said.

"Believe it or not, that's a seven shot group."

"You put seven slugs through here?" I asked. "That's incredible."

"Don't I wish?" Wes replied, warming up a bit. "That was a buddy of mine from gunsmith school. It was with the silencer, too. He offered me five thousand dollars for it on the spot."

"I can see why," I said. This was a polite lie. The fact is I don't care for firearms that much, and I never have. I would prefer to deal with criminals the way the British were able to until the last few decades, without having to rely on firearms. When it comes to shooting, which I enjoy and find relaxing, I prefer archery or precision single-shot air guns. At the standard fifteen meters, I've put five shots inside a half-inch, although that doesn't happen often. As a matter of fact, it has only occurred three times in thirty years, but on one occasion I had a witness.

"Do you remember his name?" I asked.

"Yeah, David something. The other guys called him 'Davy Crockett' because he was such a good shot, a real natural. I think he may have had sniper training in the Army, but I don't know for sure."

"Any idea where I might reach him?" I asked casually.

Miller wasn't fooled. He'd been a policeman too long. "Davy's not your guy," he said with a sardonic grin. "He might be a little hard to reach, too. He's been dead for quite a few years."

"Any idea how he died?"

"Not really. We weren't that close. Someone told me he was working for the feds and was killed on a bust." Miller shook his head. "He would still be alive if he hadn't been such a damned cowboy. Making guns was just too slow." He shook his head. "That's why I quit and started doing this. I don't miss the excitement at all, Jazz." He looked at me closely. "You ever had to shoot anybody?"

"No, thank God!" I replied.

"I did, but I was lucky. The kid lived and I heard he straightened out, too, so I guess it was worth it. It sure ruined me as a cop. I asked for a desk job and retired as soon as I could. I'm glad I don't have his life on my hands."

Miller seemed open again and I decided to probe gently. "Look, this whole conversation is off the record, Wes. I'm retired myself and I'm running this line as a favor to someone else. Is there any way someone could have gotten hold of one of your weapons? Stolen? Black market? Copied parts? You know what I'm saying."

"Oh, hell, yes! I can't keep up with my orders. I'm running six months behind. I've put out almost seven hundred of those things now, and I don't enjoy working on them the way I did. All of them went to law enforcement agencies, but you know how that goes." He shrugged. "What I can't figure is the .357 angle. Are you sure about the size bore?"

I nodded and Miller continued. "You know, I heard there was another guy who fooled with this type design. I think he was before my time, but he ran into the same problem I had with the .357. Accuracy wasn't all that bad, but it wasn't quite what I wanted." He laughed. "I got the idea he was more interested in the other side of the law. His called his rifle the Warden's Favorite, but I think he had poachers in mind."

"Any idea what happened to him?"

"Yeah, he's dead, too. Down in Florida is what I heard. Went after one 'gator too many." Miller grinned. "It was a classic case of firepower over accuracy. The game warden had a Mac 10."

# 12. Filling In Gaps

I was back in Ft. Smith the following week working on something else when my cell phone rang. I answered and it was Jack Keller, though it took me a while to figure out who he was. Then I realized this was the bishop's son from Ft. Worth.

"Thanks for calling, Jack," I told him. "I really appreciate it."

"I called Detective Kowalski, but my mom said I should call you, too."

"Well, tell your mother I appreciate it. I haven't had a chance to talk to Kowalski in a while. Would you mind telling me what you said to her?"

"I told her the whole thing was a hoax." Somehow the last word didn't sound quite right coming from Jack Keller. "I made the whole thing up."

"You mean the calls from Wally?" I asked, just to be sure.

"Yeah," Jack replied. I waited for him to go on, but he didn't.

"Why would you do that, Jack?" I asked.

"I guess it's what I wanted to believe. I thought that believing it was true would make it be true." Again there was something about the way he said this that didn't sound like a teen talking.

"Jack, is this what you really think or is this what your counselor told you?" I asked.

There was silence for a long moment. "Why do you ask?" he responded. "What difference does it make, anyway? What I told you wasn't true and that's what matters."

"Well, it matters quite a bit, Jack. When you were talking to me at home, it sounded to me like you were telling us the truth. I know when people are lying and when you said you had talked to Wally, it sounded like you really believed what you were saying."

"Well, I did. Now I know I was wrong."

"Wait a minute. Help me understand. Why were you so sure it was Wally at first?"

Jack hesitated a moment. "It sounded like Wally. He said some things nobody else would remember. You know what I mean."

"I might think so, but I really don't," I said. "Tell me what you mean."

"Like the way he used to greet me. 'Hey, Jack-bird, how they hanging?' That's what he used to say."

"That must have really been strange to hear from him after your dad died. How often did you hear from him after he left home?"

Again Jack hesitated and I knew there was something he was holding back. "Well, more than I told Mom. At first it was three or four times a year. Then I didn't hear for a long time and I was afraid he was dead. I had a hard time believing it was him at first when he called, but he told me some things nobody else could know besides Wally."

"So what made you change your mind?" I asked. Jack was silent and for a moment I thought he'd hung up. "You still there?" I asked.

"Yeah," Jack answered but said nothing else.

"Look, Jack, as far as I'm concerned, you're not in any trouble over this at all. I just want to know the truth, the whole truth. What are you not telling me?"

"The guy called me."

"Who called you, Jack?" I insisted.

"The guy pretending to be Wally."

"When did he call?"

"Yesterday," Jack said.

"Let me be sure I understand," I told him. "This is the same guy you thought was Wally when he called after your dad died?"

"Yeah, that's who I'm talking about."

"OK, let's take it from the beginning. Wally didn't call for a long time. Then this guy called and convinced you he was Wally? Right?"

"Right. It was the same guy that called after Dad died."

"He called you at home?" I asked. "Or do you have a cell phone?"

"Dad wouldn't let us have cell phones," Jack told me. "He called me at home."

"All right. Who answered the phone?"

The question surprised Jack. "I did. Who else would it be?"

"Your mother or one of your sisters could have answered," I replied.

"No, he called my number, not mom and dad's."

"Every time?"

"Yeah. Why are you so interested?"

"Details are very important," I answered. "Sometimes the most insignificant detail can turn me in exactly the right direction. This one tells me the caller didn't have to worry about anyone else answering the phone. He knew he would get you."

"Why is that important?" Jack wanted to know.

"I'm not sure it is at this point, but it may turn out to be a key to solving the case."

"Weird!" Jack said.

"So he called you on your private line. Did he give you a name?"

Jack was silent for a moment. When he spoke, he was excited. "I see what you mean. He never actually told me he was Wally. He just let me believe it. Then he told me to call him Quinn when he called yesterday."

"This is where details can be really important, Jack. Can you remember exactly what he said to lead you to believe he was Wally?"

"I think so, but if it wasn't Wally, how did he know those things?" Jack answered.

I laughed. "You're catching on fast. That was the next thing I was going to ask. Let's stick to the first question for now. What made you think it was Wally?"

Jack mentioned a number of things that came up in the early

conversations that only Wally would know. One was Jack's music, which was not limited to marching band. Jack had followed his older brother by taking up clarinet, but his real passion was jazz piano and his favorite performer was George Winston. The imposter had mentioned both and even asked if Jack had Winston's latest album. He had also made reference to family pets, now dead many years, and asked about family friends.

I found myself impressed with the depth of the con, and wondered why the imposter went to such great lengths to con Jack. There is always a motive behind a con, even if this is nothing but the dubious thrill of successful deceit, and I couldn't see why the sham had picked Jack. There was no obvious pay-off.

There was a second question that came to mind as I thought about this. Having completed the successful deception, why did the imposter finally come clean? This didn't make any sense unless the payoff was reveling in the victim's pain. I decided to see what Jack thought.

"Any idea why this guy Quinn did all this?" I asked.

"Not a clue." I could almost see Jack shaking his head.

"Did he rub it in or tease you about it?"

"No, the dude apologized. I didn't believe him at first but he kept telling me how sorry he felt and I think he really meant it."

Suddenly I felt a cold stream of fear run down my back. This Quinn character was a most unusual con artist. Not only was he very thorough, he was subtle, and in my mind this made him extremely dangerous. Yet I was very careful choosing my words. I didn't want Jack to panic. "Have you noticed anything out of the ordinary lately, Jack? Anything at all?"

"You mean besides my dad getting shot?" He quipped. "Sorry," he added quickly. "It just sounded funny."

"Yeah, like asking Mrs. Lincoln how she liked the play," I shot back and Jack laughed for the first time that day. It really wasn't funny, but teens have a good sense of the absurd that they often lose later in life. They seem to like gallows humor in particular, maybe because none of them are convinced they will ever die. "Seriously, Jack, I want you to really think about what I asked. Did Quinn ever suggest getting together with you or anything like that?"

"No, and when I asked if I could see him, he told me it wasn't a good idea. That was when I still thought he was Wally."

Damn! I thought. There is nothing that will avert suspicion like getting the victim to suggest the set-up and insist on it. I could see nothing else to do but grasp the nettle firmly. "I don't want to scare you, Jack, but this guy may be after you. Has anyone been following you or hanging around? Especially someone you don't know."

The thought was new and I could tell it scared him. "No, I haven't noticed. I haven't really been paying attention. Geeze."

"Have you had any feeling you were being watched?" I asked.

"No, but I'm listening to music most of the time," he said. "Even when my pod is off. I play it over in my head. I guess that sounds dumb."

"Not at all. I used to do that with Smiley Jones' piano music."

"Why did you quit?"

"I investigated his murder. When I did I found out what kind of creep he really was. He stole some of his music from other people. That sort of ruined it for me."

"Wow!" Jack said. "Did you catch his killer?"

"With the help of some good people I sure did. How it turned out was the guy who killed him was the guy Smiley stole his theme song from." We were getting away from the subject, so I asked, "Listen, do you have any idea why this guy Quinn pretended to be Wally?"

"He said they were friends and he promised Wally he would look out for me."

I thought about this for a minute. "That doesn't make sense," I said. "Why would Wally ask him to do that?"

"I don't know," Jack answered. "I never thought about that. Unless Wally thought he couldn't do it himself." I could almost hear the gears spinning in his mind. "Or unless Wally knew he was dying."

*Or was in prison or a mental institution,* I thought, but I didn't say this. I decided to go in a different direction

Then another thought hit me. *Why couldn't the caller be Wally, pretending to be Quinn?* Again, I said nothing but I made a note to myself to give this more thought and to talk with Dee about this. As I was writing it out, I missed Jack's next question and had to ask him to repeat.

"Do you think Wally's dead?" Jack asked.

I decided to be candid. "I don't know," I told him. "The question in my mind is why he would stay hidden now your dad is gone. That was why he left in the first place. At least, that's what your mother said."

"I wondered that, too," Jack sighed. "I think he's dead. I think Quinn was telling me the truth."

"Why do you think that?"

"Because if he was really Wally, why wouldn't he want to come back?" There was a great deal of vulnerability and pain in Jack's voice.

"There might be a number of very good reasons," I told him. "He might be sick and not want to be a burden to the family." While I was thinking of AIDS, I didn't say so. I know of several instances when a prodigal coming home with AIDS has created a living hell for his family. I can think of nothing in the world worse than seeing someone you love wasting away until death is no longer dreaded but welcomed as a gift. Cancer is bad enough, but I would think the stigma of AIDS would make it even worse.

Jack seemed to be reading my mind. "You think he has AIDS?" he asked.

I decided to lie. "I was thinking of cancer or MS," I answered. "I lost my wife that way and it's not something I'd put my family through. Why did you think it might be AIDS, Jack?"

"You know," he replied. "You've seen his picture. Didn't you think he was gay?"

"I wondered," I admitted. "I didn't say anything because I wasn't sure. Was that why he and your dad were at odds?"

"I don't think he ever told Dad," Jack answered. "When he told me, he made me promise not to tell dad."

"How about your mother?" I asked. "Did she know?"

"I don't know and I'm not going to ask!" Jack shot back. "I'm not about to get Mom in any trouble!"

"I'm not after your mom," I assured him. "All I wanted to know was if Wally had come out to your family. Your mother might know who this Quinn is."

"You mean he's like Wally's lover?" Jack asked.

"That's not what I was thinking, though it is possible," I said. "Then it would make sense for Wally to ask him to look after you if Wally had AIDS."

"Or if he's dead," Jack added, finishing my thought.

"Listen, Jack," I said. "I know you want to know about Wally one way or another, but I want you to just put all this out of your mind as much as you can for a while. In the meantime, I'm going to talk with your mother about getting you a cell phone."

"Cool!" Jack said. "All my friends have them."

"That's not why I want you to have one, Jack. When you get it I want you to set a speed dial button to 911 and another for Detective Kowalski and Detective Adams. I want you to put in one to my cell phone number too, the one you just called. If you see anything that seems scary, I want you to call Kowalski or Adams immediately. And if you can't get them, then call 911. All right?"

When he responded I could hear the fear in his voice. "You really think someone is after me?"

"Look, Jack, I don't want to scare you," I told him. "So, no, I don't really think that Quinn is a creep who's stalking you. But I don't want to take any chances, either. I want you to be safe. So I want you to carry that phone with you wherever you go."

"I can't take my phone to school," Jack said. "It isn't allowed."

"Kowalski will clear it with your principal," I assured him. "I want it with you all the time, so keep it charged when you're at home. Now let me talk to your mom."

Jack called his mother to the phone and I gave her a brief rundown of my concern for Jack's safety and what I wanted. She was alarmed at first, but I was able to assure her this was just a precaution. She thanked me for the warning when we signed off. More important, she agreed to make sure Jack kept the phone with him and to see that he kept the battery charged.

I called Kowalski when I was done and brought her up to date. She was in the car with Adams, but he pulled over and she somehow put the call on speaker-phone. I'm not sure exactly how they're able to do such things these days, but there's a part of me that wonders if it isn't through arcane rites and dire covenants made in cemeteries at the stroke of midnight.

"This doesn't make a bit of sense, Jazz," Adams said at one point. "Why would this Quinn character give up the con?"

"I don't see the payoff, either," Kowalski added.

"I don't know, either," I answered. "But I'm beginning to think Wally may be alive after all. I had a case like this a couple of years ago in Arkansas. I'm pretty sure we're dealing with a serial killer and I think it may be Wally."

There was a long moment of silence as they absorbed this. "Well, if the killer really is Wally, he certainly has motive, at least for shooting his dad," Adams observed.

"Telling Jack he was being conned would make sense, too," Kowalski pointed out. "He may be feeling some heat and trying to throw us off."

"Someone needs to go to Arizona and check things out," I said. "Wallace is closest. Could you talk to him?"

Again, there was silence. "Thing is, Jazz," Kowalski said. "To do that we'd have to reopen the case. I don't think our chief will go along with that."

"Maybe I can talk Wallace into it," I said. "He doesn't seem too enthusiastic about a trip to Nogales."

"I've been there and I can see why," Adams laughed.

I was about to ask something else when I heard the radio in their car go off. "We've got to take a call, Jazz," Kowalski told me. "We have an officer down." She must have been reaching for the siren switch even as she said this. I heard it whoop once before the line went dead.

Since I was already on the case, I made another call, this time to

New Hampshire. I'd tried to reach the bishop there several times before, but with no luck. Nor did the right reverend sir seem inclined to return my calls, though I knew he was supposed to be in the office all week. This time I decided to push a bit.

"This is Dr. Phillips, again, the FBI consultant," I told the secretary. I'd talked to her each time I called. "I need to speak with the bishop."

"Oh, he's in a meeting right now, Dr. Phillips," she told me, just as she had each time before.

"Well, he's not returned my call," I told her. "I guess I'll have to have a couple of agents come out and pick him up." I was very careful to keep any tone of threat out of my voice. I've found this is far more effective than yelling. "Is he scheduled to be there all afternoon?"

The casual tone had its desired effect. When the secretary responded, she sounded scared. "Can you give me any idea of what this is about, Dr. Phillips?" she asked. "Let me hand him a note."

"Well, yes, I can. It's about the murder of one of your priests. You might tell him I prefer to handle this by phone rather than sending someone for him."

"Oh, you mean.... Oh, goodness, just a moment." I'm sure the thought of her boss being escorted from their office in handcuffs was uppermost in her mind.

Thirty seconds later a deep tenor voice came on the line. "This is the bishop," it declared. "Who is this?"

I game him my name and told him I was involved with investigating what looked like a serial killer who was after Episcopal clergy. I also told him I'd left several messages and had not heard back from any. I mentioned the name of the priest who was shot and told him I needed more information.

"How do I know you're for real?" He asked. "We've been pestered to death by the press with this affair."

I suggested he call the Ft. Worth medical examiner's office and ask for Dr. Simon Smyth. I also gave him a name to call at the FBI office in Washington, DC. To give him credit, the bishop had every right to be suspicious and when he said he would take my word for it, I insisted he at least call Simon. I gave him my number to call back.

Ten minutes later my phone rang and the bishop was on the other end. "All right," he said. "I'll tell you what I can."

"I appreciate it," I told him. "I'll be as brief as I can. Were there any hints, rumors or allegations that the priest who was shot was ever involved in sexual abuse?"

"You get to the point, don't you?" he answered. "There have been several things along that line that have come up since his death that suggest he may have. We certainly didn't know about it before. Believe me, I'd have kicked his ass from here to Texas if I'd known. Why do you ask?"

I decided to be candid, hoping it didn't come back to bite me. "What I've to tell you is for your ears only, sir. All right?"

"Fair enough," he replied.

"There looks like there may have been several cases of priests shot like this within your denomination," I told him. "They all went to the same seminary about the same time, and it looks like there was sexual abuse involved in every case."

"Jesus!" said the bishop, and it sounded like a profound prayer. "I had no idea. So you think someone is hunting down abusive priests. Have any Roman Catholic priests been killed?"

"Not so far. At least, none we know about. However, there may be some cases in other denominations. We're looking into that, too."

"My, my," the bishop said and I could almost see him nod. "I suppose Rufus Keller was one of the people you're talking about, wasn't he?"

"Yes, his death is what started our investigation. Why do you ask?"

"I couldn't help missing the similarities," the bishop replied. "Then, too. Rufus was very.... I don't know, intense is not exactly what I'm trying to say. He always seemed to be on edge, even in the most relaxed circumstances. Amanda seemed to fit the profile of victim, too, though I never asked. So did their children."

"Why do you say that?" I asked.

"I wasn't always a priest," he told me. "I worked as a social worker in Chicago for many years before seminary. There are days I wish I was still there, but not many. Anyway, how else can I help you, Dr. Phillips?"

"I understand Bishop Keller was very homophobic, too."

"Yes, but that's a matter of public record. Rufus shouted it from every housetop and with every media that would give him time."

"As a social worker, would that have suggested to you he might have some of his own issues there?" I asked.

The bishop chuckled. "You're very delicate when you want to be, Dr. Phillips. Just between me and thee and the fence post, I always wondered if a lot of his behavior was not simple self-hatred. It usually is when people get so full of rage."

I thanked the bishop for his time and told him I regretted having to push my way into his afternoon. He assured me it was all right and invited me to stop by for a cup of coffee if I was ever in his neighborhood. I believe the man really meant it.

I was wondering whether to go back to work or to call Jeanne when my phone rang again. It was Wallace. "Damn, you're hard to get hold of," he said. "I've been getting a busy signal from your number all morning."

This didn't make sense until I remembered the time difference. "I'm not surprised," I answered. I told him who I'd been talking to and what I'd learned.

Mike listened patiently but I had the sense he had news of his own. Sure enough, he told me he had traced down his seminary sources and his victims were not only tied to one another, they were tied to mine. This made at least eight deaths tied to the same killer and it was time to call in the FBI. I said so to Wallace and he agreed. He also agreed to make the call, which was best. While I'm well connected with the FBI as a consultant and could raise their interest, a request for assistance from a state law enforcement agency would carry more weight. The important thing was to nail this guy before he killed again.

When I suggested someone needed to go to Nogales to check out Wally Keller's death, Wallace was in complete agreement. He asked me if I would be available as a consultant on the case and didn't flinch when I told him my contract rates. There was apparently more wiggle room in his budget than he was willing to first admit. He told me he would send a letter of agreement by fax and would meet me at the Phoenix airport at my convenience. He told me to be sure and bring a jacket and hat. Even though it's on the border and can be quite hot, Nogales is high desert. It can get very cold there in early December and snow is not that rare.

My right ear was feeling like the phone receiver had taken root there, but I called for a reservation and then called Jeanne to let her know where I would be the next few days. "My goodness, Dr. Jazz, you do get around, don't you," she teased, but I could hear disappointment in her voice. "I don't suppose you need a girl Friday to carry your bags, do you?"

"This is different from Ft. Worth, Jeanne. Where we're going is not a nice place at all and I don't know what my schedule will be. I'd love to have you along but I'm afraid we wouldn't have much time together. I'd rather plan a trip to Phoenix together when this is all over."

"I'll take that as a promise, sir," she said. "When do you have to leave?"

"I've got a flight out of Little Rock Monday morning," I told her.

"Oh, good! That gives us the whole weekend. I'll drive up tonight and take you to the airport." Then she chuckled. "Assuming, of course, you're in any shape to fly."

# 13. Nogales

When I stepped outside the airport in Phoenix, I was immediately aware of how dry it is there. I could feel the moisture being pulled out of my body, though I didn't find this unpleasant. It felt good, like those rare mornings in northern Arkansas when the air is clear and perfectly still and the temperature stands near zero. My grandfather would have said it was bracing.

I was also glad I had brought a warm jacket and had thought to bring shades. Even at ten in the morning the light wind had a raw edge and the desert light was intense. I was glad when Wallace and I got to his car and out of the wind. Yet when I saw the car I had to laugh. It was a standard white police Crown Victoria. "I thought everyone in California drove an SUV," I said.

"That's pretty much true these days," Wallace answered. He was dressed western style, complete with a string tie, cowboy boots and a soft felt Stetson. He also wore a blue western cut dress shirt tucked into western trousers, and his wide leather belt was buckled with Hopi silver. The only indication he was a lawman, other than his manner, was a badge on a leather flap over his belt. I couldn't see his pistol until he took off his Navajo design jacket, but when I did I recognized it as the standard .45 Long Colt revolver once used by the cavalry.

On me the getup would have looked ridiculous. I'm far too short and stout to pull it off, and when I carry a weapon, my jacket looks like I've something growing under my arm. On Wallace, however, it all looked perfectly normal. There was no question he was a western lawman, tall and lanky with an air of quiet authority. I was sure his intense gray eyes missed nothing.

We drove in silence for a few moments as Wallace negotiated traffic and got us onto the freeway headed south. The light on the mountains around Phoenix was stunning and I found myself wishing I had time to spend there with my camera. "Personally, I wouldn't have one," Wallace said, startling me. "The things are just too unstable. We see a lot of fatalities with them that wouldn't happen with a car like this. Mostly families."

It took me a moment to realize he was still talking about SUVs. "That's what I hear," I answered. "Nice light out here."

Wallace chuckled. "It sure is. It's nice to look through air you can't see."

Again we rode in silence, but I didn't find it uncomfortable. Wallace seemed to be one of those rare people comfortable with holding his peace and I was happy to watch the play of light and shadows against the mountains. I'd seen Southwestern colors before, but they seemed different around Phoenix and I suspected the light might be hard to catch. I thought it would be nice to bring Jeanne here to see them.

I was thinking about this when I realized Wallace had asked me something. "No," I said, "I'm fine." He gave me a strange look and I realized I'd answered the wrong question. "Sorry," I said, flustered. "I was a thousand miles away."

Wallace nodded. "I don't like being away much, either," he said. "That's the only thing I don't like about my job, too much travel. Don't get to see enough of my family. You got kids?"

"No," I said. "Only grandkids. My wife died a while back," I told him.

Wallace nodded. I could see he was trying to figure this one out. "My wife and I sort of adopted a younger family in Ft. Smith," I told him. "The kids call me Grandpa Jazz. We never had children."

"Sorry to hear that." He gave me another searching look and I knew he knew I'd not been thinking about grandchildren. I decided to let him wonder a while. "Hmm," he said noncommittally and I knew he had figured out I was seeing someone new.

"You never told me what the FBI had to say," I reminded him.

"You have quite a reputation there," he answered. "They told me you're the best man in the country for serial cases." He gave me another look.

"Yeah, I seem to have them fooled," I said. "Did they have anything else in their database? Any other cases like these?"

"No, and that surprised them," Wallace laughed. "Seems like you and I saw the pattern first. They searched when they saw your query, the same one I did, but no cases popped up. It shook them."

"It's good for their souls," I answered and Wallace laughed again. Like most state and local police officers, I suspect he was ambivalent about the Bureau. Humility is not a vice the Bureau seems to cultivate, and its special agents stir up a crop of resentment with the way they deal with local agencies.

"They did tell me they could get Keller's military records for us, though," Wallace added. "They didn't have any information on him except for his firearms license. They got that from Treasury. Their information is that he is dead, and his firearms license hasn't been renewed."

"So he was a licensed dealer. How about the gunsmith school? Has anyone run that down yet?"

Mike shook his head. "No, not on my end. We're sort of short staffed right now. Not looking for a job, are you?"

"The State of California doesn't have that much money," I laughed. "I've been there and done that. I even got the tattoo and T-shirt."

"I figured you'd been vaccinated," Wallace nodded. "I have my twenty years and some days it's all I can do to go to work. Things are so different than when I started, real different." He shook his head. "My youngest graduates high school in two years. After that, I'm gone."

"So tell me about Nogales," I said. "I know it's a major point of entry for illegal drugs, but not much else."

"Nogales, Mexico, is a real border hell-hole," Wallace told me. "Whatever you want, you can find there. Drugs, hookers, contract killers false documents, it doesn't matter. If you have money, you can find it." He chuckled. "Or get killed being ripped off. That's a real cottage industry there, too. God only knows what the homicide rate is on the other side of the border, and no one is really sure what it is on this side, either. The state of Sonora is Mexico's equivalent to cartel areas of Columbia. They have direct business ties to Columbia. The point is that drugs are everywhere and are tied into everything that happens, and there's almost no real law enforcement on the Mexican side. They're all bought off or killed, just like in Columbia."

He gave me a sardonic grin. "Of course, that's one man's opinion, but the whole border area is set up for smuggling operations. For one thing, there's ninety miles of border along the Tohono O'odham Reservation and nobody lives out there. It's rugged country and, honest to God, they use burros and backpacks to get the stuff in. Back in Nogales, they use the tunnels."

"The tunnels?" I asked. "You mean like the ones across the DMZ in Korea."

"Even worse," Wallace told me. "Smugglers use storm drains like interstates. They tunnel in from the Mexican side and move the stuff to Phoenix and Tucson to break it down for wholesale distribution. They've found drugs from Nogales as far away as Seattle. Next to Laredo, it's probably the biggest inland port of entry. The DEA has closed down at least twenty tunnels in the last fifteen years. That's a lot of drugs and wetbacks." He laughed. "That's what they call illegals coming across the Rio Grande, wetbacks. Around here I'm told they call them dusty-butts."

"What about guns?" I asked. "That's how Wally Keller was involved."

Wallace shrugged. "Well, Jazz, you know how it is. Anywhere you find drugs, you're going to find guns, too, but that's not all. There's a strong market for smuggling people into the country, too. The tunnels are very good for that and the coyotes run very low risk. A lot of people die trying to get in. Some of the illegals are shot by the same people they paid to get them across. Like I said, it's a real hell-hole."

"I wonder why anyone chooses to live there?" I asked. "At least, those who have a choice."

"You hit the nail on the head," Wallace answered. "A lot of them don't have much choice. I guess for the rest it's the same reasons people choose to live in LA." He shook his head. "Sacramento is bad enough. Sometimes I get the feeling being a cop is like being a Roman centurion, watching Rome go down while the emperor fiddles." He looked at me to see my response.

"Yeah," I answered. "But it's like my partner, Dee, says. All we can do is take down one asshole at a time." Wallace was still smiling when we got to Tucson and stopped for lunch.

We found a little place to eat just off the freeway. It was called La Taqueria Linda, something little known in Arkansas. The place was filled with Hispanics and their conversation died when Wallace and I walked in. We took a seat at an empty booth at the back and a pretty young waitress brought us water and took our order. After a couple of minutes, the conversation started up again, but was very muted. Most of what I heard sounded like Spanish with an assortment of English nouns mixed in. One phrase I heard several times was "mi chingada Chevy." I suppose the speaker was a Ford fan.

When the food came, Wallace asked if I minded if he said grace. I told him to have at it and he mumbled something I couldn't understand until he said, "Amen." I said the same, and we dove into the fajitas.

While I know we ordered beef, I also know the meat could also have been rat, but if it was, I'll settle for rodent. I've never tasted anything quite like it and Wallace told me part of the flavor was from the mesquite wood used in the grill. "It's probably full of all kinds of nitrates and other stuff that isn't good for us, but I could care less," he told me, signaling for more flour tortillas.

I told him I was flatly jealous. "You skinny guys have it good," I complained. "If I ate like you do, I'd be wider than I'm tall."

"I wouldn't be eating like this if my wife was along," he admitted. "When I'm off the reservation I eat what I want."

"Same here," I said. "At least, it was when Nellie was alive. When I traveled it was chicken fried chicken and lots of potatoes and gravy.

It was worth every heartburn."

"Oh, I'll pay for this later," he assured me. "It's fizz tabs for me for supper." Yet as he said this he reached for more refried beans. "I can't seem to decide which is better, the beans or the Spanish rice."

True to his word, Wallace stopped at a drugstore to pick up some antacids before we got back on the freeway. I offered to help him drive, but he shook his head. "This is a rental," he told me. "They get sticky about that." I nodded, but then I wondered why he rented a car that looked so official. For the same money we could have looked like drug dealers. On the other hand, that image might not help us much dealing with local law enforcement people.

The road atlas says it's 101 miles from Tucson to Nogales. The whole route is four-lane highway and Wallace poured the coal to the Crown Vic. I avoided looking to see how fast we were traveling, although I never felt unsafe. We had apparently used up our quota of conversation and Wallace drove with both hands on the wheel, his eyes constantly monitoring every side. The only time he slowed down was when traffic increased near the few towns we passed, and at some point I dozed off. When I awoke we were taking a Nogales exit. I glanced at my watch. Just over seventy minutes had passed since our lunch stop.

Wallace drove directly to the sheriff's office without calling for directions, and this surprised me until I thought about it. Some people do ask for directions. Nor is Nogales, Arizona, that large. About twenty thousand souls live on the American side, compared to eight times that number south of the border, and while the streets run every which way, the town is not that hard to navigate. We left most of the traffic near the port of entry, which is always busy, and once we left the main roads, we could have been in almost any small town in Arizona or New Mexico.

My phone rang as I was getting out of the car. I looked at the display and punched the answer button. "I better take this call," I told Wallace. "It's Kowalski." He nodded and settled back into his seat.

"I need some advice, Jazz," Kowalski told me. "Something's come up. I don't know how to handle it and neither does Jim. The janitor called me back."

"The fellow from the church?" I asked.

"That's right. Something's really been bothering him ever since the shooting and he finally gave me a call. The bottom line is that he was on his way into the sanctuary to clean up the glass from the broken window when he found the body."

"My, my. So much for accidental homicide," I observed. "When did he call?"

"Late yesterday afternoon, but I didn't get the message until this morning. Then I had a hard time getting anything out of him. He was scared he could be in trouble for not calling sooner. It took me a while to convince him he wasn't."

"The man was in shock," I replied. "I don't imagine the trip to the emergency room helped his frame of mind, either."

"Exactly. That's what I told him."

"Did he say when he saw the glass?"

"That's the problem. It was about an hour before he found the body. He left to get a broom and a dust pan to clean it up. Something else came up and he didn't get back right away."

"When had he last cleaned the floor in the transept?"

"A floor crew was in the night before. The janitor was making sure they had done it right when he saw the glass. He saw the scratch in the floor, too."

"You think he's telling you the truth?"

"Yeah, I do. I can't tell you why, but I do."

"I call it cop sense," I said. "Trust it. By the way, what does the janitor look like?"

"I'd call him small and wiry. He's five seven or five-eight, weighs maybe one-forty. He's bald with a gray fringe around the sides. I'd put him in his early sixties. Why?"

"Some of the other victims were found by janitors, but none of them match your description. I'm just making sure. So what did Joe McClellan say?"

"Before or after he got done cussing?" Kowalski quipped. "That's what I don't know how to handle. He won't let us reopen the case.

What do we do?"

"Protect yourselves," I told her. "This is what I was afraid would happen. So make your report and be sure a copy gets into the file."

"That's it?" she demanded. "You're telling us to roll over for this?"

"Not at all," I corrected. "I'm telling you to protect yourselves. This case has gone national and sooner or later Joe McClellan will have to get on board to cover his own ass. He may find himself in an awkward position and you need to make sure he can't blame you. So do the shuck and jive 'yazzah, boss!' for now and stay as far out of his way as you can. Have you reported any of this to your immediate supervisor?"

"That's you on this case," Kowalski reminded me.

"Yes, but let your regular supervisor know what's going on, too. Like I said, this may get nasty and I don't want you or Jim hurt by it. As a matter of courtesy, tell Dr. Smyth, too. He's a good man to have in your corner."

We talked for another minute or two before Kowalski had to go. After I hung up I looked at Wallace. "I imagine you caught the general drift of that?"

"Yeah, but why don't you fill me in a bit more?" he replied. When I was done, he nodded and said, "We have problems with that kind of thing, too. I know it's about turf 'issues' but I'm damned if I understand them. There's ways of handling things so no one gets the dirty end of the stick."

I was about to agree when my phone rang again. I looked at the display and it was another call from Ft. Worth. "I seem to be popular in Cowtown this morning," I said.

The call was from Joe McClellan and I had no trouble hearing what he was saying. I turned the volume up and turned the phone so Wallace could listen in.

"Have you heard from Kowalski?" McClellan demanded.

"Yeah!" I said with a lot more enthusiasm than I felt. "It sounds like you caught a good break in the case, Joe. Congratulations!"

McClellan broke into a stream of profanity and I was glad he couldn't see my grin. I glanced over at Wallace and he was smiling, too. When the chief wound down a bit, I broke in. "I don't understand, Joe. I thought this would make you happy. It's going to reflect very well on you and your department."

"How the Harry Frigg is it going to do that?" McClellan demanded.

"You have a national case," I said. "I'm in Nogales working with a senior investigator from California. We're on the guy's trail, Joe. We're going to nail this bastard and the people who broke the case open were two rookies from Ft. Worth. That's going to speak well for their chief."

"Who broke the case was one ornery asshole from Arkansas," McClellan shot back, but he was getting calmer.

"One ornery asshole you had the wisdom to hire in the first place, Joe," I pointed out and Wallace started laughing silently. "Seriously, there's nothing to worry about here. This is a win-win situation for you. You can always blame me if it goes south, but it won't."

"So what's the body count now?" McClellan wanted to know.

"Eight almost for sure, but I wouldn't be surprised if we find others once the story gets out," I told him. "Right now we're keeping it pretty much under wraps until we have exactly who it is."

"Might help to break it before the papers get it first," McClellan suggested.

"I don't know, Joe," I replied. "I'm not so sure about that. It could cut two ways."

At this point, I think Joe McClellan was already in the middle of a full-bore press conference in his mind. I silently asked forgiveness of Whomever Might Object for my part in leveraging him there, and Wallace knew exactly what I was doing. It was one way to get the man to reopen the case and cooperate with other agencies.

"Well, keep me posted," he said. "I can't promise anything, but I don't want the press to get it before we tell them."

"I understand completely," I told him. "I better get going. We've got a meeting."

Wallace shook his head after I hung up. "I'm not a betting man, but if I were I'd bet he calls a press conference tomorrow morning."

"I think you'd lose," I answered, glancing at my watch. "I think it will make the ten o'clock news tonight."

The deputy assigned to talk to us was name Ruiz and it was clear from the get-go that he didn't like having to deal with us. Wallace was very patient, explaining our need to make sure our suspect was dead, and after a while Ruiz relaxed a bit. He was not the case officer who investigated, but he was the first one on the scene after it was called in, and he had the file for us to look over. He even agreed to take us out to the crime scene after we had read through the file.

"Who called it in?" Wallace asked, picking up the case folder and opening it.

"We don't know," Ruiz told us. "As you'll see from the file, it was an anonymous tip. Most of them are around here." Once again, Ruiz seemed a little defensive and I wondered if there was something more than turf involved.

"We got a lot of that up in Arkansas, too," I said. "Murder's a pain in the ass. Can't blame people for not wanting to get involved."

Ruiz gave me a sharp look, but I wasn't being sarcastic. The fact is that any kind of major crime investigation disrupts people's lives, and sometimes witnesses feel like they're being treated like criminals. "I've been on both sides of an investigation," I told him. "It's not pleasant."

Wallace looked at me with new interest. "What in the world did you do?"

"I busted the governor's cousin," I laughed. "I made it stick, too. Grand larceny."

Ruiz told us he had a couple of things to do and showed us to an empty room with an iron table and two iron chairs. The furniture was bolted to the floor and a mirror was set into one wall. There was no question this was the county interrogation room, or that the mirror was one-way. Nor was there any question in my mind that the room was wired for sound, or that Ruiz would be watching us the whole time. I wondered who else might be behind the glass with him.

"You can make notes but no photocopies," Ruiz told us.

"How about copies of crime scene photos?" Wallace asked.

"We'll see," Ruiz answered.

"Where's the washroom if we need it?" I asked.

"Second door down the hall to the left. Anything else you need?"

Wallace told him not and we settled on either side of the iron table. I don't know who decides the size of such things but the table was on the small side. There wasn't much room to spread out the file. "How do you want to do this?" Wallace asked.

"I prefer to look at photos first," I said. He nodded and handed me a sheaf of black and white glossies.

I was surprised by this and by the quality of the photos. Black and white was the standard years ago, but these days most departments use high resolution 35 millimeter color film. Yet there is good argument for both, particularly if the black and white is in medium or large film format. Medium format film has approximately four times the surface area of standard 35, which means enlargements contain far greater detail. The optimum, of course would be medium format color film, but that gets too expensive. Even a simple crime scene can involve a couple of hundred shots.

"These are first class work," I told Wallace, mostly for the benefit of viewers behind the mirror. I was the one facing the mirror and the observers could not see him smile. There was little chance of getting anything past this man. I was glad I was not in the hot seat with something on my conscience and him as the investigator.

On the other hand, what I said was true. It was quite clear what the photographer intended each photo to show and the incidental details were in sharp focus. The notes on the back of each photo were clear and concise and perfectly hand printed. While we still needed to visit the scene for a general sense of geography, I doubted we would find much there not covered in the photos. There was even a panoramic series of shots covering a full circle around the entire scene, and the photographer had chosen the point of view well.

"I see why the coroner didn't need a body," Wallace remarked. "With that much blood loss, I don't see how anyone could survive."

I got the impression that he, too, was speaking for the benefit of our unseen observers.

"I wonder where they took the sample?" I asked. "What with that trail down to the water it almost looks like too much blood. He must have been still alive when he went into the water."

Wallace nodded and I knew we were on the same train of thought. Human blood is hard to come by but looks exactly the same as animal blood to the naked eye. It would be natural for an investigator to take blood samples from the car and not from the dirt. Ground samples would be more likely to be contaminated, and if we were right, then the trail to the water might be mostly animal blood. Nor would many investigators think to check this out given all the other evidence at the scene.

As the photographs made so clear, whoever was sitting in the car was shot twice from the driver's side and dragged out the passenger's door. The driver's window had apparently been open and two slugs were recovered from the passenger door. They had been fired from an unknown weapon chambered for .357 ammunition, and I wondered why the shots had not traveled completely through the passenger door. A .357 magnum load would normally have done so.

*Unless it was hand loaded for a silenced weapon!* With that thought I found myself getting excited. Keeping my voice calm I looked up and said, "Funny how the bullets didn't punch through the door, isn't it?"

Wallace looked up and nodded. "Strange how nobody at the park heard the shots, either," he replied and once again I knew we were on the same track. A silenced shot would not be heard more than fifty feet away, particularly if there was any wind.

The rest of the file was normal crime scene material, written up in the stilted legal style adopted by law enforcement these days. Again, I recognize the need for this but I also find it puts me to sleep very quickly. After about thirty minutes I told Wallace I needed to wash my face and headed for the restroom.

Coming back, I bypassed the interrogation room in favor of the very next door on the same side of the corridor. It was locked, so I knocked and the door was opened by a very surprised Ruiz. Over his shoulder I saw a man I recognized as the county sheriff from his photo in the foyer. There was another well-dressed Hispanic man who I had never seen before standing next to the sheriff. "Oh, excuse me," I said, giving them a smile. "Wrong door." Ruiz stepped out, shutting the door behind him and followed me back to the interrogation room.

Wallace was waiting patiently, the file closed on the table in front of him. "You need to look at anything else?" he asked.

"Maybe later," I answered. "I think I have a pretty good picture. One thing I did wonder, however. It wasn't clear if the lake was dragged for a body."

"I don't know," Ruiz answered. "I heard it was but I wasn't there."

"There's nothing about it in the report," Wallace pointed out. "Maybe we should ask the sheriff."

"He's tied up right now," Ruiz answered. "Maybe you can see him when we get back from the lake."

"I hate to tie you up all afternoon," Wallace answered. "Why don't we follow you out there in our car? That way Jazz won't have to shift over his equipment."

This was news to me. The only equipment I had along was my camera bag and my suitcase, but I didn't blink. "That would be best," I said. "I hate to have to recalibrate."

Ruiz didn't like it, but there was nothing he could say so he nodded. "All right," he said. "You can follow me. We'll head out 82. The state park is about eight miles this side of Patagonia." He scooped up the file folder. "I'll meet you out front."


"So who else was in the observation room?" Wallace asked once we were in the car and on the road.

"The sheriff and one other man," I told him. I don't know how he knew what I had done, but this was no guess on his part. "Judging from the clothes, I'd say one of the local doctors or maybe the county judge. He was dressed too good for a lawyer."

"Could be the coroner, I guess," Wallace replied. "Any idea why they're so uptight?"

I shook my head. "Maybe they're just worried about being embarrassed," I said. "I think it's more than that, though. There's no question they're hiding something."

"I'd guess the sheriff is dirty," Wallace observed. "Being on the border like this, I'd guess he's very dirty. You know that old proverb."

"Something like, 'The wicked flee when no man pursueth?'" I asked and Wallace nodded. "You don't think they had something to do with the killing, do you?"

"Could be," he answered. "Wally Keller might have gotten in their way. I think maybe we better make our visit short and sweet. We can stay in Tucson tonight and drive back in the morning if we don't get done."

"You think we may be in danger?"

Wallace shrugged. "You may not give it credence, but in Vietnam I always had a sense of danger whenever we were about to be attacked." He looked at me. "It wasn't just once or twice, but every single time. I learned to trust it."

"You've got that feeling here?" I asked. Wallace nodded. "Then maybe we better clear out after we visit the crime scene," I added. "I've got the name of the doctor. We can pay him a surprise visit tomorrow morning. Or not. I don't think we're going to get more information than was in the file. We can write them for a copy of the photos and the coroner's report if we need those."

Wallace looked embarrassed. "There's not any real need of that," he said. "I've got the whole case file."

Suddenly I understood what he was saying. "Call me sneaky!" I told him. "No wonder you wanted to sit with your back to the mirror."

"I just hope they don't have a hidden video camera on the other side of the room," he answered. "That's why I don't want to go back there." He reached in his pocket and pulled out a flat digital camera about the size of a calling card case. "A friend of mine got me this. I tried not to be too obvious."

I took a shot in the dark. "I don't suppose your friend is named

Cowboy, is he?" I was watching Wallace closely and knew I'd scored a hit. He gave me a searching look. "It's a small world," I said. "I consult for a lot of people."

"You certainly, do," Wallace told me. He looked like he was about to pursue it but changed his mind. I felt certain that we had a common friend in Sam McKee. Even so, I might be wrong.

"So what's your bottom line thinking?" I asked. "About this case."

"I imagine it's pretty much what yours is. I think there's a damned good chance Wally Keller's still around and taking out preachers."

"So how did he fall off the radar screen?" I asked. "That's hard to do these days."

Wallace nodded. "Like I said, you can get anything you want in Nogales, including a whole new identity and the papers to go with it."

"I guess being officially dead is a pretty good start. You don't think they sold him the papers and then killed him, do you?"

Wallace's answer was cryptic. "I think we better stay in Tucson tonight and talk this through."

# 14. Patagonia State Park

We met up with Ruiz at the entrance to the state park. The place looked desolate and deserted at the moment, but I figured it would fill up with snowbirds within a few weeks. What I thought might tell us something was the fact we were there at the same time of year Wally Keller was supposed to have been killed.

Ruiz took a side road to the west before we reached the park headquarters and we drove for about a mile before he stopped. The sign at the intersection told me we were on something called Blanca Road, and as we crossed the dam I could see the main park about a mile away across the lake. Then the pavement ended and we drove on to a spot near a small cove beyond the dam. Finally, we came to a spot near what looked like a deserted campground and Ruiz stopped. When we got out, I recognized the place from the crime scene photos. From where I stood I could no longer see the main park.

"This is it," Ruiz told us. He walked to a point above the water and pointed. "This is where the victim's vehicle was parked."

"Killer must have been someone he knew," Wallace observed, looking around. "Or someone he expected."

Ruiz nodded. "Personally, I think it was a drug deal gone bad. There's a lot of that around here with the border so close."

"Is this the only road out?" I asked and Ruiz nodded. "Seems like a pretty risky place to do business. No alternate escape route."

"Oh, there's ways," Ruiz assured me, "Particularly if you have four wheel drive."

"Keller's car looked like a family sedan," Wallace said. "Or did I miss something?"

"A lot of guys around here put a car body on a four-wheel truck frame," Ruiz told us. "That gives them plenty of ground clearance."

I nodded but I thought Ruiz was tossing us a red herring. The crime scene photos showed a standard passenger car, not a rig like Ruiz suggested. Nor did the photos of the interior appear to be shot from a ladder, which they would have had to be to show what I'd seen in the crime scene photos.

I got out my camera and tripod and set up for a panoramic shot like the one in the case file. As far as I could tell, I was very close to the exact spot the original crime photographer chose. When I was done I took down the tripod and tried to duplicate as many of the original shots as I could remember.

At some point, Ruiz figured out what I was doing and asked why I didn't just wait for file copies from him. "Those are all black and white," I assured him solemnly. "I needed to catch full color, too." I could see this didn't make any more sense to him than it did to me, but he nodded. I could also see Wallace, standing behind Ruiz, smile and turn away.

We poked around for a while longer, but there was not much there. Too much time had passed for any physical evidence to be positively tied to the shooting, even if we found something. Yet being there did give me a sense of how it might have happened and filled in some critical details. Not that these got us anywhere.

The case file said the car had been seen early in the morning by fishermen in a boat and that a deputy had driven out to check out the anonymous tip that afternoon. The file also indicated a five-hour time lapse had occurred between when the tip came in and the time the blood was discovered. When I asked Ruiz about this, he told me there had been a series of false alarms over a period of several months. So the tip was not taken seriously and the deputy hadn't expected to find anything. He had waited until he was headed this way on another call. Once he had called it in, the response was swift. Even the highway patrol was involved.

Despite the delay, the blood was still fresh enough for them to determine it had not been there longer than twenty-four hours. Some of it was still slightly damp. This seemed to indicate the shooting had occurred the night before. Yet, there were no witnesses found and no one in the campgrounds had heard shots or seen anything suspicious. Since the car was parked a good way off the dirt road, it was not surprising no one had noticed the blood earlier. It would have not been spotted by the fishermen and it was hidden from the dirt road by the incline.

It was clear to me that whoever was responsible for the blood trail had chosen this site carefully, but I didn't say anything until Wallace and I were alone. I also wondered if the victim was driven here at gunpoint. The blood trail led directly to the edge of the lake and crime scene photos showed blood on rocks sticking up from the water. These rocks were missing and I asked Ruiz if they had been taken to the lab for testing.

Ruiz laughed for the first time that day. "No," he told me. "We don't have that kind of budget. We were going through a drought and the lake was a lot lower. What you saw was the top of some damn big rocks."

"I'm surprised you didn't drag the lake," Wallace told him.

"I heard they used a cadaver dog," Ruiz answered. "Guy around here trains them. Didn't find a thing." He didn't seem to realize his answer was inconsistent with what he said before. Or maybe he just didn't care.

"How far out did they search?" I asked.

"I'm not sure. Maybe this bay and a good way along the shore on either side." Ruiz answered, pointing vaguely in both directions from where we stood. "What I'm telling you is what I heard."

I looked at Wallace. I could see he thought we were being fed the official line, and a pack of lies, too. Yet, I didn't push it. "Well, dogs are supposed to be the best way to find a body," I said. "I sure wish they had."

Wallace nodded. "Yeah, it would have saved us a trip. Anything else you need to know?" he asked me.

"There was one thing I was wondering about." I replied, looking at

Ruiz. "Do you know what happened to the business?"

"What business?" Ruiz asked. It seemed to me he was a little uneasy.

"The gun shop," I answered. "Keller was a gunsmith around here, wasn't he?"

Ruiz thought a moment before he answered. "Yeah, he was."

"What happened to his shop?" I asked. "I imagine he had an inventory."

Ruiz shrugged. "It was sold. There was a sheriff's sale after he was ruled dead."

"When was that?" Wallace asked.

"A year or two after he was shot," Ruiz answered. It was clear to me he didn't like this line of questions and I was sure this was equally clear to Wallace.

"What about his family?" Wallace asked. "Why weren't they notified?"

"Sheriff didn't know he had one. They couldn't find anything in his stuff." Ruiz's face was a closed mask. "No next of kin information."

"What about military records or fingerprints?" I asked. Wallace nodded.

"Sheriff didn't have any prints for him on file," Ruiz answered. "Without a body...." he shrugged.

"What about his ATF firearms license?" Wallace asked. "Couldn't you trace him through that?"

"Sheriff couldn't find it," Ruiz answered. "Couldn't find any personal papers. Not even bills."

"Didn't that make you suspicious?" Wallace bored in. "No personal papers?"

"Things are different down here," Ruiz answered. "There's a war on, a drug war. We don't have time to run stuff down. We don't have the manpower or the money."

"Any idea of who bought the shop?" I asked.

Ruiz nodded, but took a moment to answer. "Yeah, a local guy."

"Does this local guy have a name?" Wallace wanted to know.

"Yeah, his name's Joe. Changed the name to Joe's Gun Shop."

"What was it before he changed it?" I asked.

"Davey's Gun Locker," Ruiz answered. "Strange name."

"Does this Joe have a last name?" Wallace put in.

The deputy nodded. "Ruiz."

"Any relation to you?" I asked gently. Ruiz looked like a cornered rat and I didn't want to push him over the edge. "A cousin?"

"Brother," he said and Wallace nodded.

"Do you think Joe would let us look at Keller's records?" I asked. "I guess we could do a subpoena, but I'd hate to do that."

"There weren't any records," Ruiz told us. "Like I said, there weren't even any bills. Nothing."

I looked at Wallace. "I'm surprised the ATF didn't nose around. They're real touchy about firearms records."

Ruiz shrugged. "They sent a guy around. We couldn't tell him any more than I've told you. Besides, around here they're as short handed as anyone else."

"Could it have been a gun deal?" I asked. "I didn't see any evidence of drugs in the case file."

Ruiz was clearly uneasy. "Drugs, guns, what's the difference? Some asshole comes in from out of town to make a quick buck and gets himself killed."

"Oh, I thought Keller was here for a number of years," I said, taking out my notes. "Yeah, here it is. Four years." I smiled at Ruiz. "At least that's what the ATF tells us."

Wallace looked at Ruiz. "What about phone records? Or bills coming in afterward?"

"Sheriff checked all that out. Keller used a cell phone. It was a service company out of Nogales, Mexico. They don't play ball with us. I don't know about other bills. They weren't mentioned in the file."

"What about inventory?" I asked. "Wasn't that registered?"

Ruiz shook his head. "There wasn't anything left but tools and some worn out parts. Not even any ammo. Joe didn't get much."

"You think someone cleaned him out?" Wallace asked.

"Could be. Like I said, we don't have time to waste on cases like this." Ruiz's eyes were cold and hard. "Drug dealers shoot each other every day around here. So do gun runners. As long as they don't kill a cop or anyone else, the sheriff doesn't like wasting time." He glanced at his watch, clearly telling us we were wasting his.

"Well, that's one way to solve the problem," Wallace nodded. I wasn't sure if he was agreeing or not, but Ruiz apparently thought he was.

"I can't think of anything else I need to know," I told Wallace.

"I can't, either," he said. "We appreciate your time. Please thank the sheriff for all the help." He held out a hand and Ruiz shook it and then mine. "I don't think we'll need copies of the crime scene shots, after all. Sounds like you people have done about everything you could."

*About everything they could to cover up,* I thought. Yet, I smiled and thanked Ruiz, too.

"So what do you think?" Wallace asked. We were headed north on Arizona 83 to catch IH 10 at Vail. Rather than double back through Nogales, Wallace had turned left on 82 at the park junction, taking us through Patagonia and Sonoita. While neither had a thousand residents, both obviously catered to the seasonal snow birds. Wallace told me he wanted to see new country, but I think the real reason we came this way was so we could get out of Santa Cruz County as quickly as possible.

Even so, the drive was more picturesque than the freeway and I was fascinated by the play of colors across the high desert. We were traveling close to three thousand feet elevation and the air was very dry, making distant mountains seem quite close. I'm told it takes hunters time to adjust to the clear air here, wondering why their shots at easy targets hit the ground half way between. I wished Jeanne were there to see it, too, and decided to send her a subscription to Arizona Highways for Christmas.

Wallace's question startled me and it took me a moment to shift mental gears. I looked at him and he chuckled. "I don't know where you were, but it must have been nice," he said.

"I was chasing light," I said, pointing to the passing landscape. "This is a photo nut's heaven. Everything I read tells me it's hard to catch on film."

Wallace nodded but said nothing. I focused on the question. "I think we have a suspect," I said. "Everything I saw screams set-up and cover-up. I think Wally was who set it up. How about you?"

"The same here," he answered. "So how do you think we need to proceed?"

"The first thing is to find out everything we can about Walton Davis Keller. I think he's the guy the gunsmith in Arkansas told me about. You know, the guy who put seven rounds through a hole the size of a quarter."

"How do you make that connection?" Wallace asked.

"The starting point is the weapon. It's the unique thing in all these cases. Consider the fact no shots were heard out at the park. You know what kind of bark a standard .357 revolver makes. I think it's entirely possible the shooter was using a silencer, one of those 'poacher specials' Miller told me about. I don't know any of this for sure, but it's what my gut tells me. Call it a working theory."

Wallace thought about this for a moment and nodded. "It's a good starting point," he said, glancing my way. "There's something else on your mind, isn't there?"

"Yes, but it's in the realm of pure speculation. Look at the name shift. Walton is an unusual name, and it becomes Wally. Walton sounds like an East Coast lawyer. Wally is just one of the guys." I paused and looked at Wallace. He was with me.

"Here's the leap. Wally goes into the Marines. I'm guessing he goes to sniper school. When he gets out he heads for gunsmith school in Colorado. That's where Wes Miller meets him. He's the friend I told you about in Arkadelphia. Our guy drops Wally and becomes Dave Keller in the process. He calls his place Davey's Gun Locker. While he's here, Keller develops a sniper design based on Miller's weapon, but using the .357. He runs into some accuracy problems like the ones Wes ran into, but for some reason he sticks to the .357. Once he solves the accuracy problems, he arranges the scene of his own 'murder' and changes identity. He starts hunting Episcopal clergy at that point. I think that's the tie, Episcopal. Taking out a bishop is major league."

"What about my preachers in California?" Wallace asked. "How do they tie in?" He didn't have to remind me the Golden State was footing the bill for this trip.

"I think those were practice runs," I said. "I may be wrong, but the dates fit. Up to the time he perfects his design, he has access to a large number of weapons, most of which are probably untraceable. It's not much trouble to cut down the barrel of an old Mauser or Carcano and thread it for a silencer. I'd even bet a lot of his business along the border was selling silencers as 'kits' to whoever had the cash. Even if word got out, it's like selling switchblade 'kits' in New York. It may be wrong but it's perfectly legal."

Wallace nodded. "Yeah, I see how it might work. 'Davy Crockett' Keller becomes the silencer king of Nogales and makes his bundle. He doesn't put much money into his shop or stock. Or even his wheels. The car at the lake looked like a junker. He's saving his money for later. That would explain staging his death."

"Exactly. Once he's got his design and stalking technique perfected, and money to live on, it's time to go hunting. So it's time for the silencer king to be murdered."

"Too bad we don't have the original blood samples," Wallace said. "Forensics could tell us a helluva lot in a hurry."

"I'm guessing the original evidence has been destroyed," I said. "I think that may be one reason why the sheriff and Ruiz and the other guy are so tense."

"I think it's a lot more than that," Wallace replied. "I think they are all very dirty."

"Oh, I do, too," I answered. "I think you were very right to head north. We might have been caught in the crossfire of a drug bust at our motel tonight. It would raise a stink, but one that could be managed."

"Particularly if a few low life types ended up dead, too." He shook his head. "Here I thought LA was bad."

"I don't have much experience of border towns, but they seem to cater to the worst elements of both sides," I observed. "There's so much money involved it's hard for any decent soul to stay clean."

"Ain't that the truth!" Wallace said. "I like your theory. The death dates of my guys fit perfectly. They all occurred in the four years before Wally 'murdered' himself. He could have easily driven to California for each hit. Any idea of where he might have gone from Nogales?"

"I think he ended up in the Dallas area," I said. "There are several million people in the surrounding counties and it's an easy drive to all of the shootings except the one up in New Hampshire. That one has me wondering."

"Maybe we ought to start there," Wallace said. "I can't get away anytime soon. How about you?"

I thought about this. There was nothing pressing I needed to do back home and I had never been to New England this time of year. I wondered if Jeanne had and that was the thought that sold me, the thought of spending a Currier and Ives Christmas with Jeanne in New Hampshire. "Sure, why not?" I said. "The bishop offered me a cup of coffee."

Wallace dropped me off at a motel near the Phoenix airport that evening and after supper, decided to head back to California. There was a meeting in San Bernadino he wanted to attend the next day and he told me it was faster to drive than fly.

"There's a difference?" I asked. "I'd swear we snagged cactus with our landing gear." He laughed.

Over dinner we divided up specific areas for each of us to follow. I was to talk to the police in New Hampshire and poke around there for a couple of days while Wallace checked out the gunsmith school in Colorado. I gave him Wes Miller's number in case he needed more information there, and Dee's number to call if he couldn't get me.

Wallace also agreed to do a full background query on Wally Davis and coordinate our efforts with the FBI. After talking it over, we decided that for now, it might be best to avoid asking Amanda Keller directly for more information. I would talk to her later if there were no other sources.

"You know, it might be worth looking into his biological family, too," I said. "We might get a line on him there. Adoption records are more open than they used to be. With Wally as old as he was, they might not be sealed."

"Are you thinking of anything specific?" Wallace asked.

"Yeah, I am. I'm thinking family names. This guy doesn't choose names casually, but he doesn't stray far, either. Maybe it's a stretch, but I keep thinking about Davis Keller becoming Davy Crockett. He was a sharpshooter, too."

"What about famous snipers? You think he's that obvious?"

"Not really. I'm grasping for straws and trying to teach granny to steal eggs. I don't have a clue where to start."

"That's two of us, but I'm sure if we look around, we'll come across something."

"I'm also wondering where he got all that blood," I said.

"Who knows? Maybe he robbed a blood bank."

I called Jeanne that night and we talked for a couple of hours. She was delighted with the idea of spending Christmas together in New Hampshire and family obligations were not a problem. "We get together at Thanksgiving and Easter," she told me. "With the grandkids it works out better that way. I usually don't do much."

"Speaking of Christmas," I asked, "what does a guy give a girl who seems to have everything?"

"It depends on what his intentions are," Jeanne giggled. "There are some things money can't buy. You could start with a kiss."

"That's a nice ending, too," I agreed. "I was thinking of something a little more, ah, sentimental?"

"As opposed to passionate?" Jeanne shot back. She was in a giddy mood. "There's always Victoria's Secret, you know. A woman can't have too much intimate apparel."

"I'm not sure about sizes. I mean, what do I say to a sales clerk when she asks for sizes? I can't exactly hold up my hands."

"You're the detective," Jeanne giggled. "You figure it out."

After hanging up I called to schedule a flight out of Phoenix. The fastest, most direct itinerary called for a two-hour layover in Albuquerque. On the spur of the moment I decided to make it an overnight stop and reserved a hotel room near the airport. One of the things we had not done was to follow up on the shooting of the priest in New Mexico and I wanted to see the case records. I called Wallace and told him what I planned and he agreed it was a good idea. He told me he'd phone the Albuquerque police department and set things up.

I lucked into a direct flight on Southwest at a ridiculous hour the next morning and was at the police department by nine o'clock. Once again I ran into a detective who had read my book and was glad to meet me. When I commended him for checking my credentials to make sure I was who I claimed, he grinned. "Well, you know Rule 78, Dr. Phillips," he told me, cheerfully citing my own words back at me. Rule 78 is never assume anything.

"That's right, detective," I laughed. "Please call me Jazz. Now show me yours."

I was kidding, but the man took me seriously. "Which one do you want?" he said pleasantly, handing me a leather case. It had his badge and a laminated card not unlike my Arkansas credentials. These told me I was talking to Detective Sergeant Juan Martinez. "I also have some beautiful undercover docs," he added. "So what can I do for you?"

I brought him up to speed quickly and told him what I needed. Ten minutes later I was seated at a table with a comfortable chair and a cup of coffee. The case file was in front of me and I was pleasantly surprised to find the coffee was excellent. Martinez told me he brewed it himself. "Don't drink the other stuff around here," he told me. "I know for a fact it dissolves plastic."

When I read through the file I became more convinced than ever this was tied to the Keller shooting. I also discovered lots of loose ends that should have been followed through but weren't. I made quite a few notes, including the address of the church where the priest was shot, and when I was done I went looking for Sergeant Martinez.

I found Martinez in the crime lab, talking to an attractive young woman in a lab coat. When I first spotted them, I had the distinct impression the sergeant was not there on official business. This was confirmed when Martinez turned around and saw me approaching. His posture changed and he became politely official, first introducing me to the technologist.

Once again, I found my reputation had preceded me. "This is embarrassing," I confessed as I autographed the technologist's copy of one of my manuals. "You know Casey—Dr. Jones—wrote most of this, don't you?" I asked.

"That's exactly what he told me about you," the tech said, blushing and showing me a familiar scrawl on another page. "He was in Denver last year doing a workshop."

I asked Martinez if there was a quiet place we could talk and he led me down the corridor to an empty conference room. Like the one in Nogales, this one had a mirror on one wall, but it also had a line-up board on the facing one. Martinez laughed when he saw me glance toward the mirror. "There's no one there," he said. "At least I don't think so." He took out a key and turned a lock on the wall by the door. The lights dimmed enough in the conference room that I could clearly see that the room behind the mirror was empty.

"It's nothing that sensitive," I told him. "I just didn't want to talk in front of the lab tech. I have some questions about the investigation."

"Don't we all?" Martinez answered. "I reviewed it when the first query came in. To be honest, Dr. Phillips, I was appalled how shoddy the investigation was."

"I've seen a lot worse in Arkansas," I assured him. "Any idea why?"

"Yeah, the lead detective was very sick at the time, though he didn't know it. He took a medical retirement a couple of months later. It was cancer and he was gone pretty fast. I think he died a couple of months after he moved to Oregon."

"What about his partner?" I asked. "I understand he's dead, too."

"Herb was not a forceful guy," Martinez told me. "There was some evidence he had a drinking problem. I'm not sure how much it affected his work, but I don't think he cared enough to go against his partner. They were pretty tight and I think Johnson covered for him a lot." He shrugged. "It happens. What the file won't tell you is that Herb had a .06 blood alcohol level when he was killed in the wreck."

I opened my mouth to ask how he knew, but it was none of my business. "Thanks. I appreciate your candor."

Martinez grinned. "You're dying to know how I know that, aren't you?" I nodded. "I was on my first Internal Affairs rotation then. We rotate by halves every year. It went down in my second year. I'm not going to say much more than that."

"So you would have been on IA when the priest was shot?" I asked. "There must not have been any question about the case at the time, then, was there?"

"There was, but we were overloaded in IA just then. One of our senior cops turned out to be a major drug distributor and we were after his network. By the time we got to the Johnson investigation, he was already dead." He shrugged. "You know how it is."

I nodded. "There are always plenty of live ones that come first," I answered. "That's probably Rule Four."

Martinez counted on his fingers. "Rule One must be protect yourself and your family. Two would be protect your partner. What's Rule Three?"

"Don't embarrass the department," I said and Martinez nodded.

"I expect you'd like to see the crime scene, wouldn't you?" he asked. I nodded. "I'll drive you there."

"Thanks, but I don't want to take you away from what you need to do," I told him.

"It comes under Rule One," he told me. "Self care. Always take time to loaf when visiting dignitaries drop in."

# 15. Local Martyr

I found out later that the reason Martinez could drop everything and squire me around town was that he was on rotation as the senior officer in Internal Affairs that year. "It makes things kind of pleasant," he told me. "Even my bosses are nice to me."

"So the ass chewing you hand out today may come back tomorrow with interest?" I asked. "Interesting concept, but it would never fly back home. It makes too much sense for the Arkansas legislature."

Martinez laughed. "That sounds like New Mexico, too. You know what we say here about the former governor we sent to the US Senate, don't you? It raised the IQ level of Santa Fe and Washington both."

Albuquerque is an interesting city, far more than Santa Fe in my mind. Too many wealthy refugees from California have changed the feel of Santa Fe, which seems very plastic and New Age to me. The Santa Fe I visited as a child was full of mystery and charm and its culture revolved around a strong sense of history. That's gone now, or has been driven underground by the onslaught of a rapacious consumer economy driven by hunger for the accoutrements of wealth and power.

The same process has been at work in Albuquerque, but with much less success. There's a raw edge to Albuquerque that's carefully hidden among the cedar canyons of Santa Fe, and poverty is still allowed there. One gets the sense that being poor has been outlawed in Santa Fe, and I have always wondered where the service workers live in such places. Poor folk cannot afford normal housing or transportation, and they are not allowed to live on the street. So where do the clerks and the janitors and the cops and the school teachers live?

There is no doubt where such folk live in Albuquerque. The neighborhood which Martinez drove us into was clearly such a place. Most of the houses were post-war vintage, World War II. They were small and set close together on tiny lots. The cars I saw parked in the streets were much older than the ones downtown and many of them were unique. There seemed to be a preference for bright primary colors on both the houses and the automobiles, and there was a feeling of vibrant life there that's not evident in wealthier areas. The houses looked like most of the people who lived there had lived in them for a long time. I suspect their inhabitants were as well known to one another as people who live in small towns.

The church we stopped at looked like it had been built in the same period as the houses. It was a traditional small chapel with white siding and a wooden bell tower to one side in front. There was a simple cross on top of the tower and the sign in front was in Spanish. It told us this was the Templo Apostolica De La Gente, Pentecostico, which I translated as People's Apostolic Temple, Pentecostal. What I found intriguing was that the People's Apostolic Temple had a bright red door, a symbol of the Holy Ghost also favored by many traditional Episcopal churches.

Since the priest had been shot in front of the building, there was no reason to go inside. Martinez parked on the street and we stood on the sidewalk as he explained the layout of the crime scene. I found this helpful since what I'd seen of the crime scene photos was very sketchy. While these were in full color and focused on details well enough, the photographer had not included a shot of the whole scene. I found myself wishing the photographer had taken at least one wide view from the street. A wooden deck with an access ramp had been added since the shooting. This made it hard to visualize things as they were when the priest was killed.

One thing I noticed was that there was a small, well tended white cross to one side of the entrance to the new ramp. Around it grew a bed of roses, now trimmed back for winter. I pointed this out to Martinez, but he didn't know what it signified. In a Catholic setting it might be a shrine, but it seemed out of place here.

We were about to leave when a well-dressed Hispanic man came out of the church and approached us. He introduced himself to us as the pastor and asked if we needed assistance. Martinez showed him his badge and told him why we were there.

The pastor told us he had been at the church only a short while when the shooting happened. "It was so sad," he said. "There were two gangs killing each other off here in the neighborhood and a group of us were working hard to get them to stop. Father Lee was interested in our work and came down to see me that day. Unfortunately, I had to go to the hospital. Someone was in a car wreck and very badly hurt. I left a note on the door but I don't know if he saw it. He was apparently leaving when he was killed."

Martinez looked at me. This was new information, not in the file. "Did anyone ever mention seeing what happened?" he asked.

The pastor nodded. "About a year later a young man came to me. He was scared and very troubled. He told me he had seen the shooting. When I called the detective in charge of the case they told me he was retired and the other one was dead. I asked to see someone else, but no one was around and no one ever called me back. When I tried again later, I was told to forget it."

"Do you remember the names of the people you talked to?" Martinez asked. He had taken out a notebook and pen.

"No, but I have it written down here somewhere," the pastor answered. "I'll have to dig it out."

"Can you tell us the young man's name?" I asked. Martinez gave me a sharp look but said nothing.

"Yes, but he was killed in a shootout six months later. It was so sad because he wasn't even a gang member. He was standing next to someone who was and the killer missed."

"What did he tell you about the priest's shooting?" I asked.

"Only that he saw it happen. When he did he hid. He was afraid the man with the gun would shoot him, too."

"Did he get a license number?" Martinez jumped in.

"No, but he said it looked like a police car. It was a dark blue sedan, a new one. He saw the shooting because he was looking at the car. It didn't belong here."

"What about the shooter?" Martinez asked. I was glad to see him getting involved and  let him take the lead. "What did he look like?"

"All Tino could see was his head and shoulders. He never got out of the car. He told me the man was a grin..." The pastor stopped suddenly and glanced at me. "He said he was an Anglo, an older guy. The man had a blonde beard and was wearing sunglasses and a cap. Tino said when he saw the man turn the cap backwards on his head he knew what was going to happen and hid."

I wondered why Tino didn't shout a warning, but I knew the answer even as the question crossed my mind. Tino didn't want to get shot, not for an Anglo stranger. Had the priest been Hispanic, Tino might have taken the risk. Then, too, there was no way Tino could know the stranger was a priest. All he would have seen was a man dressed in black with a green handkerchief, the colors of one of the warring gangs.

"Did he say anything about the gun the Anglo used?" I asked.

"Yes, he did," the pastor said, surprised. "He said it looked funny, not like any gun he'd ever seen. The barrel was short and very fat, like this." He held his hands apart about twelve to fourteen inches and made a circle about two inches across with his fingers. "He said he never heard the man shoot, but he saw Father John fall down. Tino ducked after that and hid himself until he heard the car drive off. Then he ran away."

I looked at Martinez and nodded. There was no doubt in my mind this was our man. "A very unique weapon," I said. "It all comes back to that."

The pastor clearly wanted to know what I meant, but Martinez diverted him with more questions. I listened but there was nothing else the pastor told us related to our serial case. One thing I did learn was that the white cross was a memorial to the priest who was shot. Apparently his death was a very significant event in the life of the church and eventually played a role in the ending of the gang war. I found this ironic given the padre's history. I wondered what the congregation would think if they knew their local martyr was a child molester.

"So what are your thoughts?" Martinez asked as we drove back to his office. The question startled me and I realized I had said nothing since we left the church.

"I'm ninety-nine percent sure this is our guy," I said. "The MO is slightly different but it's the same custom made weapon. I bet the ballistics will match."

"Do we need to reopen the case?"

"Not really," I said. "Just alert whoever needs to know so it won't be a surprise when the case breaks. I think the killer is from north Texas and we've got Ft. Worth, the California state police and FBI all working the case. Let me send you an update in a few days."

"I'll be watching for it," Martinez told me. "How about some lunch? You can give me an overview while we eat."

I left on the earliest flight from Albuquerque to Little Rock the next morning and Jeanne picked me up at the airport. The plan was for her to spend a few days with me in Ft. Smith before we took off for New England and we stopped for a late lunch at a little place I know just west of Conway. It's owned by a family who's been there three generations, starting just after World War II. When we sat down, we were waited on by a young woman who looked like the cook's daughter. I said as much to Jeanne and she pointed toward the table where our waitress was seated when we came in. There was a wicker bassinet next to the table and I could see a tiny hand lying quietly on a pink blanket. No doubt this was the fourth generation.

The food was plain, very Southern, and excellent. We both ordered the roast beef special and were treated to side dishes of pickled beets, black-eyed peas, and candied sweet potatoes. The breadbasket held fresh baked biscuits and cornbread muffins, and we were given a choice of coffee or iced tea. What was most amazing was that the cost for both of us was less than what I'd pay eating alone in Dallas or Washington, DC.

We talked more about our plans over lunch, debating whether to drive or fly. Little Rock is just over a thousand miles by interstate from Washington, DC. Where we were going in New Hampshire was several hundred miles more.

The biggest issue was not distance, however, but time. I didn't think I should be out of touch the extra days driving would take. I also had a lot of work I'd promised to get done before the first of the year.

Yet air travel presented its own challenges. Since we'd be flying at the height of the Christmas holidays, air tickets would be very difficult to get, even with a law enforcement priority. Then, too, the priority would only apply to me.

"Oh, my," Jeanne said when I mentioned this. "That's no problem. Couldn't I be your prisoner? Then I could seduce you into giving me my freedom."

"I don't think you'd like the bracelets," I laughed. "They're sort of clunky and might not match your earrings."

"Well, if it's too far to drive on business," Jeanne suggested, "why don't we take the company plane?"

"I didn't know you had one," I said. "Are you sure it's all right?"

"I don't see why not," she answered. "It spends most of its time on the ground in Hope. I'm sure it's not going anywhere over Christmas."

I thought about this for a moment. Then I had another idea. "You know, we could always take the land yacht," I said. "Are you comfortable driving that?"

"Are you kidding?" she asked. "I was driving a hay truck by the time I was ten."

"Would you mind me working while you drive?" I asked. "I could bring my laptop along and I can stay in touch by cell phone."

"You can stay in touch by computer if you want to," Jeanne said. "I'm sure most campgrounds have some sort of arrangements for that. We can probably connect it to my satellite phone, too. I read something about it in the manual."

"You read manuals?" I shook my head. "I forget sometimes we are living in the twenty-first century. This is all very new to me."

"It is to all of us," Jeanne answered. "I don't think the kids can keep up any more. Not even Tom and Rebecca, and they're in the business."

"You know, there's a lot about you I don't know," I observed. "I never imagined you knew how to drive a hay truck."

"Well, think of the fun you'll have finding out," Jeanne shot back.

My cell phone rang about then. The display told me it was Kowalski and when I answered, she was excited. "The chief did it," she said. "He held a press conference yesterday afternoon and announced he's reopening the Keller case."

"What did he tell the press?" I wanted to know.

"Not a whole lot more than that," Kowalski said. "No specifics. I sent you a copy of his statement by e-mail. Haven't you gotten it yet?"

"I've been in Arizona. I haven't logged on for the last three days." I told her what Wallace and I had learned in Nogales and what we were thinking. "We need to keep this as quiet as possible," I said. "Amanda and her kids don't need the hassle if we can avoid it. It's going to be hard enough to handle if we're right."

"What do Jim and I need to be doing?" Kowalski asked.

"Why don't you stop by and check on Jack Keller?" I suggested. "We need to know Wally's family name, his biological family. I told Wallace we should wait, but I've changed my mind. Can you do it without alarming Amanda?"

"I'll tell her it's one of those bureaucratic details we need for the file," Kowalski said. "You want us to trace them if she knows?"

"Sounds like a winner," I replied. "Just do basic police work like you would with any other case and keep in touch. Let me give you another number, just for you and Jim to use if this one doesn't work."

I turned to Jeanne. "Do you mind if I give them yours?" I asked.

She shook her head and I told Kowalski the number and who it was registered to.

"Well, tell Jeanne 'hello' from me," Kowalski answered.

"Tell her yourself," I replied and handed the phone to Jeanne. From what I could hear of her end of the conversation, Jeanne and Kowalski spent most of their time laughing about me. I guess it's one of the ways women bond.

On the other hand, I really didn't mind. It's a compliment to be cared for enough to be teased by two intelligent, good-looking women.

Our road trip to New England and back was simply wonderful. When I gave it any thought, I felt strange taking another man's wife on a road trip in his land yacht, so I simply didn't dwell on it. I told myself that the RV was half Jeanne's, anyway, and if she were divorced from Henry we'd already be married. Most of the time this worked, but it took a long conversation with Grant Forster, the old chaplain, to put it to rest.

"Who the hell are you to judge God's gifts?" he challenged. "Why are you still hanging on to that legalistic crap? Whose rules really matter, ours or God's? What makes you think God even has rules?"

Faced with this barrage, I simply saluted and took delight in the grace given, at least most of the time. Every once in a while the hell-fire preacher voice inside my head started harping again, but when the did, I told him to talk to Forster. It seemed to work

One of the wonderful things about the trip was that we could take our time. With my laptop hooked up to Jeanne's satellite phone, I was never out of touch, though there was little for me to do at this point in the investigation. Once we knew we were looking for Wally Keller, running him down was a matter of standard police work by the FBI and the various jurisdictions involved. Even Wallace moved on to other cases, keeping me informed as developments turned up.

At some point early on, it became clear to me that the search for Wally Keller could be a long one. I guessed it might take years to find him, if we ever did. It was equally clear he had severed his ties with

Jack and the Keller family, and that little would be accomplished by letting them know he was still alive. Maybe we were wrong, but I would hate to live with the thought a child of mine was not only a serial killer, but also the subject of a national manhunt.

So I put the file on hold and enjoyed our trip to New England. I told myself I was still on the case since the purpose of the trip was to gather more information on the killing there, but I knew I was just filling in the file. The fact is, I was tired of the case and there were other things more pressing on my mind. When this became clear, I called Wallace and told him there wasn't much point in me following in the footsteps of the FBI, and he agreed. I also told him I wasn't billing the Golden State for my trip east. He said his comptroller would appreciate it very much. The State of California was running in the red that year.

This all took place as we were traveling through the Appalachian Mountains, but we decided to continue our trip north. This was not the best time of year for travel in New England, but we stayed on the interstate network and stopped in motels when we wanted a real shower. The land yacht was well equipped, but the bath facilities were cramped and there was no hot tub, something I'd never experienced much. Jeanne considered them high on the list of necessities of life and I have to admit she converted me in short order.

We also decided to change our itinerary a bit to allow a side trip north before our promised pot of coffee with Bishop Hopewell, the man from New Hampshire. Our intent was to travel east beyond Montreal and then turn south on IH 91, which follows the Connecticut river separating New Hampshire and Vermont. Yet Mother Nature and the delights of Ottawa intervened. We never made it east of there.

We arrived in Ottowa on December 24 and celebrated Christmas by attending a moving candlelight service at an Anglican church that evening. Some of the carols weren't familiar, but they were led by a full choir and after a couple of verses I could hum along. Nor am I sure an angelic chorus could have sung them better or with more gusto. When it comes to Christmas, no one celebrates it better than

Anglicans. Forster tells me that Good Friday is the day that gives the church year meaning for Roman Catholics, who seem to emphasize suffering and sacrifice. Yet for Anglicans, who focus on God's Word becoming embodied in human flesh, he says the meaningful day is Christmas, and their music reflects this. One of the hymns I heard that night was a new one, written by an American priest and set to the tune of an old hymn I knew well.

> Oh, lift up your voices, my dear friends, and sing
> To God our Creator who sends us a King,
> A child born this morning with glory and grace
> Oh, come to the stable and gaze on his face!
> Allelu, allelu! Let the Earth lift its voice,
> Allelu, allelu! Every creature rejoice
> With God our Creator who gave us a Son,
> And whose Holy Spirit now makes us all one!
>
> Oh, come to the stable, rejoice in the Light
> Which breaks through our darkness on this holy night
> Oh, come to this table and join in this feast
> With angels, archangels, the great and the least!
> (Refrain)
>
> Oh, come, all you broken who dwell in the night,
> Come all those who hunger, be filled with this Light!
> Drink deep of this Cup and delight in this Bread,
> Oh, join with glad dancing, rejoice and be fed!
> (Refrain)

We took a week to explore Ottawa and then turned south, leaving just ahead of a major winter storm. We made it as far as the Pennsylvania border before the storm caught up with us and we spent New Year's Eve holed up in a motel. At the stroke of midnight, as we watched the ball descend in Times Square, we uncorked a bottle of champagne and made a toast to our first New Year together. Yet when we sang along with the words of *Auld Lang Syne,* I almost lost it. Robert Burns was Nellie's favorite poet, and she particularly liked the second and third stanzas:

We twa hae run aboot the braes
And pu'd the gowans fine.
We've wandered mony a weary foot,
Sin' auld lang syne.

We twa hae sported i' the burn,
From morning sun till dine,
But seas between us braid hae roared
Sin' auld lang syne.

When I tried to apologize, Jeanne wouldn't have it. "She was my friend, too, Jazz. I may not miss her as much as you do, but I grieve her passing. I always will." Then she smiled. "Did you know she wrote me not long before she died? She told me to be sure to take good care of you."

"She wrote me, too," I replied. "I still haven't been able to read the letter. I suppose Lindy told you that."

"No, she didn't," Jeanne answered, nodding. "She wouldn't. She's a counselor."

"I'm not exactly one of her patients, Jeanne."

"No, but she doesn't carry tales. Did she mention our conversations about you, hers and mine?"

I shook my head. "Didn't she call you the night I called you from Ft. Worth? She threatened to."

Jeanne laughed. "She tried all right, several times. She told me about it later. She kept getting a busy signal and figured I must have been talking to some man."

Since we were almost there, we decided to stop in Washington, DC, for a few days. I had some things I needed to discuss with McKee and we had promised Willie and Liz Dill we would stop by the next time we were nearby. As it turned out, the McKees were throwing what Sam called an Epiphany party to celebrate the old Christmas and we ended up there, as well.

It was at the Epiphany party I got the unexpected break that helped us track down Wally Keller. One of the things I do for McKee is to help identify multiple killers and track them down, not serial killers but professional assassins. This is normally a long, involved process much like putting together a jigsaw puzzle. Part of it is developing a profile pulled together from wisps of information gathered over a wide range of sources, and another part is figuring out what they look like so they can be identified before they are able to get to their next target.

This last challenge was what a group of us were talking about at McKee's party. I can't remember exactly who was involved in the discussion. I do know it was Angelino who spoke up when I told them about the trouble we were having finding Wally Keller. "We have facial recognition software for that now," Michael told me. "I'm surprised you haven't tried using that."

"I've read about that, but what I've seen isn't that good. It's sort of like the old layover transparencies. All it gives is a generic likeness. Except on cop shows."

The group laughed, as did Angelino. "We're way beyond that now, Jazz. We really can do reconstructions from skulls."

"Well, if I had his skull, I wouldn't worry about the rest of him," I answered.

Angelino would not be put off. "Seriously, Jazz. We can now take a picture and age the person, just like they do on cop shows. It's phenomenal."

"That's right, Jazz," Sam McKee agreed. He had joined the group to see what fat was being chewed. "We took an early picture of my dad and Michael ran it through the works. Except for a couple of scars, it looked like my dad the week before he died."

"All I have is a Marine Corps Band portrait," I said. "It's quite a few years old."

"Age doesn't matter much," Angelino told me. "Is Wally wearing a hat? That could make it harder."

"As a matter of fact, he's not," I answered. "He doesn't have much hair but he's not wearing his service hat."

"Even better," Angelino told me. "Without hair we can get a better idea about the shape of his head. Do you have it with you?"

I laughed. "Not on me," I told him. "I think it's in the file in Jeanne's RV."

"Then bring it in the next time you come to the office," Angelino suggested. "Let me scan it into our computer and see what happens. I think you'll be surprised."

Surprised I was three days later when Angelino told me he had something to look at. I followed him down the hall to the photography lab. The lab contained all the normal photography gear, but most of the equipment now was digital. Even film photos were reduced to digital images by high resolution scanners and the quality of prints was so good I had a hard time telling the difference.

"All right," Angelino said, tapping a few keys. "Here's the picture we started with." A sharp image of Wally Keller in his Marine Band uniform popped up on the wide LCD screen behind the keyboard. The clarity of the image was incredible.

"Now, let's age him the right number of years," Angelino said. He tapped a few more keys and the image began to change, aging at about a year every two seconds. When it stopped, it was the face of a mature man with broader shoulders. My sense of having seen him before was even stronger.

"How about some facial hair?" Angelino asked and tapped a few more keys. At first a moustache appeared, morphing into different shapes every three or four seconds. Then chin hair was added in increments until the face was fully bearded. Next, the beard changed shape, growing quite bushy before receding into well trimmed mutton chops. Angelino adjusted something and we were looking at a well groomed man with a beard.

"What about the uniform?" I asked. "It's distracting. Can you take it out?"

"Sure can," Angelino told me and the man on the screen was wearing a dress shirt and tie. "What about hair?" He typed in another sequence and different styles of hair began taking shape on the screen.

"Hold it!" I told him suddenly. "Back it up a couple of steps if you can." Angelino did so and my sense of familiarity was even stronger. I almost knew who I was looking at. "Try removing this." I pointed at what I wanted changed.

Angelino made a few key strokes and hit the enter button. A strong featured face showed up on the screen, one I recognized instantly. "Oh, shit!" I said, grabbing for my phone. "I must be going blind!"

"I think you just convinced the man," McKee said dryly, and Angelino laughed.

"Can you send that image directly by e-mail?" I asked.

"Sure can," Angelino replied. "All I need is an e-mail address."

I dug through my wallet and came up with a couple of business cards. One was from Wallace and the other was Kowalski's. I dug deeper and came up with one for Simon Smyth and Sergeant Martinez. "I'll call them and tell them what it's about."

"No problem," Angelino said. "I'll just write 'Jazz serial suspect' in the subject line. That will get their attention. I'll also send a confidential cover page."

"You think that ever stops anyone from looking?" McKee chuckled. "All that does is invite attention. Did it ever stop you?" Angelino flushed and became very busy with his computer.

# 16. Set-Up

I immediately made several phone calls but had trouble getting through. The first person I reached was Wallace. I caught him just walking out of his office, but when he heard what I had to say, he told me he would check his e-mail and make the call to the FBI before leaving.

I was able to track down Dee, who said he would take care of calls to the appropriate people in Missouri and Oklahoma. I also asked him to call Martinez in Albuquerque and bring him up to date. "Let him know there's an age-corrected picture of the suspect coming to his e-mail," I added. "I'll ask Angelino to send you one, too."

Then I tried Kowalski and Adams for what must have been the fourth time, but there was still no answer. So in desperation I called Simon and finally got through to someone in Ft. Worth. When I told him what I had, he whistled. "Cool customer," he said. "Not many people could pull that off."

I agreed. "Any idea where I could find Kowalski or Adams?"

"They've been sent back to car patrol," Simon told me.

"What? What happened?"

"I don't know. There was a flap over homeland security and our chief of police said we needed more uniformed officers on patrol. He pulled a lot of people back into squad cars and Adams and Kowalski were the junior members in homicide."

I sensed Simon was not telling me something. "Come on, Simon. What gives? It's just us chickens."

He chuckled. "And no rooster in sight! The thing is, Jazz, I think most of this was just for show. Their national poll numbers are down right now so the dumb butts in Washington are back to using scare tactics again. The whole thing was very vague but the chief couldn't ignore it. He even has our crime scene van out driving around, burning my fuel budget for visible presence."

"It could backfire," I said.

"It already has," Simon told me. "Nobody takes it very seriously when they raise the alert level these days. Too much crying 'Wolf!' What's going to happen when real trouble comes, already?"

"Could you reach Kowalski and ask her to give me a call?" I said. "I need to get her and Adams a copy of the picture," I said. "We need to work out a strategy for bringing this guy in."

"I guarantee you, she'll be delighted," Simon assured me. "So will Adams. They split them up, you know. They wanted one 'seasoned officer' in every car."

"Seasoned, as in barbecue?" I quipped.

Simon laughed. "Something like that. Now hang up and let me make some calls. I'll rescue them from durance vile."

I looked McKee up in his office and told him I'd need to be gone for a few days. "I thought you might," he answered. "Anything we can do to help on this end?"

"I don't know," I said. "You might." I outlined what I needed to know and he told me he would put someone on it that evening.

As any child who watches detective shows on television can tell you, figuring out who committed a crime is one thing. Proving this in court is another and police have to be very careful with evidence now. Nor am I one to bash our higher courts for insisting that police follow proper procedure. The Constitution is there to protect me and thee from mob injustice and official stupidity, and I see no honor in resorting to perjury or criminal activity to make a case. Such tactics corrupt justice and erode the freedoms so basic to our whole way of life. We depend on such freedom to live together in peace and prosperity, and sacrificing them for expedience is the first step on a slippery slope into the abyss of totalitarian rule.

Knowing who committed the crime tells us where to dig, but it is only the first of many steps in building a successful criminal case. At this point I was reasonably sure Wally Keller was our shooter, and I was almost certain of who he had become after arranging his own 'death' in Arizona. What remained was connecting the dots but this was not a simple task. Even knowing what we did at that point, we could still blow the case to bits if we weren't careful.

What McKee had promised to get us were Wally's military records, assuming these were available. Sometimes they are not, depending on what missions a former soldier had been given. A lot of material gets classified to save political embarrassment, and if he was trained as a sniper, Wally could have been involved in gray or black operations. Were this the case, the Pentagon might either deny that he had ever been in military service, or release only an expunged record. They might tell us his duties were limited to guarding embassies and playing in the band. There was no way we could force them to tell us more than they felt necessary.

Yet there were other avenues of inquiry open to us, and knowing Keller's new identity would be quite helpful. To get the ball rolling, I went online and sure enough, there was a website that told me where to dig. Since Dee is better at these things than I am, I called and asked him to take it from there. When we hung up, I could tell he was as excited as a bloodhound that's just caught scent of the trail.

Having done all this, there was not much I could do but wait until the information I was after came in. As much as Jeanne and I like visiting Washington, it was time to be getting home, so we took a leisurely trip back to Arkansas, following the coast line all the way to Pensacola and past Biloxi before turning north. One of the more memorable stops was the week we stayed over in Myrtle Beach, living out of the land yacht and playing on the seashore. The water was too cold for swimming, at least for us, but we spent a lot of time building sand castles and sitting together quietly watching the surf.

As we sat there, we talked of many things. Jeanne wanted to know everything I could tell her about myself, and especially about my life with Nellie. When it was my turn to listen, she told wonderful stories about her kids growing up, and included any number of things I suspect they would have preferred she never mention. As a matter of fact, so did I, but I don't think Nellie would mind. There is no question she wanted me together with Jeanne once she was gone. When I finally read her letter, which broke my heart all over again, this was very clear.

An interesting thing happened during this period. We made a transition from coffee to tea. I became quite partial to green tea, which Jeanne told me was full of antioxidants and lots of other things which were good for me. Yet what I liked most was the delicate flavor and somewhere or other I found a backpacker's stove I could rig for the beach to make fresh tea there. And while there was quite a bit of physical intimacy, too, most of our lovemaking was in the wonderful time spent sharing tea and gentle conversation while we watched the winter surf. I could have gladly stayed there until the spring break migration.

Even so, Jeanne was fretting about her responsibilities back home, so we headed west until we came to Lafayette, Louisiana, and turned north for Shreveport. Though this was a bit out of our way, it was mostly interstate, which kept us off the back roads of Louisiana. Those are worse than the ones we have in Arkansas, and I felt much more confident driving the land yacht on four-lane road. Even this far south, there is always a chance of freak ice storms in January, and the drainage ditches along back roads in Cajun country are called sloughs in drier climates. They've been known to harbor alligators and large channel cat.

As much as I enjoyed our time together over the weeks, I was feeling the call for keeping my own company for a few days. I may be guessing, but I think Jeanne was feeling the same way. We'd both been away from our normal haunts for quite a while and cooped up together in the land yacht. It had been years since Jeanne had lived with a man on a regular basis and like me, she is a pretty self-sufficient soul. Cats are like this. When they are in the mood for affection, they can't get enough, but then they reach their quota and it's time to sit in the sun and absorb it all.

We got into Hope late Saturday afternoon and I spent the night there before heading out for Ft. Smith. The Crown Victoria had been parked in Jeanne's garage for almost a month, but it started right away and I headed north. When Jeanne kissed me goodbye, she was wistful. "I wish we could go to church together before you leave," she told me. "I'd really enjoy that."

"That would really give them something to talk about around here, wouldn't it?" I laughed. "On the other hand, I think it would be begging trouble down the road."

Jeanne got a stubborn set to her jaw, the kind that says "Flank speed ahead and damn the torpedoes." She started to reply but I held up my hands. "Seriously, Jeanne. We better not."

She sighed. "God, I hate small towns!" she declared. "We should be able to worship God together without causing gossip."

I glanced at my watch. "Well, you could follow me up to Oak Grove," I said. "Albert Jones gives a good sermon and they have a wonderful gospel choir."

Jeanne grinned wickedly. "Now wouldn't that twist their tails around here! Let it be known Miz Big-shot Schmidt is attending a black gospel church. Let's do it! No one from here will see us together, but I'll make sure word gets out that I attended." She dropped into a wonderful imitation of Southern belle gush. "Oh, don't you just love gospel music! Why, I was up at that little Baptist church in Oak Grove a couple of Sundays ago and they have the most marvelous gospel choir."

Believe it or not, Jeanne was ready to go in ten minutes, dressed to the teeth in a demure blue suit and feminine white blouse that revealed her figure but not cleavage. We arrived separately about ten minutes before the service started and we sat with the pastor's wife, who I'd met on another case a few years before.

As I expected, Emma Jones insisted we come to lunch after the service, and we were given a polite third degree grilling. Albert simply listened, obviously amused. As we were leaving he took me aside. "I'm glad you found someone, Jazz. I've been a little worried about you since Nellie died."

"Thank you," I said, touched by his words. "It's a little irregular, I know. I hope we didn't offend you by coming up today."

"The thing is, Jazz, I get the sense God has brought you together and God doesn't seem to always play by the rules." Albert smiled. "You understand what I'm saying?"

"I think so," I told him.

"Well, let me be very blunt. When Adam and Eve produced kids, there wasn't any such thing as a marriage license." Albert smiled and pulled at one ear. "Nor did God abandon Ishmael, Abraham's son by Hagar, Sarah's maid. They were his children and he cared for them just like he did for Isaac. The point is, I know of a lot of marriages that are full of sin where the people are technically faithful, at least sexually. I also know of a lot of unions like yours with Jeanne that are very blessed. If God blesses these, then who the hell is anyone else to condemn?" Then he grinned. "Of course, I could get tarred and feathered for saying that from the pulpit. Or if it were rumored."

"Thank you, Albert. I really appreciate it," I told him. "It goes no further than us, Jeanne and me."

Jeanne and I politely shook hands when we got to the parking lot. I don't think we fooled anyone, but we both knew a public display of affection was unwise. "God, I love you, Jeanne," I told her softly as we parted.

She smiled back demurely. "Consider yourself ravished, Buster," she whispered, nodding her head as if I'd said something funny. "I hope you know it's all I can do to keep my hands off you."

The drive to Ft. Smith that afternoon was bittersweet. The sun came out and there was a little snow among the trees, but this only accented the desolation of winter. The light was wonderful and I stopped for a number of good photo shots.

Yet, even the bright light seemed to carry an edge of melancholy and I wondered for the thousandth time about asking Jeanne to simply walk away. I worried that waiting for Henry to die would poison the beautiful thing we had, and I resolved to talk with Jeanne about this the next time we were together for any length of time.

The next morning I was awakened quite early by the phone. It was Jeanne and she was in tears. "I can't stand it, Jazz," she told me. "I want to be with you and this place gives me the willies. How would you like a permanent house guest?"

"What would you like for supper?" I asked, and she laughed. I spent the rest of the morning cleaning house and shopping for groceries, as giddy as a teenager whose first crush has just agreed to their first date. Time to oneself may be wonderful, but it's even more wonderful to know there will be someone there at the end of the day to tell about whatever has happened.

There was not a lot going on that needed my attention, and we spent the next two weeks getting Jeanne settled in. The Keller case was developing slowly, mostly because we had trouble getting military and academic records. We could not reasonably invoke the Patriot Act since we were not dealing with a security threat, although I know there are those who have. While my main concern was the erosion of civil liberties, my own personal liberties, in particular, the point I stressed to others was the possibility of losing the whole case to a sharp defense lawyer down the road. Violating the intent of the Patriot Act by invoking it for the wrong reason could give a competent attorney lots of material to build a strong "fruit of the poisoned tree" argument. With as much effort as we were putting into the Keller case, I wanted to make it stick.

So I spent a few hours each day clearing my desk and keeping in touch while Jeanne prowled around Ft. Smith. One of the first things I did was to hire a packing crew to completely clean out a couple of rooms and take most of the stuff to the local thrift shop. I had been through the rooms myself, sorting out the small amount of stuff I wanted to keep, and I asked Jeanne to supervise the job. There were a few items she wanted to keep, but the thrift shop got almost everything.

When the job was done, I took Jeanne to the empty rooms. "Now you get paid," I told her, handing her a credit card. "This is your personal space. Do whatever you like with it. Once you're done here, we can move on to the rest of the house."

Jeanne smiled and handed my card back. There were tears in her eyes. "I've got my own money, Jazz, and I want to use that," she said softly. "Henry would never let me use my own money. So most of what I have in Hope is his, at least in my thinking."

"I want this to be your house, too," I said. "So have at it. The only things that are off limits are my office and the library next to it." I hesitated. "Maybe the garage, too. I have a shop out there."

"Well, the first thing I need is a car," she told me. She had arrived driving the land yacht filled with some of her things and had been driving Nellie's old Buick. "A new life needs new wheels, but I can't decide between a minivan or a sports car."

Jeanne ended up writing a check for a brand new Caravan that afternoon, mostly because the seats folded flat into the floor. "The furniture stores deliver," she said, "but I like to do auctions and garage sales, too. I need room to haul stuff."

A couple of days later I heard voices in another part of the house and went to investigate. They were coming from the bare rooms and there I found Jeanne talking to Zilpha and her oldest daughter. Not knowing anyone else in Ft. Smith, Jeanne had called Zilpha, who was only too glad to help her decorate. "It's about time, Grandpa Jazz," Zilpha told me, but I had my hands full. Zilpha's granddaughter had broken loose from her mother and came running to give me a hug.

Jeanne took a couple of weeks decorating her personal rooms and when she was done, I was impressed. "You should be a professional decorator," I told her.

"Zilpha has a good eye," Jeanne told me. "I think she could do this full time."

"She seems happy at the real estate office," I ventured.

"That's all right for putting bread on the table," Jeanne said. "I'm thinking about hiring her and setting up our own business here. Would you mind?"

I took her hands in mine. The emerald ring felt warm to my touch. "One thing you never have to do is ask my permission," I told her. "Except for dinner parties with boring people."

A couple of months later the redecorating was done, except for the kitchen. It was at that point Jeanne told me, "I'm going to sell the house in Hope, Jazz. I may need to spend a few days clearing it out."

"Would you like me to come with you?"

"Yes, I was hoping you would. It may take two or three weeks. Can you be away that long?"

"Sure, if we can come home on the weekends," I answered. "Dee can handle most of the routine stuff."

"Come home on the weekends," Jeanne whispered with tears in her eyes. "I like that, Jazz, coming here as coming home."

It was a couple of weeks after Jeanne started moving in that I got a call from Lou Wallace. "We finally got the military records," he told me. "Thanks to our mutual friend in Washington. He seems to know where a lot of bodies are buried."

"His father-in-law ran the shop before Sam did. He helped start the place during World War II and he's still around. He has better files than Hoover had."

Wallace chuckled. "No wonder Sam was able to get the information. Well, the Army records show that Wally was a sniper in Special Forces and he served in Panama and Grenada, among other places. They were pretty vague about that. Wally was later treated for post-traumatic shock by the VA, but didn't complete his course of recommended treatment after they gave him a medical discharge."

"What about gunsmith school?" I asked.

"They're harder to get information from than the Army," Wallace said. "But your guy from Albuquerque helped us out there. Martinez got a warrant and drove up and went through their records. Keller registered under his original birth name, Charles David Ember. That's the name he used for his ATF license, too. I haven't been able to run it down, but I bet he had it legally changed at some point. He got a new Social Security number before he applied to gunsmith school."

"That's not what he's going by now," I said.

"No, he changed it again. When he went to school in Phoenix it was under the new name, and that seems to be what he's been ever since."

"I bet he has another identity he's never used," I said. "One he can use to bolt with if we get too close."

"Yeah, but this guy is good. I don't think we'll be able to find that one until after he uses it, if then. We need to be really careful going after this guy, Jazz."

"We also need to track him somehow," I said. "He's probably already setting up his next kill."

"Maybe we should bring him in," Wallace suggested. "We know he's been in the vicinity at the right time for every case we have. I certainly have enough for a warrant to hold him. Maybe we can get him convicted of something to give us time to dig."

"We don't have enough to convict unless we can prove fraud with the name change. I want us to nail him down, Mike, not just scare him underground. What we need is the weapon and we need him tied to it. Let me talk to our friends in the District. They may know some way we can track him without his knowing it."

"We could always put a GPS bug on his car," Wallace suggested. "Thing is, he never takes his own car on his hit trips. That's how we placed him on site. He rents a car and drives himself there."

"Yeah, but I'd imagine he has a legitimate reason for being there," I observed. "I would bet he planned his hits that way."

"As a matter of fact, he does, every time. It's all work related. So his lawyer could claim it was pure coincidence."

"Yeah. Any lawyer worth his fee could get our evidence of seven other correlations suppressed, too." I sighed. "I think our best strategy is to wait him out."

Wallace gave a wry chuckle. "It's not like he's taking out anyone but predators, is it? I might be comfortable ignoring it for years."

"On the other hand, he might shoot the wrong person," I said. "That one guy really bothers me, the one who was getting his life turned around."

"Yeah, there is that, isn't there? I was just talking through my hat."

An idea began coming together in my mind. "On the other hand, we could bust the hell out of him and warn him off," I said. "We could let him know we are on his trail in a big way and hope he quits or makes a mistake. Sooner or later they all do." Even as I said this, I knew Wally would never quit. I don't know of a serial killer who has ever stopped voluntarily. On the other hand, how would anyone know if such a killer did?

"How would you go about that?" Wallace asked, very interested.

"I'd hit him with a full court press. Arrest him on suspicion, extradite him to the place that has the strongest case, and get search warrants for his home. While he's being held for extradition, grill him around the clock."

"His lawyer will put a stop that," Wallace told me. " I bet he'll ask for a lawyer right away."

"It doesn't matter," I said. "We don't have to let him see a lawyer for seventy-two hours. So long as we don't use any evidence we may get from him, we're all right. All we need is some time to plant GPS tracking bugs. We can put three in his car, one he's sure to find and a couple of others he won't. We can also use an angel tracking system. I have a friend named Angelino who was telling me about those the last time I saw him. The new ones are pretty sophisticated."

"Well, Michael knows his business," Wallace told me, confirming his connection with the McKee organization. "But how do we implant one of those? Keller will never give consent and doing it without his knowledge would poison the tree."

"I was thinking shoes," I said. "We could implant a responder in his shoes."

"His shoes?" Wallace asked. "How could you be sure he was going to wear any particular pair of shoes when you wanted to know where he was?"

"Not *a* pair of shoes," I said. "*All* of them. We set things up ahead of time and when we bust him and search his place, we embed a bug in every pair of shoes he has."

"Do those things really work?"

"So I'm told. Scary thought isn't it?"

My next call was to Michael Angelino and I asked him to patch Sam McKee in on the call since Sam would have to give approval. When I told them what I had in mind, McKee chuckled. "You've got a devious mind, Jazz. How many of the things are you going to need? A couple dozen?"

"I would guess so," I said. "A dozen would do it for my closet."

"Why don't we ship you three dozen just to be safe? The things aren't all that expensive and you can send back what you don't need."

"Wouldn't a personal implant be better?" Angelino asked. "You're assuming he's going to use the shoes in his closet."

"It's a good bet," I answered. "The hits are all tied to his professional work and he probably would wear shoes from his normal wardrobe."

"There's also the issue of how we get the implant in him," McKee responded. "This isn't Russia where we can nail him with a dart from an umbrella. There's a wee matter called the Constitution that stands in the way of doing that without consent."

"There's the Patriot Act," Angelino argued.

"This guy is a domestic killer," McKee said. "He's also a US citizen. No way can he be classified as a terrorist."

"There is evidence he was involved in gun running," I said. My heart wasn't in it, but Angelino might have a point. "That might do it."

"Do you want to risk your case?" McKee asked. "How do you implant it without his knowledge? Who do you get to do the operation? No, it's cheaper and much less risky to do it the way Jazz suggested. The only clinker might be if he flies somewhere and the airport security scan picks up the device in his shoes."

"Not this device," Angelino assured him. "Jack and I have tweaked it. It might show up on a medical X-ray or CT, but not a normal scan."

"See, there?" McKee answered. "The KISS principle always works best."

"The kiss principle?" I asked. "That sounds interesting."

"Steady, there, stud horse," McKee chuckled. "KISS is a reminder to myself. It's an acronym. Keep It Simple, Sam."

I talked to Kowalski to let her know what was up and she was enthusiastic about moving ahead. The possible problem she saw was getting Joe McClellan's approval of a joint operation. "He's pretty territorial, Jazz," she told me. "When the television crews show up, he wants to be out front. He's still torqued about reopening the case."

"I noticed he seemed a little huffy the last time I talked to him," I said. "I hope he hasn't taken it out on you."

"Well, we were sent back on patrol, though we weren't singled out. There's been a lot of other stuff going on in town, too and he's pretty conscious of how things look." She chuckled. "He didn't like it when Dr. Smyth asked for us back on the case, but he didn't dare say no."

"You know, I noticed that when I was there on the Keller case," I said. "His being so careful with the media. Only, I didn't realize it at the time. It took me a couple of weeks to realize there weren't any reporters on the scene when the bishop was killed. I never got around to asking why."

"That was his doing," Kowalski told me. "The media didn't get wind of it until late in the day and it took them time to make it there through traffic. They showed up a while after we left for the water tower. It was the chief who called them in and he was who talked to them. I guess you missed the evening news."

"I guess I did. How in the world did he keep them away? Most of them have radio scanners now."

Kowalski laughed. "New tactics. We all have cell phones now and our standing instructions are to phone in anything that looks like it may be politically hot. They also know we're told not to talk to them, so they've pretty much given up trying. I'm here to tell you, all this gripes the hell out of them."

"I can imagine," I said. "Listen, let me talk to Joe first. I think I can put it in a way that he'll want to play along."

"Care to run it by me?" Kowalski asked.

"Sure, but you may not want to know until after the fact," I replied. "You damned sure don't want the chief to know you were in the picture ahead of time."

"I think I'll take your word for it," Kowalski answered. "Just be sure to let me know what happened."

# 17. End Game

The way I brought Joe McClellan around was very crude and very effective. I called to let him know I'd caught wind of a major FBI operation to take down a serial killer in Ft. Worth. After he got done swearing, Joe was anxious to hear just what I knew, and when I was done, he got on the line with the right people in Washington. They were waiting for his call and allowed themselves to be persuaded to let the Ft. Worth Police PD run the show so long as Ft. Worth stayed within the FBI's game plan.

When the special agent in charge hung up, he looked at me and chuckled. "I'd hate to play chess with you, Dr. Phillips."

"Checkers is actually my game," I told him, putting away my cell phone. "Chess is way too complicated."

"Right. Do you think McClellan will keep in line until this goes down?"

"You made it pretty clear how embarrassing it might be for him if he didn't," I said. "I think you can probably count on that. I'm eighty-seven percent sure."

"What's the other thirteen percent?" the agent wanted to know.

"About half of it is general uncertainty in dealing with an egomaniac, and the rest is the random stuff that can go wrong that might cause him to plunge on in."

I could see I was not being understood. "Suppose some local stink happens that puts a lot of political heat on Joe. Maybe a white officer shoots an Hispanic suspect who turns out to be a model citizen.

Everybody is up in arms. Joe might go ahead with busting a serial killer to distract the press and take some of the heat off the police department."

The special agent in charge laughed. "Yes, we're familiar with that around here. I just had never heard it so precisely calculated."

I shrugged. "I could be wrong, you know. On the other hand, doing things this way puts any embarrassment on Joe if things go south."

"You think they may?"

"We're dealing with a pretty level-headed killer," I said. "He's insane but he's very well organized and very shrewd. No one knew what he was up to until eight people were dead, and maybe more. I think when the case finally hits the news you're going to get a lot of inquiries from all over the country."

"He's crazy all right," one of the newer agents said. "You'd think killing the guy who abused him would be enough."

"We don't know who all abused him," I reminded him. "These guys were all in the same clique. Maybe one of them used to baby-sit for his dad and abused him sexually, too. It could be his dad beat the shit out of Wally when he told on the guy. This is one very sick group of people."

"All of them clergy, too," another agent spoke up. "That's what gets me. A rotten apple every once in a while is what you'd expect from any basket, but eight of them from the same school? What the hell are they teaching there?"

"They're supposed to be weeded out before they go there," I replied. "Remember, these guys all came from different areas of the country. Not all of them are predators, either. There's no evidence Bishop Keller was. He was just mean as hell to his family. A lot of police officers are as bad as he was. Look at Rampart in LA. God only knows what all went on there."

"Ouch, now you're getting personal," Wallace chuckled. He had flown in for the meeting with the FBI, as had Martinez, who had taken a personal interest.

"Little Rock has its share, too, Mike," I assured him. "What these guys did to protect each other is not that different from what police do. At least, some of us."

The group nodded. "You seem to be assuming you won't find the gun when you do the search," one of the federal agents pointed out. "How come?"

"We might get lucky and find the gun when we search Keller's place," I answered. "My sense of the man is that he is too careful for that. I think he probably changes his clothes completely when he goes out to kill."

"So the shoe implant may not help at all?"

"Yes and no. It will help us track him at home, and if he has a hideout somewhere, it will lead us to that."

"This sounds pretty complicated," someone said.

"We're dealing with a very sophisticated killer," Wallace answered. "There's a reason no one heard of him until after his eighth hit. Jazz just happened to get lucky."

"I think Jazz makes his own luck," Martinez interjected. "This guy is damn good."

"Yeah," I said derisively. "Jazz can walk on water in Minnesota in January." It took them a moment to get it, but then they all laughed.

"Shoot, I can make water out of wine," Wallace put in solemnly. "But to get back to business, how soon can you have things in place in Ft. Worth?"

"Two days minimum, ten days at the outside," I said. "I'm not sure Joe can hold his water much longer than that. Just to be on the safe side, we're going to have a California warrant so we can hold Keller for Wallace if things go south."

"It's a done deal," Wallace added, reaching in his jacket and pulling out a folded legal packet. "I'll give this to Joe McClellan when we get to Ft. Worth."

"So what's the extra time for?" one of the federal agents asked.

"Getting the players in place," I said. "Martinez is going to be there and the guy from Missouri will be sending Kowalski a warrant, too. Keller might get a sympathetic judge and beat one extradition hearing, but not three back-to-back. We'll only invoke the other two if there's need."

"Sounds like overkill," one of the federal agents observed.

"That's what this asshole is all about," Martinez reminded him. "We don't need any more bodies."

The first phase of the bust went down three days later. Kowalski and I were in one car and Adams and Wallace were keeping loose surveillance on Keller in another. We decided to wait until our quarry was at work before moving in, and Kowalski and I met them in the parking lot behind the Presbyterian church when we got the call.

"He's in the church," Adams told us. "Kowalski and I can take the front and side doors if you and Wallace want to go in here." We were standing at the back door near the staff parking area.

When we entered the building, the first thing I heard was the sound of the organ playing. We were in a hallway and I turned in the direction of the sanctuary. This ended in a door that led into the west transept and I peeked around one of the brick columns that lined each side aisle. I could see the organist seated beside someone else at the console. They had their backs to me and were talking about something, but I couldn't tell what.

I put a finger to my lips and motioned for Wallace to follow me down the side aisle connected to our end of the transept. As we walked close to the wall, keeping out of sight, I noticed Wallace had his weapon drawn, but he was holding it by his leg. When we got to the end of the aisle there was a door leading into the narthex, and when we opened it, we found a surprised Adams standing at the foot of one stairway to the choir loft. He pointed to the other stairway and I knew Kowalski was there.

Neither the organist nor the other man heard us approaching, and when I spoke, both were startled. "Hello, Wally," I said.

Karl Mann glared at me, his Van Dyke trembling with sudden anger. "My name's not Wally," he said. "Neither is his."

"Move off the bench please, sir," I asked the man sitting next to Mann. "Take a seat back there." I pointed to the choir risers.

Mann started to rise too, but Wallace pushed him back down on the bench. "Keep your hands in plain sight, sir," he said. His weapon was not pointed at Mann, but it was quite visible. Adams and Kowalski had theirs out, too.

"What do you think you're doing?" Mann demanded.

"It's over, Wally," I answered. "Put your hands behind your back."

"I told you, my name is not Wally," Mann snapped back. His hands remained on the keyboard.

"That's right," I answered. "That's only what you went by when you lived with the Kellers. Your birth name is Charles David Ember. You changed it to Karl Mann before you attended the University of Arizona and faked your own death. Now put your hands behind your back or these officers will do it for you."

Karl Mann looked around. While none of the officers had a weapon pointed directly at him, their pistols could be brought to bear in an instant. Mann nodded and slowly put his hands behind his back. Wallace cuffed him quickly and said formally, "Walton Davis Keller, you're wanted for suspicion of murder in California."

"We also have a warrant to search your house," Kowalski added, placing a legal folder in an inner pocket of Mann's sport jacket. "You will want to look at that after you're booked."

"I want a lawyer," Mann snarled. "You'll pay for this."

"A lawyer will be provided at the appropriate time," Kowalski told him. "However, it may not be until Monday."

"I demand a lawyer now!" Mann snarled.

"The law says we can hold you for seventy-two hours without one," Kowalski told him. Not that it matters. We're also holding you for extradition to California, so there won't be bail. You can make a phone call, but there's not much your lawyer can do to get you out."

"Can I go now?" It was the man who had been on the bench beside Mann. He held his hands half raised.

"Who are you?" Kowalski challenged him.

"I'm the singer," the man said. When it was clear no one knew what he was talking about, he added. "I'm the soloist for the funeral tomorrow morning."

Kowalski chuckled. "Well, I hope you can play the organ, too." She nodded toward Mann. "You have some ID?"

The soloist handed Kowalski his driver's license. She noted the name and number, but I was surprised she called in the number. Yet, it was a smart move and I gave her points. One never knows what will show up on a routine check.

Since the soloist had no outstanding warrants, Kowalski let him go. I suggested he might want to call whoever was in charge of the funeral to let them know they needed someone else at the console. I added that it might be a good idea to notify the pastor of the church, too. When we were done talking to him, the young man took off so fast I was afraid he might tumble down the stairs.

When we got to the main police station it was obvious someone had made some phone calls because there was a lawyer waiting for us. Judging from his suit, which I guessed must have set him back a couple of thousand dollars, he was expensive, and his manner was strictly upper echelon. Kowalski took a quick look at his card and handed it to me. The firm was actually one I had heard about, and the man standing there was one of the partners. Someone was really going to bat for Wally Keller, aka Charles Ember, Karl Mann and God only knows what else. I wondered why.

As a courtesy, Kowalski invited the attorney to join us in a small conference room while Karl Mann was being booked. Adams was handling that. She introduced Wallace and me, telling the lawyer who we were, and gave him a concise outline of the major charges pending against his client. She gave him more than I would have given out, but without revealing much in terms of solid evidence. When he asked for that, she told him he would have to talk to the district attorney.

Even though he was a full partner and used to having things turn out his way, I could see the lawyer was surprised. I would not have cared to be in his shoes.

"I assume you're going to want to search my client's dwelling," he said.

"We're already have a warrant," Kowalski told him. "Your client has it in his possession. At least, he did until we booked him. We have his place secured already."

"I'll want to have someone from my office there when you search and I'll want a receipt for everything you take," the lawyer said.

"Fine, but we're not going to wait for you," Kowalski answered. "As soon as he's booked, we're going in to search."

The lawyer pulled out a cell phone and made a call. He asked Kowalski for the address and passed it along to whoever was on the other end of the line. He asked a couple of more questions, mostly about the extradition warrants, and asked to see his client. When he was leaving, he turned to me. "I've heard of you, Dr. Phillips. What I don't understand is your involvement in this case."

"I was giving an investigation seminar for the Ft. Worth Police Department when Bishop Keller was murdered," I told him. "The chief wanted my professional opinion."

The lawyer asked a couple of other questions about my status as a sworn peace officer, and I was glad to be able to tell him I was strictly a consultant. "Yes, but my impression is that you are the key investigator in this whole affair. Is that not true?"

I shook my head. The bastard was good. He was already searching for lines of defense and trying to lead me into a misstatement. "My contract with the Ft. Worth Police Department is strictly a training role. I don't carry a badge or a gun. What I do is advise and research."

"How did you learn of this case?" the lawyer asked Wallace. Wallace just looked at him. "I can force you to answer that on the stand," the attorney said.

"Have at it," Wallace replied. "Until then, that's all you get." He held up a copy of the extradition warrant, but pulled back when the lawyer reached for it. "This copy is for the Ft. Worth PD," Wallace told him. "You can get a copy from them." He gave the attorney a cold smile. "I believe that's how it works."

There was no question what Wallace thought about high priced lawyers. This opinion is shared by many police officers. One of them once described the legal profession to me as lawful whores. "They're all like hookers," the officer told me, well in his cups when he did. "The only difference between the ones in the gutters and the ones in penthouses is price and maybe the quality of service. No, make that the quality of servicing. You get screwed either way."

I was equally in my cups when he told me this and it seemed hilarious at the time. We had a lot of fun talking it to death, and the next day I wondered why. The question we had the most fun with was figuring out what might be the hooking equivalent of Legal Aid for the indigent.

Of course, Wally was out of jail by Monday noon. This was not any surprise. We barely had enough evidence to get a search warrant, much less to build a case. None of us expected the search to turn up any evidence linking Wally to the crimes, but it allowed us to place implants in his shoes. It also put him on the defensive. Up to that point he'd never even been a suspect.

We never did find out exactly who was fronting Mann's legal expenses. I suspect it was one of his gay lovers still living in the closet, and it could have been blackmail on Mann's part. Or maybe it wasn't. From what I could tell, everything must have been set up well in advance. At the time, this made me wonder if Mann had an active accomplice, or even a whole network of accomplices. I could never pin this down until long after we got Mann, but I wondered then if someone was feeding him names.

Nor was I ever able to trace the movement of any monies to fund any of this, which surprises me. This fact initially seemed to point toward revenge as the motive in these killings, but later I came to the conclusion it was vigilante justice taken to an extreme. Aside from his own adopted father, where the motive was clearly revenge, which ultimately got him caught, Keller-Mann seemed to be acting like an angel of death, cleansing the earth of sexual predators and abusers in the most direct way possible. It was only much later that I learned how right I was.

Despite our best efforts in gathering evidence, we almost lost the case. The search of Mann's dwelling and storage unit turned up nothing but credit card records we already had. These showed quite clearly that Mann had indeed been in all the right places at the right times, but they also showed he was there every time for a legitimate reason.

Nor did the monitors we implanted in Mann's shoes turn up anything but his normal routine at first. Our prey was either innocent or had gone to ground and was being careful. After a while, no one was monitoring the tracking devices but a small computer dedicated to that task. Once we had programmed in Mann's normal haunts, the thing was set to notify us only if Mann went somewhere new. When it did, these turned out to be legitimate places for Mann to be. After a while we all found other more pressing things to attend.

It was only about a week or two before the end of battery life for the tracking devices that we got a solid hit. As it was programmed to do, the computer phoned Adams when it couldn't reach Kowalski. Both were attending an FBI seminar in Oklahoma City, and the call got forwarded to me. This wasn't the first time this happened and I didn't get too excited. I made a note to get in touch with Kowalski, but it got pushed under some other papers and it was almost a week later before I got in touch.

"That's a new one, all right," she said, laughing. "Maybe Wally has found himself a new girl friend. That's happened before." Yet when she called me back an hour later, Kowalski was dead serious. "This may actually be it, Jazz. I ran down the landlady and showed her Mann's picture. She recognized him right away. It's a garage apartment and he's apparently rented the place for years. She thinks he's a traveling salesman."

"I guess in a way, he is," I answered. "Have you taken this to Joe?"

"Not yet," Kowalski answered. "Adams and I are going to keep close watch on the tracker. Our supervisor knows we're watching it and we don't have to clear routine surveillance unless there's another case. I'll give her a heads up."

"Why don't you get a warrant, just in case?" I asked. "That one judge seemed a little sympathetic."

Kowalski called back the next morning. "Bad news," she told me. "Mann's left town. He has a music conference in Little Rock this week."

"That's interesting," I said. "It will be easier to take him on my turf."

"What if he's after you?" Kowalski asked.

The thought had not occurred to me. "Why would he do that?" I asked, but I knew the answer. Sociopaths who commit serial murders have their own logic and I had ruined Mann's game. Suddenly I felt very exposed. I unlocked a desk drawer and took out my Glock, setting it in my lap.

"Just keep a low profile, Jazz," Kowalski told me. The tracker's still working and so far he's still in Little Rock. I'll call you the minute he heads your way."

"Let's take him in Little Rock," I suggested. "He may be on another clergy kill. See if Wallace can fly in and I'll pick him up. I'll call Dee and round up a couple of people who owe me a favor." I wasn't sure how legal it was to involve officers from out of state, but both Dee and I are sworn Arkansas peace officers.

The next thing I did was secure the house. Fortunately, Jeanne was in Hope that week, closing down the house there, and I didn't have to worry about her safety. Once the house was secure and the burglar alarm was set, I phoned McKee and told him what was going on.

"A team will be in Little Rock tonight," he told me. "Willie is not available but Alex is and I'll send Martha, too."

It was then a chilling thought hit me. "Would you mind covering Jeanne Schmidt in Hope?" I asked. "He might come after me through her."

"I'll send Martha there," McKee assured me. "Just let Jeanne know she's coming and why." My silence must have been eloquent because McKee chuckled. "No reason to worry, Jazz," he assured me. "Martha is plenty and she can call in reinforcements if she needs them."

"All right," I answered, not really that assured. I decided to ask George Williams to keep a watchful eye out in Hope, too.

"Jazz, believe it or not, Martha is plenty. She's like the Texas Rangers. You know their policy, don't you?"

"You mean that old 'one riot, one Ranger' thing?" I asked and McKee agreed. He also told me he would send an extra tracking machine along with his crew.

When I called Jeanne on her satellite phone, there was no answer. This was odd and I got a bad feeling about it, so I called George Williams and asked him to make sure she was all right. I explained what was going down and he was on the way. While I waited for word back, I tried to pack for the trip to Little Rock, but it was hard to focus and I finally gave up. I went to the kitchen and made myself a cup of green tea.

Twenty minutes later my phone rang and it was Jeanne. I breathed a sigh of relief. "What's going on, Jazz?" she asked me. I started to minimize the danger I felt but decided to tell her exactly why I was fearful.

"Well, goodness," she said. "I'll be happy to see Martha, of course, but you didn't have to go to all that trouble. I loaded my pistol before I called you."

I told her about the killer who came after us in Ft. Smith, the one Nellie took out. "You don't put enough faith in your women, darling," Jeanne laughed. "Nobody in his right mind would mess with us." Yet behind the bravado, I could hear the uncertainty in her voice. Knowing one is being hunted is not pleasant.

"Just humor me," I said. "Give Martha my best."

Kowalski called back a while later. "I think our guy is gone hunting," she said. "We got a warrant to search his other place and found a box of loaded ammo. We also found a lot of other hand-loading components, including partition-type bullets. There was a hand-loading press with .357 dies and some other gun tools. The bullets are the right brand."

I told her about McKee's team and asked if she would be there, too. "You bet your sweet grits," she answered. "Adams will be coming, too, but we'll be driving. Its as fast as flying from here the way I drive."

"No, you're wrong," I told her, beginning to relax for the first time in hours. "With you at the wheel, it's much faster!"

"I'll tell Adams you said for me to drive," she laughed and hung up.

I was on my way out the door when the attack came. Had I not reached back to lock the door, I would not be writing this. As it was, I caught the second round in the arm. The first had embedded itself in the door jamb where my head had been an instant before. There was no sound but that of the bullet striking the wooden framing, but I knew what it was and rolled back into the kitchen, shoving the door shut with my left arm. As I did, the second round came through the solid wood door. This diminished its power, but I still got a nasty wound.

I had my Glock out by then and it was tempting to put a round through a window just to let the bastard know I was armed. Yet there was no telling where it might land and I held my fire. *Let the bastard come after me,* I thought savagely. At that point I would have gladly emptied a magazine into him. I wiggled across the floor and took up station in the hallway behind the refrigerator.

Nothing happened. I lay there for a moment, then fished out my cell phone and hit the 911 button. When the operator answered I told her an officer was pinned down by a sniper and gave her the address. I glanced at the kitchen clock and noted the time. I called Kowalski and then McKee. Three minutes later I heard sirens blaring up my street then stopping. My cell phone rang and I answered. It was the SWAT commander asking for a status report. I told him where I was and where I thought the shot came from, and that I was wounded. Three minutes later he called back to tell me the area was clear and that he was coming in. By then I had heard the ambulance arrive.

The paramedics wanted to take me to the hospital, but the wound wasn't that bad. It had torn a long gash across the surface of my forearm, which is why it bled so, and it would be stiff the next day. At the moment it was only a dull ache and my first priority was catching our guy. I holstered my Glock and jumped in the Crown Vic. Once I was on the way, I used my cell phone to alert the state highway patrol I was under way at high speed. I said the right things to the shift commander, and he cleared the way.

Somehow, Mann made it back to his hotel in Little Rock without being spotted. To this day, I still don't know how he managed it, but he must have had help. He was dressed in a business suit and dress loafers when they stopped him in his hotel lobby two hours and thirty-two minutes after the shooting in Ft. Smith. There was no gunshot residue on his hands, face, or clothes, and the Ft. Smith police could not turn up any witnesses. A search of Mann's car and his room were fruitless. There was no ammunition or sign of his weapon. There was also a witness who vouched for his presence all afternoon at a private home in Little Rock. After holding him for several hours, the police had to let him go.

Even so, I know the shooter was either Mann or one of his boys in the band. The bullet the lab techs dug out of my doorway in Ft. Smith matched the one that killed Bishop Keller and the other Episcopal clergy. They also found the place where the two shots were fired at me, but there were no empty brass casings or any other physical evidence that tied Mann to the niche by my garage. The only evidence we had that he had even been near Ft. Smith was from a GPS reading recorded on the computer still at work sorting through the signals. The closest we could place him for sure was in Clarksville about an hour and a half before the shooting. There were no GPS readings after that and my guess is that the battery for the tiny transmitter in Mann's shoe finally ran down.

Fortunately, I was able to catch Wallace before he took off from Sacramento and saved him a futile trip to Little Rock. Since Kowalski and Adams were already in town, I took them to a little place that's famous for its ribs. They were kind enough to say the ribs were worth making the trip, but I knew they were as disappointed as I.

"Some of these guys are lucky as the devil," I said, trying to console them. "We did all the right things but we had some bad breaks."

"Oh, I don't know. The son-of-a-bitch missed," Kowalski reminded me.

"I didn't think he'd go after me," I answered. "Psychopaths don't normally go after cops unless they're cornered."

"Maybe he's feeling cornered," Adams suggested. "We leaned on him pretty hard in Ft. Worth. You're the guy who spoiled his game." I glanced at him sharply. "What?" he asked, catching my look.

"That's exactly the same thought I had when I talked to Kowalski," I told him. An idea began to form. "Let's keep the pressure on him. Do you think he's aware we know about his second place in Ft. Worth?" I asked.

"Well, if he doesn't, he will when he gets there," Adams answered. "We impounded his loading equipment and ammunition."

"Good!" I said. "We'll need another warrant and here's what we'll do."

# 18. First Blood

This time it was the pastor who was in the choir loft with Mann when we arrived at the church. Mann's face went hard when he saw us coming and the pastor glanced around nervously. Kowalski handed the pastor the search warrant and explained that it was for the church and campus buildings. "This says you're looking for firearms, among other things," the pastor objected. "We don't allow those here."

I was watching Mann closely when Kowalski was speaking to the pastor, and I saw him go tense. Adams had seen it, too, and was standing behind Mann, his pistol in his hand but concealed behind his leg. "We think someone has taken advantage of your good nature," I told the pastor, never taking my eyes off Mann. "That's why we have the warrant. May I please have the key, Dr. Mann?"

"What key?" Mann replied coldly. I could see he was having to work hard to remain in control.

Kowalski smiled. "The key to the back of the organ console," she said lightly. "Or I can use this, I suppose." She took a flat pry bar out of her shoulder bag.

The pastor looked like he was about to faint. "For God's sake, give it to her, Karl! We can't have them breaking the console."

Mann started to reach into his jacket but heard Adams move behind him. "Gently, sir," Adams told him. His pistol was now visible, though not pointed directly at Mann. I took the pastor by the arm and led him aside. I wondered if we were going to have to give him CPR at some point.

Mann handed a ring of keys to Kowalski, who took them in her left hand. The way she was holding the pry bar in her right hand told me there was no question it would quickly become a weapon if Mann made the wrong move. The organist must have seen this, too, for he moved very slowly and very deliberately.

Kowalski moved to one side and offered me the key ring. "Why don't you do the honors, Jazz?" she asked.

"Thank you," I answered, donning a pair of vinyl gloves. I don't know who chooses the colors of these things or the logic behind the choices, but these were purple. I sorted through the key ring and found two keys that might work. One had an uneven double cut, and I tried it first. The lock turned easily and I looked inside.

"My goodness," I said, removing the back panel of the console and setting it to one side. "Look at what the organ service man left behind." I took out a stubby rifle with a large round barrel. I opened it up and looked into the breech. "I see it's fully loaded, too. What do you use this for, Dr. Mann? Church mice?" I detached a magazine from the weapon and set it on the polished top of the console. Then I reached back into the console and took out a box of ammunition. The lab told us later it was all subsonic and loaded with the partition type bullets used to kill the bishop.

"What happened, Wally?" I asked him. "Did Bishop Keller recognize you after all these years?" Mann glared at me but said nothing.

"Of course, he didn't," I continued. "At least not until the last moment. You set the whole thing up so it looked like he was accidentally hit with an outside shot. The night before you put one shot in from the water tower hill. Then you put a second shot out the window with the same weapon to confuse things and enlarge the hole. But I can't believe you killed Keller without letting him know who you are." I could see from Mann's face I had it right. "You knew the acoustics of this place. You knew that all you had to do from up here was murmur softly, right at the last moment. He would hear you clearly, even if someone else in the choir loft couldn't. What did you say, Wally? What did you tell him?" Mann's face was a grimace.

"So the phone call to the insurance agent was bogus, too?" Kowalski looked at me to ask the question, which was a mistake. Quick as a mongoose, Mann ducked back and grabbed the hand that held Adams's pistol, using the leverage to throw him into Kowalski. Thank God for Adams' presence of mind, taking his finger off the trigger when the gun was yanked. Had he not, Kowalski would have been shot.

Mann used the momentum to fling himself toward the stairwell leading down into the narthex. The console was between us and there was little I could do to stop him.

Then I did the strangest thing. It's not something a policeman would normally do. Nor do I understand why I did it then, except the case had become extremely personal. The bastard tried to kill me on my own doorstep and I was damned if I'd stand there and let him get away. Had there been a hymnal on top of the console I'd have thrown that. What was there was Mann's gun.

I wanted to trip Mann, so I grabbed the sniper's rifle and threw it at his knees. My hand slipped as I let go and it flew high, spinning end over. It struck him barrel first in the armpit just as he turned to go down the stairs. There was a slight noise when the gun struck and it bounced back into the loft. Then there was silence, followed by a strange noise from the stairwell.

Kowalski took off for the other stairs while Adams cautiously took up station behind a corner at the stairwell Mann fled through. A few moments later I heard Kowalski shout, "Clear down here."

Adams quickly peeked around the corner of the stairwell, then took a longer look. "He's lying on the stairs," he called back. "I see blood and he's not moving." He kicked the sniper weapon out of the way and began to descend. "Come on up," he called to his partner. "I think Jazz shot him."

"I didn't shoot him," I protested. "The gun was empty."

"He's dead, Jazz," Kowalski answered. "You forgot to clear the chamber."

That's how I killed my first man. I thought it would haunt me, but it never did. Yes, I made a deadly mistake not clearing the bullet in the chamber. Nor am I sure I could have shot Wally with his own gun if I'd tried. By the time I had figured out how to use it, he would have been down the stairs. I was very lucky the bullet didn't hit someone else, and I am grateful the grand jury gave me a no-bill for homicide.

For a while it worried me a bit that I wasn't more troubled by this and I talked to Forster about it, but it was Dee who gave me a handle on things. "Do you remember that copperhead you killed when we were still on highway patrol?" he asked. "You know, the time we were trying to help the governor dig his Jeep out of the mud? You were mad as hell at the stupid bastard for getting stuck, and when that copperhead popped up and took a bite at you, you hollered 'son-of-a-bitch!' and hit it with the shovel. You cut its head clean off. Remember that?"

"How can I forget?" I laughed. "The governor thought I was talking about him. He chewed my ass royally."

"How did you feel about killing that snake?" Dee asked.

"I felt pretty calm." I answered. "It was like I vented all my anger with that one swipe. Then I got tickled and started laughing when the governor stepped on the snake and almost stroked out."

"Do you see what I'm saying?" Dee asked.

"I think so. I just did what I had to do and the snake died."

"That's one way of describing what happened to Wally or Karl or who the hell ever he was. You did what you had to and the snake died. You could even claim he set up himself if you push the logic."

I thought about that a moment. "No, I don't want to go that far, Dee. I'm not even sorry it worked out the way it did. I keep thinking of Amanda and Jack and the girls, and I'm glad it never came to trial. I suppose justice was served. Let's leave it at that." Then I chuckled. "I must be getting mellow in my old age."

"How's that?" Dee wanted to know.

"I didn't even holler, 'son-of-a-bitch!' this time."

That night I slept like a baby.

# Epilogue

That's the way the case ended. The irony is that if I had not been in on it from the start, Wally Keller would have been discovered sooner. As I said, local police do better with simple homicide than people like me. They have their networks and their own sources, and they know the players and the turf. So standard police procedure solves all but a very limited class of cases.

Kowalski didn't believe me when I pointed this out. "Jazz, you were the one who understood it was a serial case," she declared. "You caught on within ten minutes. We didn't."

"Yeah, but if I hadn't taken off on a serial tangent, standard procedure would have identified Mann as Wally within a couple of days at most. I pulled you away from basic procedure. Any seasoned investigator worth his salt would have run all the prints right away. We focused on the janitor and forgot Mann."

"That was our mistake, me and Jim," Kowalski insisted. Adams nodded. "You warned us to follow standard procedure and we didn't."

"Yes, but I didn't make sure you followed the checklist," I told them. "I was your supervisor and I let you down. Fortunately, things turned out all right, but I didn't do my job."

"List?" Adams asked. "What list is that?"

I laughed. "The one in the back of my textbook on investigation," I told him. "I think it's in the first index. I refer to it in the introduction and in one of the later chapters. It was what I talked about the last day while you were on the case."

231

"Index?" Kowalski laughed. "Who's got time to read those? It's all I can do to get through the main chapters."

"Well, I should have made sure you did," I told them, wagging a finger. "You need to make a photocopy of that list and put it in every case file you have. Among other things, it can keep your ass from getting fried by Internal Affairs."

There's not much more to tell. I was back in Washington six months later on a job for Sam McKee. Jeanne was with me, as she normally is these days, and we were staying in the agency apartment that has become like a second home. We were there so often I told McKee we needed to pay rent, but he wouldn't hear of it. "Then I'd have to pay you what you're worth," he smiled, closing the subject. I didn't argue, but I also didn't bill him for all my time after that, either. There's more than one way of winning an argument, especially a polite one with a friend.

During nice weather I got in the habit of walking to work, and on the way home I often stopped in at the National Cathedral for Evensong. The Cathedral is about the closest thing I have to a regular church home, though Jeanne and I drive down to Oak Grove to visit Albert Jones's church as often as we can. We go mostly for the music, and to visit Albert and Emma, who have become close friends. But I like to hear Albert speak, too. While his message is always the same, Albert seems to have no end of ways of talking about a loving Father who wants nothing more than to have all his children live in harmony, not just with one another, but with all creation.

So I visit the Cathedral quite often when I am in Washington, and I go there to find peace with questions that have no answers and issues that will not rest. Somehow, being there in the presence of the Presence of Many Names seems to help, even though I get very few answers. I guess it helps to be reminded of just how much is beyond human understanding and control, and of the possibility of One Whom It Does Concern. What I find there is what I need, not answers but solace.

One day while I was waiting quietly for the service to start, I was thinking of Wally Keller. We buried him as Karl Mann out of concern for Amanda and her children, and I guess we lied by our silence in never connecting the dots for the public. As far as I am concerned, it was not anyone's business, and I had to twist Joe McClellan's arm pretty hard to get him to agree. This probably cost me any more consulting jobs in Cowtown as long as he is chief, but I figured his days there were pretty numbered.

As I sat there in the Cathedral that afternoon, I was thinking about Wally as a child and a young man. I was reflecting on the incredible gift that enabled him to create music far beyond anything I could ever perform. I thought of him placed in the care of adults who so casually betrayed the trust given them with this child.

I was also thinking about what came of this violation of trust, of the dreadful rage and hunger for power to which this betrayal gave birth, resulting in so many dead. I thought of the waste of genius spent plotting multiple murders rather than marvelous symphonies, and I had a sense of great loss. I was hoping, or maybe praying, that if there is anything beyond this life, it is a place where ravaged children like Wally can find healing for their tormented souls.

I know this sounds strange coming from a policeman, but I don't hate the people I hunt down. There are reasons they are how they are, which means they are insane by most accounts. How can one remain angry with people who are mentally ill? As one writer put it, they did not choose their insanity, it chose them. Many of them were born that way and the others, like Wally, were raised to be the way they are. My job is not to judge these people but to stop them from acting out their insanity on the rest of us.

These were my thoughts and I was lost in them. I was aware that a couple of men sat down beside me just as the service began, but I was caught up in the music and didn't pay them any mind. When I rose to leave after the end of the service, I was startled to see it was someone I knew, but it took me a moment or two to remember the two clergymen watching me at the end of the row of chairs. I don't know how I knew they were clergy, since both were dressed in mufti, but I did.

"Dr. Phillips?" one of them asked, and I recognized it was the bishop from the National Cathedral. Next to him stood his friend, the bishop of New Hampshire, with whom Jeanne and I had shared a prolonged pot of coffee before Christmas.

"I beg your pardon, Bishop," I said. "I was a thousand miles away."

"Do you have a minute?" Bishop Hopewell, the man from New Hampshire, asked. "We were just talking about you a bit earlier. We wondered how your case turned out."

I was anxious to get back to the apartment, but I had never kept my promise to let these men know what had happened. They had both been instrumental in resolving the case and I owed them for that. "Is there somewhere more private where we can talk?" I asked.

We ended up back in the same office McKee and I visited earlier. I told them most of what had happened and how, and why there had been such little media attention. "None of them knew who Karl Mann really was, and without a trial, we didn't have to give them much more than the bare facts. The press came up with the theory that Mann shot Keller because of his violent homophobia. They liked the idea that Keller had threatened to expose Mann, and was shot to keep him quiet. We didn't do much to dissuade them."

"Thank God for that!" Bishop Hopewell said. "Amanda and the kids didn't need to be dragged through the mud."

"They were the principal reason we didn't set the media straight," I admitted.

"I'm surprised the local chief of police went along with that."

"A few shakers and movers in Ft. Worth had a come-to-Jesus meeting with Joe McClellan," I said. "They were all Episcopalians." Too late, I remembered who it was I was talking with. "Oh. I beg your pardon, Bishop. I didn't mean any disrespect."

Both men laughed "We're glad he saw the light," the cathedral bishop said. "I suspect the cherub who set the archangels on the chief was named Jazz."

"I wouldn't know anything about that," I said. "Angels are your department."

"What I don't understand is why he did it," Hopewell told me. "I understand his killing Rufus. That was simple revenge and I can relate to that. Truly, I can. But why all the others? What's the motive there?"

"There is a certain twisted logic to it," I said. "Mann was a little different from a lot of serial killers. Revenge may have started it off, but it became a mission to him and he was extremely well disciplined, even for a serial killer. He started to fall apart only at the very last, when he came after me. That was a break in his pattern, but the strange thing is that he set it up."

"How's that?" one of them asked.

"There comes a point with most serial killers that the thrill starts to diminish. Part of what seems to drive them is living out on the edge, and they get too good at what they do. To increase the risk, they start to leave signatures, which often contain clues to who they are. Very few of these are clear until after the killer is caught."

"So at least one part of them wants to be caught?"

"That's true in many cases, but what they're after is recognition. Guilt has little to do with it, although self-hatred can be a big piece of their makeup."

"Ah. 'Now is the winter of our discontent,' sort of thing," my friend from New Hampshire said softly, quoting the opening lines of *Richard III*. He chuckled dryly. "Unfortunately, that's something I can understand, too."

"What set it off in the first place?" the cathedral bishop wanted to know. "Was it the physical abuse?"

"It was that and some other things, too. One was being molested by a close friend of his dad who baby-sat. The baby-sitter was one of the first ones killed, by the way. When Wally first told his dad about the abuse, Rufus blamed him for tempting the friend and beat the hell out of Wally. Word got around the so-called Honorable Opposition and Wally was constantly shamed by them. Another part of it was seeing the abuse Rufus handed out to Amanda. She and Wally were very close but she sided with Rufus."

"I knew that Wally had run away from home," Bishop Hopewel

said. "I just didn't know why. What I still don't understand is that a lot of kids go through all that and more without becoming serial killers. What tipped Wally over the edge, Jazz?"

"I think it happened in the Marine Corps," I replied. "When he went in he had two things going for him, his musical talent and a lot of rage. He was also very good at controlling his anger, which made him a very effective Marine. There is a lot of raw energy in rage and the Corps knows how to channel it. Yet even in the Corps, he might have gone either way. He was a good enough musician to make the Marine Band, but the Corps also taught him how to shoot and Wally was a natural rifleman. Eventually, he was recruited for sniper school and sent out on a number of missions. At some point, someone recognized him as a loose cannon and eased him out of the Corps with a medical discharge."

"Further fueling his rage," the cathedral bishop said.

"Exactly," I replied. "Yet, it was probably too late for Wally to go any other way by that point. He learned to like hunting down strangers and killing them, so it wasn't much of a transition to killing people he hated. He must have given this a great deal of thought, because when he was discharged, Wally began setting up a way for doing just that. Since he didn't have a criminal record, he was able to get into gunsmith school and it was there that he learned to build silencers. These became his trademark item, and we think he made a lot of money selling them to drug dealers along the Mexican border."

"Where did the change to Karl Mann come in?"

"I don't know for sure," I answered. "I think things may have gotten a little too hot for Wally along the border. He may have gotten in trouble with some of the drug people he did business with, and maybe the law, too. I think that's why he faked his own death. He had legally changed his name to Karl Mann a year before in another state, and after he 'died,' Wally went to ground and became Karl Mann, a music student. Once he finished getting his credentials, he set up a double life and went after the people on his list, saving his adopted dad for last. He almost got away with it, too."

I shook my head. "You know, we had Mann's fingerprints from the get-go. So if we had run them through the system, we would have picked up who he was right away from his Marine Corps prints. Yet we never suspected him until we did the photo aging. Once we did, we compared prints and knew for sure who he was. We were lucky he didn't kill someone else.

"More a matter of grace than luck, I think," Bishop Hopewell assured me. His friend agreed. "You did well."

That was all I told them that afternoon. What I didn't tell them was that Wally had not quit with his dad, or about the journal we found inside the organ console. Nor would have we found the journal if I had not kept pushing, so I guess I did do well.

The thing is, I knew there must be a record of Wally's killings somewhere. One thing I have learned about serial killers is that they all keep track. Some of them do this by keeping souvenirs, something belonging to their victims. This may be a piece of clothing or jewelry or body tissue, or it may be a journal or photo book or a cryptic record.

Yet, when we searched Wally's garage apartment, we found nothing. Nor did we find any record of a safety deposit box, not even a key. The apartment he lived in had nothing related to his crimes at all. It held those things a person usually collects just living in a place. Even when we literally tore the two places apart, pulling up carpet and checking out the walls for hiding places, we found nothing. Nor did Wally's car reveal anything touching on the case.

What led us to the journal was a can of popular spray lube we found in the garage apartment on our second time through. I was there when Jim Adams tested to see if it was for real with a brief squirt in the air, and we both laughed about the smell. It's always reminded me of bubble gum, and I've wondered if the manufacturer did that on purpose.

That day the smell triggered something in my mind, and after we left the garage apartment, it hit me like a thunderbolt. I asked Adams to swing by the church were Keller was shot and told him why.

The pastor was not too thrilled to see us, but he agreed to cooperate, and the custodian opened the back of the organ console for us as instructed. When he did, I caught a faint whiff of bubble gum and knew we were in the right place. Five minutes later, we were back in Adams' car and on the way to the police station with the journal.

As a courtesy, and to protect our evidence, Adams stopped at a copy shop on the way there and I had two copies made. One was for him and the other was for me. The original would go in the evidence locker at the main police station, but things have been known to disappear from evidence rooms.

"How did you know where to look?" Kowalski asked me when we showed her what we had.

"The smell of bubble gum," I replied. "I smelled it the first time we opened the console cabinet, but I thought it was from gum stuck on one of the choir chairs. Yet, a lot of people use that particular lubricant to rustproof guns in storage, and when Jim tested the spray can, it fell in place. The smell I noticed that first day wasn't from gum but from the spray lube."

"Yeah, but that was on the gun, not the journal. What made you think the journal would be in the console."

"That was the only place I knew we hadn't searched for it," I said. "Even then, it was pushed into a corner way in the back and wrapped in black cloth. When we found the gun in there I thought the journal was a speaker."

What we found when we read Wally Keller's journal confirmed everything we knew and even more of what we had guessed. Wally's fingerprints were all over it and a comparison to Mann's handwriting confirmed this was the same person. Each of the cases we had investigated was reported in great detail, starting with the ones in California and concluding with Rufus Keller. Nor was I surprised to see details of Wally's plan to take me out.

What was more disturbing, however, was what we learned that we had never suspected until late in the investigation. For, like most serial killers, Wally Keller-Mann worked alone at first, taking out the clergy in California. Unknown to him, there was a witness to his third killing. This witness, which the journal only identified as Q, tracked him down to Nogales and approached Wally in a public place.

Wally wrote in the journal that he almost shot Q on the spot when he found out what Q knew, but Q convinced him there was no threat real. What Q wanted in return for his silence was a small service from Wally. There was a man Q wanted put down, as he put it, and it turned out, Q's motive was the same as Wally's. This man was a former employer, who learned that Q was HIV positive and had trashed Q's career. While the lawsuit Q had filed might be just as effective in getting revenge, Q wanted his persecutor to die first. A week later, Q got his wish.

As it turned out, Q survived much longer than anyone thought possible. Over the next seven years, he acted as a middleman, arranging for certain people to be killed and splitting the wet work fees with Wally. What was unique was that Q would only take cases from victims of abuse, and he would never turn down a prospect for lack of funds. What had started as a mutual favor between Wally and Q turned into a vigilante crusade, and by the time Q died, there was a loose network of victims supporting it.

While it was chilling to learn that Wally was responsible for at least a dozen more deaths than those on his personal list, what was far more chilling was to read that Wally had taken on at least two protégés in the last three years of his life. One was a client who had insisted on pulling the trigger himself and discovered a taste for murder. The other was a victim much like Wally, whose passion for this brand of justice was even more fervent. The journal told us that Wally had trained both of these young men, but insisted they develop their own networks. One of the last entries noted that G had just completed his fifth hit, making him what Wally called an "ace assassin."

Knowing is one thing. Doing something about what one knows is another, and I have spent long hours pondering what to do with this information. Nor have I carried the secret alone. McKee is sympathetic to my dilemma, but he will not get directly involved. He has bigger fish to fry and Dee tells me we do, too. Even my beloved Jeanne sides with them on this issue, though I like her way of putting it most of all.

"Gracious, Jazz! You come across enough snakes to stomp. You don't need to go looking for more!"

So I sit in the cathedral and ask the silence this question. What should I do? As always with the Presence I sense lurking there, the silence never replies to questions without answers. There is only the silence itself and the celestial comfort I find within it. So I sit and ponder these questions while I listen to the music of the spheres.

# About the Author

Joel B. Reed is the author of eleven novels, seven nonfiction books, and two collections of poetry. Six of his earlier titles are in print and available directly from the White Turtle Books website (whiteturtlebooks.com) and at Amazon. *Murder in the Kirk* is the third novel in a series of mystery stories featuring Jazz Phillips, former head of the Arkansas CID.

A former resident of Hope, Arkansas, where he wrote his first novel, *Angels Fight Dirty*, Reed grew up in the Big Bend area of Texas. He now makes his home with his wife and two furry 'kids' overlooking the big bend of the Minnesota River.

www.ingramcontent.com/pod-product-compliance
Lightning Source LLC
Chambersburg PA
CBHW032037240626
47154CB00003B/953